Weaver

A Novel

By Miriam Kelly Ferguson

Paperback Fiction
PUBLISHED BY EARTHATONE BOOKS
FIRST EDITION

THIS IS AN EARTHATONE BOOK
PUBLISHED BY EARTHATONE ENTERPRISES LLC

EARTHATONE BOOKS
EARTHATONE ENTERPRISES LLC
244 Fifth Avenue, #2643
New York, NY 10001, U.S.A.
Printed in the United States of America
Designed by Eartha Watts-Hicks
Earthatone name and logo is a trademark of Earthatone Enterprises

ISBN 978-0-991-48920-6
Library of Congress Control Number (Pending)

First Paperback Fiction Edition 2014

In loving memory of my mother, Alethia Kelly.

[13]For You formed my inward parts;
You wove me in my mother's womb.

Psalm 139:13 (NASB)

Author's Note

This is a work of fiction. Any references to actual events, real people, living or dead, or to real locales are intended only to give the novel a sense of authenticity. Names, places, incidents, titles, characters, and dialogues are either products of the author's imagination or they are used fictitiously. These scenarios, however realistic, are not to be construed as real.

Acknowledgments

It is a myth that writers create books in isolation. We have our own vision of our novels, but without a community of helpers, our visions would remain locked away. I need to thank all the friends who helped me bring forth the images in my head for *Weaver*.

The upmost thanks go to Harriet Rzetelny, who—when this work was an infant—was one of the first people to believe it deserved space on a page. The Hurston/Wright Foundation accepted me into their workshop and encouraged me to just keep going.

Thanks go to the Harlem Writers Guild, for listening to the many drafts and giving me feedback that helped me tighten this work. And a special thanks goes out to Grace F. Edwards, the best editor ever; you didn't give up on me. I shall always remember that and hope that I can encourage others as you do. You give shape and purpose to so many wannabe authors.

It would be impossible to thank all my friends and family but one in particular stands at the forefront. I so appreciate Eartha Watts-Hicks who still believes that I am an author and has pushed and pulled me down this long creative road. Her help was priceless. Monica West and Femi Lewis, who did a great job of edits, I'm so glad my work got to you ladies.

There are many to thank, and you know who you are. Thanks go out to you, for listening to me for the last six years, as I went around saying, "I'm writing a book."

Thanks for the possibilities. *Finally, here is the book!*

CHAPTER ONE
Elktown

IT WAS ONE OF THOSE HOT, SMOTHERING summer afternoons in Elktown, the kind that makes you think you got asthma. 1983 was a hard year. How I had once dreaded coming back, but where else could I go? I had been to the West Coast, East Coast, and even to a far-off country, only to be broken by life or things I didn't understand. More than anything in the world, I wanted to be whole, have children, and have a life like you see in *Life* magazine. At 33 years of age, I was back where it all started. I was still about five foot three inches tall and barely one hundred pounds, with my thick hair still down to my shoulders. I was indeed back to where it all started. Most people said I looked like a young Diana Ross when she was a teenager. I hadn't lost my smile, though. I'd just lost my way. I had come back now to live with Mama. I needed to be still.

"The world is not for people like you." That's what she'd told me and she was right. It had kicked my ass, like I was fair game for every schemer I had befriended.

Elktown was about fifteen miles outside Easton, Maryland. Once a farming community, it is run-down now. My grandmother grew string beans, tomatoes, corn, and cucumbers for the farmers who owned the land. She somehow owned a patch of land herself, about two acres. Our house had a weathered clapboard siding and rose straight up two floors. Big for this part of the country. Across the road was the seasonal workers' tract houses. All empty now. The land looked battered. There was no money in small farming. Even animals stayed away from here. So unfruitful, so overgrown with unknown plants, so unproductive and dry, but Mama was in charge of me now and I needed to be still.

Before Grandma left this world she never would have told me to be still. She believed a person should keep busy. She taught me as a child to make potholders and then she would sew them into welcome mats. We got good at mat making. She told me to keep your hands busy and your mind will follow. Rug making, you might say, came from both sides of my family. Grandma was a teaching kinda person, like many old people can be. She made me laugh too, but sometimes she got as confused as me. I get my looks from her, some people say.

As I sat on the porch swing of my grandma's big, run down house, I saw the dust of an oncoming car. *Who could that be coming up this hour of the day?* Closer the car came and crawled to a stop. A light-skinned man, dressed in a brown shirt, drenched in sweat. He sat tall behind the wheel of the dusty white car. There was even sweat from his bald head running down his face. Reaching into his pocket, he took out a white handkerchief to mop his brow and pat his cheeks. As he stepped out of the car, I could see his skin glowed neon red and his white teeth was big. His face seemed familiar. He walked up to the porch with a limping left leg and just stared at me. "What's your name, Miss Lady."

I answered him while sucking my teeth, "My name's Almena Johnstone. You lost or something?"

"No," he said. "Don't believe I am, 'cause I'm your daddy."

"My daddy!" I popped my fingers and slid my foot across the porch boards like I had seen James Brown do it. "Come to think of it, you do look like that faded picture Mama got in the drawer. Come on up here on the porch, I'll git you something cool to drink." I walked to the kitchen and said to myself, "*Lord, let it be him. I been tricked so many times.*"

Just last month a man come by, saying he was from

the health department, and he needed to check my heart. He had a bag with a listening device and all. Said, I just needed to take off my shirt and give him the state fee of two dollars. I gave it to him. Thank goodness Mama come and chased him away. He pinched my nipples too hard.

As I passed the living room couch, I reached under it and pulled out Grandma's 'make-em-do-right' stick and put it by the door where I could reach it quick. It's too hot for a trick today. He did look kinda like what people had told me. My stomach was excited. I had to tell myself to calm down before I peed on myself. Returning to the porch with some iced tea, I looked at his hands. They was rough and hard and ashy looking. He took the glass gently and didn't seem threatening at all.

"Ain't you got a hug for me?" He said.

"I do, but first let me tell you all about me. I'm about to bust if I don't tell you this, Daddy. Oh, by the way," I said, "What's wrong with your leg?"

"Long story, baby girl, long story," he said. "Why don't you just let me sit over here and hear what you about to bust about?" He limped to the porch swing. I sat on the side rail of the porch and twisted a paper napkin in my hand. This was the best day ever.

"Guess what, Daddy!" my voice eager. "I'm a weaver just like you. Since you've been gone, I've spent a lot of time weaving, but you'd never know it from my hands. Mama said my hands are smooth as a baby's bottom. I weave in fragments of myself in my shawls and my rugs, bits of other people too. I weave in lies and I weave in life and in the end, it's hard to know if one keeps me warmer than the other. All my rugs are a work of art. Oh Daddy, if you could just see my work. Maybe when Mama comes home, she'll unlock the attic. That's where they are, you know. I tell my eyes not to see so much 'cause sometimes my rugs weep like somebody's lost. They the truth and some folks can't take the truth."

"I know that's right, baby girl." Daddy shook his head and smiled.

"I can use my rugs for a blanket, a shawl, or just hang

on a wall. Most of the time I wrap one over my shoulders, wear it like a shield covering myself with whatever I see. I got a rug from when Mama and me used to live in town. I weaved that rug out of Seagram Seven gin bottles. I used the bands from the necks of them bottles. Kinda hard to walk on and even rougher to wear but a work of art, anyhow. Everybody in town said me and Mama was a piece of work. Hey, Daddy, you got yourself one hell of a weaver here. I got me a rug so blue that Persian weavers got nothing on me. My blue rug came to me during me and Mama's loving period. Her loving husband, Wallace, inspired that one. He pulled, pushed, jerked, and kicked and tried to kiss that one out of me. Nothing could stop him from making me finish that rug except death and it did. One day Mama got so tired of his loving, he went to sleep and didn't wake up. Yes, sir. He didn't know what hit him. I got me a pretty blue rug out of it though. I don't show that rug too often. It's the kinda rug you hide or just show the edges."

"Baby girl, maybe we better wait for your mama. What time—"

"No, she won't mind me telling, 'sides I been waiting a long time. It's right up there in the attic, just as blue as any blue you'll ever see. I got me a red rug too, had to go to the U.S. Air Force to weave that one. I went there to see the world and met up with the spirit of Mr. Jones, Jimmy Jones. My rug got nine hundred threads to an inch in it and during my weaving, guess what? I had an accident and spilled grape Kool-Aid on my work. I never will drink that stuff again."

Daddy didn't look too well, rubbing his fingers across his temples and staring off in space, but I continued anyway.

"Daddy, I got me a yellow shawl. It came to me during my Power-to-the-People years. See, all you had to do was suck on this paper or sniff up this powder and just like magic, California Sunshine! My shawl's got a kinda white foggy border all around it, but it's pretty though. Don't know how long that shawl took to weave, but it's a good piece!"

"My favorite rug I was afraid to weave. But I'm a weaver, Daddy, and you can't stop a weaver from weaving. I was inspired at a place called Barswell. No, I didn't go back to the service, but sure enough I was still government property. This rug's got every color you can imagine in it. Like a mosaic kinda thing, if you look at it long enough, you'll see the bars and guards, and women pretending to be queens, and broken women, and women who looked like kings, and orange uniforms, and barbed wire fences, and right in the center, if you look long enough, you'll see the picture of a woman finally trying to catch her mind. A piece of work I tell you. Took me almost five years to finish that one.

"Yes sir, you've got yourself one hell of a weaver, Daddy. Ain't you proud of me?" I looked up at him and his sweat had dried and turned his skin a faded gray. Seem like he didn't want no hug no more. *My weaving does that to people sometimes. I must remember this color.* There was stillness. He didn't say a thing, and we sat there watching a bumblebee buzz around the rim of his glass of sweet tea. I stuck my thumb in my mouth and took a delicious suck. *Something I hadn't done in years.*

Finally I couldn't stand the silence any longer, and I whispered loud enough for him to hear, "You come for me? I bet you could teach me how not to see so much." I searched his face and saw he was struggling with my last question. *Oh Lord, I did it again. I ask for too much. Mama's always telling me not to want. Stop wanting Almena. Stop seeing. It ain't coming. That's like telling a weaver not to weave.*

After a few more minutes of silence, I said, "Does your leg hurt?" Thumb back in my mouth.

He cleared mucus from his throat and said, "Almena, I lost the full use of my leg in Memphis, Tennessee. Did your mother tell you I was in the Air Force?"

"Of course, she did! And that's why I went. We just alike."

"That's my baby. But one night in Memphis, I was

down on my luck and decided to switch decks with my marked deck of cards. I won big time for the next three nights, so big that the prettiest lady in Memphis went out with me. She and I went to her house and between the liquor and the loving, I told on myself. Her man didn't take highly to that, me cheating him out of his money or being with his woman. Four men with crowbars took me out back of the gambling house the very next night. They beat me and destroyed my hip, and yes, baby, my leg does hurt. It hurts when I move too quick. It hurts when it rains. It hurts when I see a deck of cards, but most of all it hurts right now. I should have been here so you didn't see so much."

I gave him a hug, a light one. I don't rightly like touching too much. *Lord, I'd been tricked so many times.* Some folks in town took me for slow or strange. I gave people a wide spacing. Maybe I was strange, but I was also a weaver, a damn good weaver. *My thumb taste good today. Mama better not catch me sucking it. She say we done with that.*

I could hear the sound of the bus coming way before it got to our lane, and I knew Mama would be walking up the road shortly. She was going to be happy tonight. Daddy was home. I usually would run to meet her and either hold her hand or hug her around her wide waist all the way to the house. Not today. I could see her hotel maid's uniform at the end of the lane; she walked slowly like she was very, very tired today. The closer she got to the house the louder my heart was pounding. It had been a long time since Mama smiled. Closer she came. First, she looked at the car and after a few more steps, she looked at me, as if to say, "Are you ok?"

I ran down from the porch and clung to her side. "I bet you can't guess who's here!"

"No, honey. I can't guess. Who is it?" She peered over at him and when realization set in, her whole being come to attention. Her face seemed to contort, like when I miss a whole row of stitches in my weaving. The big brown eyes I loved so much squirted water and it looked like fire was coming from her small perfect nose. She told me to go inside. She said she wanted to talk to this man alone. I went inside but I sat down by the window so I could hear every word. I wished I had my weaving needles with me; I'd never weaved forgiveness before. I shut my eyes real tight and prayed that my ears could see what my next rug would be.

There was a howling, wolfing sound coming from Mama. *Is she crying? No, she's mad.* No, she was telling him to git off her porch, but I could tell she didn't really mean it. She just wanted to be in charge of whatever was going to happen here. That was my mama, always in charge. She told him every way he had failed us.

He said, "Now, Georgia, after all this time, can't you just listen. There's some unfinished business we have to talk about. Then if you still want me to go, I'll go. You sure are still a firecracker and just as pretty, too. I done you wrong, I know. But I always meant to come back for you and Almena. Please, let me have my say. Life has a way of letting you down and you can't come back to where you been 'cause you can't git enough of what you left to go git. I always loved you best, but I never had enough to give you. You and my daughter deserved better."

I thought to myself, *Oh daddy, he sure can talk sweet, can't he?* Mama wasn't saying nothing now. He was going to have to do better than that. Mama could be mean when she wanted to be. They talked for almost two hours before I saw the screen door sneak open and Mama told me, "Your daddy's going to stay for dinner, so git cleaned up and help me in the kitchen."

"Yes Mama," I said with a smile the size of a watermelon creeping up on my face. Weaving this rug was going to be a joy and I was determined to make it my best.

That night we cooked everything we had in the house. Mama was humming. Good smells was coming from everywhere. Daddy was swinging on the porch talking 'bout the work that needed doing around here. Dinner that night was fried chicken, sweet potatoes, quick greens, cornbread, fresh fried tomatoes, and lemonade. We had not had that kinda meal since Grandma died.

I wanted to hurry up and finish dinner so I could show Daddy my rugs but he kept saying, "Baby, we got plenty time. In fact, we got the rest of our lives."

Daddy went to his car and came back with a stack of blues records. He played them on our old record player. Songs that made you sad, but in your sadness, you have to laugh, 'cause some of the predicaments the singers got in was funny. I mean, what was they doing with the milkman's woman anyway. Then him and Mama started dancing. Now, that was funny. Him being a little lopsided and her being a little shy. Daddy told me to come join in but I told him, "No." I had to just see this. My rug was shaping in my head. A weaver is a thinking kind a person, you know.

I fell asleep right there on the floor that night, watching them dance to the blues. Somebody put me to bed. As daylight broke through and the rooster crowed the next morning, I jumped up and ran to the living room. The house was still. There was no Mama, no Daddy, and no car outside. My rugs was spread out over the couch as if someone had inspected them all. On the record player was a white envelope with my name on it. It read:

My dearest darling, Almena,

Your daddy and me have gone for a while. We will be back someday. Enclosed is the deed to the house and most of the insurance money your grandmother left for you. You'll be just fine. Your daddy loved your rugs but they hurt. We both want you to be free, free in your head, free in your mind, free in your spirit and free in the way to see your next rugs. You are a weaver, a damn good weaver, and if we leave now you won't see no more sadness brought on by us. The colors we see are dim, but you still have a chance to see light and good.

Mama

P.S. Almena baby, I didn't ever say your father was a weaver. You misunderstood me. I called him a no good lying deceiver.

As I put the letter down, I said bye to Mama, but didn't she know that all I ever loved is gone? What I know about free? Free seemed lost. Only God knew the emptiness of my heart. Looking at my rugs usually helped. This time, as I eyed them, they was ugly. It's a shame for a human to know nothing but hurt and disappointment in her life from birth until her Mama leaving; but I know I'm a damn good weaver and knew I'm going to weave just what I see.

That was two years ago, such a long time ago. Someday never did come for Mama. Her and Daddy run off the road in Allentown, Pennsylvania and died in a car collision. They're gone. The first six months after Mama left, I didn't weave a thing. I couldn't see anything. I think it's called grieving. I was broken once again. The cold of winter came and it made me see death, too. I wondered, *what color is death to a weaver?* It's not black, because it wasn't like I was in the dark. It just don't sound like free to me either. I hope no one ever has to feel that kinda hurt. It ain't nothing but misery.

This was too complicated for me, made my head hurt, made it match my heart. Mama and Grandma started talking to me in my head, not all the time, just when I felt like I couldn't go on. So, I wasn't lonesome, just lonely. Folks in town used to cross the street when I came by. I guess it was the way I studied them. You git mighty down, even ill, when people treat you like a retard, and then you start to believe it. I needed a subject to weave, a feeling, a doing, but if I told them that and that my dead kin talk to me, I'm sure they would've sent me to the unsteady house. *I'd betcha I could find me some subjects in there. Oh Mercy!*

I thought about leaving again, figuring if I wanted to find myself some happiness, I'd have to be around some happenings. Grandma kept telling me, "You miss too many opportunities and anyway girl, don't you leave my estate." Death must expand your vision, 'cause this here was more like a spot than an estate. Grandma did have a big old rocking chair that would hold you and rock all your cares nearly away. That chair was estate worthy. I rocked myself dizzy some days.

Grandma and Mama would be talking or coaching me through my days till one of those arguments of life would pop up and then bang, it was like a hurricane went off in my head. Grandma usually won these arguments. Like the one they had 'bout whether I should go to Salisbury and work in the canning factory. Oh my, how they carried on through the night! Mama said, "Go" and Grandma said, "Stay." Me, I just rocked and swung my head from side to side. Head listening is hard; it can grasp a person's wind.

Sometimes I had to quiet them down. Sometimes I had to make some homemade dandelion wine and take to drinking it when they got on my last nerves. That helped. Yes...and when it did, I didn't even know I had a nerve.

CHAPTER TWO
Neighborly

Spring was coming and I heard the sound of hammering just across the road. There was a new family moving into one of the track houses. Them houses had long been abandoned. Some of them sagged in the middle almost to the ground they was built on. As far as I see, it is six of them coming and going, a deep mocha man, a bright yellow woman, two older boys and two young girl children. *Now, why a family would want to live out here, I'll never know.* They came with a flowered brown couch strapped down to the top of they blue and white station wagon. They had plenty of boxes too. They wagon looks like it is down on its knees. They move quickly, putting things in and out of sight like ants. The woman started sweeping her porch as soon as the boards was taken off the windows. I watch them, didn't have nothing else to do, for about a week. "If you look at something long enough you'll find some use for it," Grandma used to say. I started weaving them. One of the young girls was going to be a challenge to weave; she kept moving and shaking her head like she saw too much, too.

The two young men rode the bus in town on Saturdays. That's the day I always go git my foodstuffs. It took a little while but we started talking one day when they held up the bus for me. I came running down the road and thanked them. And that's when I found out they names, Melvin and Percy. Now, Melvin was the talkative one, while Percy just seemed to moan and stare down at the ground. Melvin was the color of dark maple syrup, with medium pink lips, and slanted eyes. He was about average height for a man but had a real high voice and talked with his hands. They flopped from his wrists like they was made of rubber, always moving, they was the limpest wrists I ever did see. The way Melvin's hair was parted on the side; you could tell it took him all morning to git it just right. He looked to be about 23 years old. Percy was the color of fine copper with hair that was nappy and separated like a dry riverbank all over his head. I had no idea what his facial features was 'cause he kept staring down toward the ground. I thought maybe he shy and maybe his hair hurt and that's why he hadn't combed it. I guessed he was about 19 years old. I was guessing a lot, but a weaver is a seer, and anyway it didn't matter, my rug would capture just who he was. Percy was taller than Melvin but his body frame let me know he was younger. He hadn't got over his lankiness yet. Melvin told me not only they names but that they had come here to live on they mother's land. Well, I thought to myself, it ain't much but that's not my business.

Downtown Elktown had five stores and a post office. There was the grocery store, the feed store that also sold farming tools and gasoline, the material store, the beer garden and the barbershop, and our one-person post office. Now there was a school but it was about fifteen miles away in the next county. For all other needs, a person would go to Salisbury, Maryland. I got my hair done once in Salisbury: I didn't care for it at all.

"Is the post office open today?" Melvin ask

"It is honey, but you be careful in there." I know he did not understand the warning and I hoped he would not need to.

Sadie, the postmistress, ran the post office like it was holy ground. She had rules to follow in her post office or you would be waiting a mighty long time. A person better be still, ask softly, and have an "I'm begging you" attitude. She injected pain in you with her nosiness. Mama said she the queen of signifying. Sadie is ugly inside and out. Her black ash complexion, graying hair, fish-like eyes and large peeling lips surpassed the thirty-eight years she has been on this earth. I tried to weave her once but I gave up. I couldn't git that I-know-your-business-and-your-life-is-messy look she always had on her face.

This particular Saturday, I was looking for some yellow material to weave the boys' mama. She was a mountain of a woman, so I had to make her overshadow her family. I wanted to meet them up close so I said to Melvin, "Do you like sweet potato pie?"

"Yes, ma'am, I've always loved it." He outstretched his hands and then gently placed them across his heart.

"I'm going to make you and your brother one. It's the least I can do. If I hadn't caught this bus, I would have to wait till evening and the stores would be closed by then, I really thank you."

"It wasn't a problem at all. How long you been living here?" Melvin asked.

"All my regrettable life." I smiled as I said it. I knew young people didn't like the country. This town was going to be too slow and too quiet for them.

As we reached town, I told Melvin I would bring that pie over one day. Well, both of them looked at me, as if I had slapped the taste out of they mouths. Percy even moaned and took to coughing. When coughing, he looked up quickly and although it was a fast glance, I saw a long scar ran down the left side of his face. Kinda like boiling water had once resided there. His left eye was cloudy but the right eye was bright, although you could tell it was overworked. Melvin and Percy went in the direction of the post office and I went down the street to the material store. A simple thank-you would have been enough, but no...a weaver has just got to see. I mean, how can I know if my stitches would be right or not?

I knew I was overstepping my bounds, but I baked that pie as soon as I got back home. I planned on taking it to them on Sunday morning. Morning light is best for seeing every detail. I oiled myself down real good the next day. Didn't want to be ashy when I went to meet the new neighbors. I put on one of my two church dresses, the blue one with little yellow flowers on it. I crossed the road to they house with a smiling face which was to make out like I'm coming to be your friend; I ain't come to see a thing. In fact, I had already made up my mind not to tell them about my weaving, and as hard as it might git, I was not going to discuss my rugs. Now, that was going to be difficult.

Pie in hand, I stepped up on the porch of my new rug and rapped lightly on the door. At least five minutes went by. I heard a lot of moving around inside but no one came to answer. I knocked louder. Just then, the door swung open and there she was, the big yellow woman.

"Good...good morning, neighbor. I...I...come to welcome you, and this is a pie that my grandma use...use...to make and your boys...boys will like...like it. My...my name is Al...Almena." I was struggling to talk. That's so strange for me, cause I've always been able to talk. "I met your boys on the bus. They so mannerly."

I was talking so staggered-like that I forgot to breathe; it's a wonder I didn't just fall over on top of this woman. At last she spoke.

"Thank you so much. My, it does smell so good." It was the sweetest voice I ever heard. It was warm and sing-songy. "What did you say your name was? Take your time now, I don't bite."

"I'm Almena Johnstone. Live right across the road."

"Almena, I'm Coral. Sit down on that stool over there and catch your breath."

"I'm not usually so winded. I'm just so happy to have somebody out here to talk to."

She had hazel eyes, the kind you could see yourself in. Her hair was what they called good hair, which was slicked back and held with a rubber band. Her face was oval with perfectly arched eyebrows, and I know she was every bit of six foot tall. She looked right through me and said, "You been wondering about us, ain't you?"

I could feel I was being watched from behind. A shadow fell across the porch that wasn't neither one of us.

"No," I lied. "Just want to be kind to my neighbors."

One of her legs was the size of the oak tree in my yard.

I did not want to stir this woman up at all. She smelled like coconut and she was about 40 years of age. She called the girls out "Glory and Grace! Come meet Miss Almena, the lady from across the road."

They was twins. Coral introduced them and it was easy to tell them apart. Glory was the one who was shaking. She also seemed to be hypnotized by her feet. Grace was like her mother, small voiced, pleasant to look at and going to be big. They said in unison, "Hello, Miss Almena."

"My goodness they look like angels," I said. Of course, one was a quivering angel.

When Coral caught me looking at Glory, she simply said, "Been that way since birth. She's my warning child. She knows something before it happens. She's got plenty of sense, just too anxious about it."

I had been right. She saw too much. It's painful to see life coming at you and you can't get out of the way. They still was pretty little girls about five, six years old.

"I want your family to feel free to come over anytime. I know how it is to just move in. You bound to forget something and I betcha I got one if you need it. I'm always open for company, being by myself. I even got a sturdy swing in my yard that the girls could play on, and women folk need to be around each other sometime. My mama and grandma gone to glory, so it would help me to have a friend."

"Ain't nothing I'd rather be than a friend. I can tell you a sweetheart, and if we need anything, I'll take you up on your offer." She looked at me as if she understood my longings. I never did see the dark man and she didn't mention him. I lied again, saying, "I have a pot of greens on the stove and I better be going."

"We'll be over soon, and thanks again for this pie."

I had seen enough to work with. My rug was shaping but now I needed the feelings. I can capture feelings, too. Weaving's a complicated thing. This will be my best work yet. This is a new way of life for me. I had a family to weave. The woman was big; the son was scarred, and they even have a seer. I could feel the love. Coral gave off love signals. My hopes was that we would be best friends. I was doing things I might not have ever done. My past wasn't so much on my mind. Things seemed to be working out just fine. I was so caught up in my good feelings that I forgot about the dark one, but I shouldn't have.

In less than a week the twins was coming over to play on my swing every morning. Glory would watch me from far off, but in her busy eyes, I knew she knew that we was of the same spirit. Grace on the other hand was full of adventure, chasing birds and butterflies. Doing half summersaults and laughing as she fell flat on her behind. Life was pretty normal. Coral even came over twice a week, and we would sit out talking, sometimes cooking and laughing about our country ways. I love kindness.

My rugs was in the attic, even the one I was working on. Every night I could, I stitched with love. These strangers didn't think I was strange. Melvin had found a job in the neighboring town in a lumberyard, and every morning about 5 a.m., a truck would pick him up to ride the thirty miles to work. Coral was real proud of him. Percy was working the small track of land in back of they house; that boy had planted lima beans, green beans, cabbage and who knows what else. Coral said, "I'm going to open up a roadside farm market and sell Percy's Perfect Vegetables. My Percy is my gardener. He knows that inside every seed is a miracle waiting to happen." I admired the way she made each one of her children feel so special and they was. If I had me some children, that's the way I would talk about them, proud like. People called me borderline retarded when Mama wasn't around. I always did wonder which side I was on.

I never went into they house and Coral's husband, Malcolm, never came across the road. In fact, he never let me see his face. He just watched us from behind the painted dark screen door. I always knew when he was standing there. He had a long set of key chains that clang as he stood listening, and there was always the strong smell of *Camel* cigarettes. Coral and them children always remained silent or changed the subject when I asked if he liked the pies or cakes I sent over. I did not press the point, but I could always tell a person with a secret, especially one who stayed away like he did. I used to hide myself. Malcolm only moved around after the sun goes down. I could hear Mama saying, “Stop seeing so much!” I tried to heed. Maybe Malcolm just wasn’t neighborly. All things can’t be perfect and besides with five other people to weave, my hands was full.

CHAPTER THREE
Coral

Coral Lee Jackson is my name. I'm the baby girl, of the plump, good-looking, and statuesque Jackson girls. There had been three of us, Mary, Bernice and me. We was born in Maryland but our mother moved when she was young to Mississippi. Mama wanted to be a blues singer. That never did happen. The closest she came was having three daughters by three different, lowly-talented men. Folks called us "Brick House Mamas." I never did like that name. On the other hand, my sisters loved it. They would smile and whirl their behinds more at the mention of this name. I'm the biggest of Mama's girls; I have big arms, big legs and big breasts. Being shapely in the South was in style, so I caught all the young men's eyes. Chile, I'm fine. Anyway, I haven't seen my sisters in fifteen years. The last time I saw either one of them, I was down home at my grandmother's funeral and like all home goings, it ended in a big fight. Mama had died two years before this from much too much to drink. She really did have the blues. I would give anything to see them now, but it's a shame somebody always had to die before we'd see each other.

Now here we are leaving Mississippi in the middle of the night. I could hear the sirens coming toward our house on South Point Road. Police was always around our way except when we needed them. Malcolm's jaw is set in a tight clench, and any wrong move would bring a lightening backhand slap. The thought of it makes me cringe. That and his .357 Magnum next to him on the front seat. Who is Malcolm? He's my husband, or better yet a very good friend of Satan. In the back seats, is the air I breathe, my children.

We have been driving for more than four hours from one small dirt road to another, creeping along at just under the speed limit. Although it was dark, you could still see a great deal, shadowy forms of dense woods, big trees, and hills reaching to the sky. Night was the time I dreaded most. We had loaded up our life in our old rusted out station wagon. The car turned onto Route 301 heading north. And then, my bladder began to scream. Just when I thought I am going to explode, Malcolm pulled off to the side of the road. Me and the children, jump out of the car to relieve ourselves. It sounded like a heavy rainstorm. I began to laugh at the five of us coming out of the bushes. Laughter can hide your fears; I needed to show no fear. Malcolm's jaws had relaxed a little, but his gun was still close and still just as big.

Once we got back in the car, out of weariness came semi-sleep and drifting into memories of what was behind and how life with Malcolm had gone so wrong. Scenes of the last seven years flashed in my head.

I would do anything for my children. I was a lone woman with two growing boys, working twelve hours a day in a nursing home. It paid most of the bills if I juggled it right. I didn't need a man but the day I saw Malcolm at the gas station, I lost my head and my heart. He entered the scene with a bang. He was tall and husky with jet-black hair and dark eyes that always danced. His skin was moist looking and he smiled a lot. Everything about Malcolm was good back then. He was my Nat King Cole. He took my boys to ball games and barbecues, and that made them happy. My boys had never had a father. I thought Malcolm was perfect for the job. Lord knows my boys, Melvin and Percy, sure needed one. Malcolm understood their needs. He enrolled them at the boys club and every other weekend the boys went camping or hiking. A time for them to learn manly things. Stuff I couldn't teach them.

After two months of I-love-you(s), tongue kisses, fancy dinners, and long walks, it was time to test the waters; the boys was away. I knew it was time 'cause Malcolm had started getting that pleading look on his face. Tell the truth about the matter, I was ready too. Chile, I had the Avon Lady bring me a big bottle of Rose Water bath salts. That Saturday, I laid out in the tub planning how I would rock this man right to sleep. Stepping my big ass into my red short satin gown, I called Malcolm at work and told him to pick us up some dinner 'cause the only thing cooking over here was me. He got to the house so fast I thought he quit his job.

Malcolm started at the heels of my feet, sucking and licking them like they were neck bones. His hands ran up and down my legs, stopping every once in a good while to massage the top of my thighs. That man started munching on me clear up to my breast and by that time, I was whimpering hallelujahs. His tongue was precious, I tell you. When he took my breast into his mouth, I heard myself moan from a tribal place. I grasped the sheet and mattress and pleaded for him to never stop. By the time he entered me that night, I had sung, *Oh Come All Ye Faithful* many-a-times. Malcolm took his time...and he did me till he was done and could no longer move. Chile, when I come to myself, I had pulled some of the stuffing out of the mattress. That following Monday morning, me and Malcolm stood before the justice of the peace.

Nine months later came the twins, little girls, named Grace and Glory. People would stop me on the street just to see the beauty of my babies. I was so thankful or more like grateful 'cause it's a wonder I didn't have a litter the way we were going at it.

Eighteen months later, things got messed up. Malcolm got injured at the job; a tire-jack hit him in the face and took off half his jaw. His Nat king Cole profile was replaced with a sunken hole of a scar that had a keloid. Having half a jaw made it hard for him to keep his mouth closed and even harder to keep salvia from oozing out. He became so ashamed of his face that the Malcolm I knew disappeared into a shell, like a turtle protecting itself from anything unfamiliar. He poked around the house. Something died in him the day his face was crushed. It would be a lie if I said it didn't make a difference to me. Sometimes I couldn't look him directly in the face. He needed to wear a bib or something, Lord, he was a juicy frightful sight. The light had gone out of his eyes too, and most days I ignored him.

Then the fights started. If the girls cried too much, it was a fight. If the girls took too much of my time, it was a fight. The fights got more and more vicious, like the last one we had. When it was over, I had a broken nose and two cracked ribs. Malcolm beat me until he was tired.

I can't say that I was an angel 'cause sometimes I was the one who started the fussing, wishing he would leave us. But after the fights, he would always cry and beg me, saying he didn't mean it. Most of the time, he'd tell me he would kill me if I ever left him. I took that to mean he really loved me. I know, I know, I should have been left him, but your heart say one thing and your mind say another. The beatings were bad but there are some beatings people give you that are worse. It's not with their hands, but with shame, that destroys your very core. Women can be so stupid. Well, I got us into this mess and it was up to me to get us out.

Going over a set of railroad tracks both startled and interrupted my thoughts. I wanted to ask him where we going, but silence was safer. I didn't want the children to know this really wasn't a planned trip or that their father has said he would blow our heads off if we didn't go with him. The look on his disfigured face told me he meant every single word of it.

Turning to look at my children in the back two seats of the station wagon I could see that they were covered up in the blankets I had given them. *Patience.* That's what my pastor used to preach on. *Coral have a little patience.* Of course my pastor didn't know what hell we were going through. Nobody knew. I had no choice but to patiently wait on Malcolm to leave us alone, 'cause that's a big gun and Malcolm was sick in the head and no amount of love or patience could cure that.

I must have fell asleep ‘cause when I woke, we were in front of my grandma’s old house in Elktown, Maryland. The way I was feeling was strange. Familiar but lost. I woke the children up and said, “We home!”

This was my old family home, and we were going to make it ours without any of the troubles we just left. We were in the country for sure. Nobody was out here. We started to move our stuff in right away. It looked like all the houses were empty but across the field, I did see some clothes hanging on the line to dry. We had to take down the boards off the windows, and to my relief, it ain’t that bad on the inside. Melvin, my oldest is a good cleaner. He was always so tidy even as a small child. I hate to admit it but he favors a woman in many ways; but I just know he’ll grow out of that once he meets the right girl. I got a big bucket of bleach and we went to work, scrubbing from front porch to the back bedrooms. Percy found an old rusted lawn mower and he clean it up so he could cut down the overgrown weeds around the house. My girls were running around choosing their bedroom. Malcolm looked more steady than he had in months. *I wish he’d just disappear, drooling everywhere. I’m going to keep my mouth shut though, no need to fight tonight. I swear on my mama it’s impossible for me to ever love this man again—First chance I git, we gonna run. Look at him standing up there just taking up space.*

CHAPTER FOUR
The Perfect Business

In about six weeks, just like Coral said, that vegetable stand was up and running. Percy's Perfect Vegetables was a big hit. We put a grill out there to make sandwiches for the men from the lumber yard. Coral would git up at 4 o'clock in the morning and start working. Melvin helped out before work, acting like a real server. He set up a wooden table off to the side of the house and covered it with a red and white table cloth, placing forks and spoons neatly on it. Melvin sang us into business every day, *Love and Happiness.* That boy loved to sing anything by Al Green. *Love and happiness....hey.* Percy began to lift his head up just a bit, and his moaning turned to an umph. Everybody started stopping by our stand, if not for Percy's vegetables then for my pies, cakes and lemonade. The Lord will surely make a way, now won't He? We was proud! My nights was filled with weaving and life was turning.

Spring turned into summer and fall was threatening. Coral was still busy as a bee at the farm stand but every once and a while I would catch her deep in prayer, pleading for something, saying, "Not again, not this time." Glory was trembling so much I asked Coral if she had to go to the doctor. Coral dismissed this and said she just needs more soothing tea this time of year. When the leaves began to change, she don't take to change well. Being happy had made my extra seeing ability blurry. Usually I can foresee a mess. For the first time in my life, I could buy almost any color fabric or yarn I wanted. Money from the farmer's stand was the favor. I was reaching out of my lonely life, reaching into something else. My face hurt from smiling I was so happy.

My new rug was full of happiness. Too.Before they was full of anger, hurts and craziness. The day was coming when I would show Coral my rugs and she would see why I loved her and them children so much. I didn't stitch her to overshadow them as I first started to. I stitched her within them, branching off her as beautiful buds. In later years it was called my intense piece. Whatever that is, to me it is, what it is. Happiness.

The days was getting shorter and night seemed like it was always around us even before Melvin could git home from work. Lord knows, that boy still went to work before the sun was up. One evening Melvin came swiveling over right after work and said he wanted to have a word with me. He said, "Ms. Almena, I'm so glad Mama got a friend like you," his hands still moving all over the place.

"I'm happy to have a friend like your mother." I meant what I said too.

"I've met someone at the lumber yard that I think I could make a life with." His face lit up with that statement and he clapped his hand while grinning at me.

"I'm so happy for you," I laughed up at him.

"Don't tell Mama yet I still have to save up a little more money and put things in order first. Ms. Almena, this man makes me so happy," he kinda whispered.

"Well that is wonderful Melvin!" I gave him a hug. *It wasn't until later as I sat weaving did it come to me what he meant. Mercy! He sees the moon up real close. I wish he hadn't told me that, but loving is loving, ain't it?*

Coral had talked about sending Grace to school, the first grade, but she didn't want to separate her from Glory. She didn't think the smart people at the school would understand Glory. Besides, Glory was having a hard time right now. I convinced her that Grace needed schooling to help her become that doctor she was always talking about being. Even I knew you had to learn what other people didn't know. Coral caught the bus down to that school with Grace in tow. Oh, they gave her a hard time about her not having a birth certificate or medical proofs, but my gentle Coral, simply used her pleasant ways and kindly persuasion to make them smart people see that they needed her child there to be an example of how committed they was to they profession. She showed them how Grace could read, write, and count already and they could take the credit for it. Who don't want something for nothing? Coral came back with news that Grace was going to that school, and a bus would pick her up.

Glory liked to had an earthquake when she heard the news and had to be put to bed. That child shook for two days and wouldn't eat for three days. From that day on, Glory stayed glued to my side, always with one hand grabbing on to my skirts. She even wanted to go home with me after we would close the stand in the evening. I had my weaving to do so I'd just give her a big hug and promised her she could help me make pies the next morning. My seeing was slipping. One day, I overheard Grace whisper to Glory, "Go to our secret place. Just go. I'll be home before you know it." Even then, I didn't see.

I wanted my rug to be finished in time to present it to them at Thanksgiving Day over the dinner table. I wanted this to be my gift, thanking them for they kindness, thanking them for giving me a purpose, thanking them for they direction in my life. Every so often, I'd hear Mama say, "Sometimes you can be so thankful for yourself, you selfish." But I didn't know what that meant.

What became most important was my rug and keeping it a secret. News almost got out one evening, though. I caught Percy peeping in my side window. I was weaving away when I felt a stare boring into my face. At first, I thought maybe it was a bird or something else outside the window. I slowed my movements down and then, whipped around, still holding my needles in my hand. And there was that boy looking at what I was doing. I said, "Percy, you want to come in?"

He mumbled, "Just walking by."

"Well," I said, "keep walking, 'cause you could scare somebody if you pause too long. You got my screen all wet as it is, and blow your nose! You hear me?"

"Yes, ma'am," he said.

There are all kinds in this world, but I have learn that most of them lonely and looking for something. Some folks don't even know what they looking for, cause I was once wandering and searching myself. Now of course, I never was no peeper.

Maybe that's what happened to his eye. Somebody caught him peeping and threw some hot water on him. It looks like he had a stocking cap over his face with a big old wide run going down his face. Oh Mercy!

CHAPTER FIVE
Storms

The first Monday in October, the skies over Elktown became angry. It wasn't raining yet, but thunder roared. Lighting lit up the sky, and it wasn't even three o'clock in the afternoon. We decided to close up the stand before the rains did come. No amount of hugs or promises would make Glory turn loose my skirt. I didn't like thundering either so I ask Coral if I could keep her with me just for the night. Turning toward me Coral said, "Girl, them twins is a package deal, chile. They share what Grace learns in school everyday and they can't sleep without each other. You think this storm coming is something them twins might keep you up all night."

"No we won't Mama, we'll be the bestest." Grace and Glory sing-songed.

"That's what you say." Her eyes searching me, she asked "Are you sure you can handle them?"

"Of course I can," I told her, "We going to make us a bunch of pies and git our lemons nice and soft for tomorrow's lemonade." My weaving would just have to wait tonight. Besides, all that noise and lighting would make me drop a stitch anyway. My nerves wasn't what they used to be.

"Okay, okay, give me some sugar," she said and bent down to kiss the twins. "Have a good time." Coral was smiling and waving us on across the road. We hurried, like three kids going to the fair or something.

Me and the twins mashed sweet potatoes, rolled dough, licked spoons and generally made a mess until about eight o'clock. I realized that they hadn't brought anything to sleep in with them. So, I figured, let me go git them girls some nightclothes. “Listen, my little sweet potato chefs, we forgot your pajamas, so stay right here while I go git them. I'll be right back.” and I started for the door.

Glory laid down in front of the door and in that deep voice of hers, said, “Please don't go!”

Grace pouted. “We don't want you to leave us here by ourselves.”

Well, since we all female I thought, they can sleep in one of my worn out t-shirts. Walking across a road in a thunder and lightning storm ain't sensible anyway. My mama ain't raise no fool. “Okay, I won't leave you but you got to take a bath and git all that flour, potato mash and sugar off of you.”

I ran water in my grandma's claw foot tub. Grandma was sure proud of that tub. She was one of the first people around here to have inside plumbing. Before that, she used a chamber pot. She had told me that at least a hundred times before she went on to life everlasting. I had some lavender bath salts and the girls laughed and giggled when I told them to go on and git undress and bathe themselves while I cleaned up my messy kitchen. The storm got worse, wind howling, thunder now marching louder and louder, and the lightning flashing up the sky. This was the worst I'd ever heard, but the two girls upstairs happily played in the water.

When I had the kitchen under control, I knew I better take a mop into the bathroom, ‘cause I had heard the splashing of water. I opened the door with two towels and a mop and slipped on that wet floor sliding right into the toilet, head first. Well, I started laughing and pretty soon all three of us was laughing...hard. *Oh Mercy!*

I reached with a towel in my hand and caught Grace by surprise and lifted her up and out the tub. What I saw made my insides twist up and my breathing raced from my chest at the horror I saw between that child's legs. The Lord sent a round of loud thunder to mute the sound coming from my soul. It looked like Grace have been bruised up and down her legs, and her little private parts was swollen up. Chile, this child even had some kinda puss seeping down. I dried her off, as she tried to hide the mess with parts. She knew it wasn't right, poor baby. Who tricked her like this? I put my old-shirt on Grace and told her as calmly as I could, "I got some salve for your accident." I had forgotten Glory was still in the tub. I told her to git out of the tub but she just sat there, as if in a confused state. Once she looked over at Grace with pleading eyes, as if she wanted her to tell her what to do.

"Now Glory," I said, "You and me are the bestest friends. I love you and nothing will stop that." I couldn't hold my tears any longer. They rolled down my face onto the floor.

"If there is a secret, it will be safe with me. Love keeps secrets safe." Grace nodded her head and Glory stepped out. Nothing could have prepared me for what was in front of me. Glory was bruised, too, from mid thigh to her privates. There was a swelling look to her bottom too. Someone or something had visited her lately. I needed to faint. But they eyes was on me, and I didn't want them to see me be judging, like some people had been about my strangeness. I silently asked the powers that be to give me strength.

I put loads of salve on both of them, told them to git in my bed, things was going to be all right. "Your Auntie Almena loves you. You safe here with me."

Grandma had two old fashion dolls upstairs that she never would let me play with. They was in perfect condition. I gave the dolls to the twins and told them to hold them for me tonight. I didn't have any children books to read them a story but I did have an old book of maps, so we made pretend we was going to all the pretty places in that book until they finally nodded off.

I knew not to question them about what happen to them, 'cause until this day I don't rightly want to talk about that part of my life. I dropped it in my blue rug. I suffered: first the stinging and then the pains like a bee sting followed by a toothache in your middle. I can remember putting my hand down there to hold the scream in when I peed. During that time I had many nightmares and many night sweats.

I'm going backwards again. It's happening all over. I've got to get control of myself. Please...I don't want to go to that dark closet in my head. It's crammed full of old things and old pains. I won't go there. After all this time, I'm still tender...This is them children's nightmare and they need me....I've never been needed before. Walking back up to the bathroom, I was still fumbling in my mind. *I wish I could just flush this away.*

In Grandma's medicine cabinet was a bottle of pills for the curing of infection. I once used them when I had stepped on a rusty nail, and I decided I would give the twins one half a dose each day and give the bottle to they mama. To let her know I had seen the problem. *Robbed of they innocence, scarred, and shamed at six years old, these little ones was tricked. They lives would never be like other little girls. At least, I had my weaving to air out my ugliness. What did they have? What was I going to do about it?* Mama always did say I had common sense. I sure hoped it was enough 'cause this was more than just common to me.

I wish I hadn't seen that. I went back down to the kitchen. Passing the mirror on the wall, I saw a great big vein swelling up on the side of my head. *Please....*My head is killing me with a skipping pain. My knees are weak and I cry til past midnight. Pacing back and forth, from the kitchen to the front room, seem like my life scars are filling with pus again. *Not now...*

I washed them kid's clothes especially they underpants over and over on the washboard, as if that would make they wounds go away. But I seen them and nothing would do that. Nothing.

Still, the thunder roared and the rain came down like all heaven was weeping. *Where was my mind?* Gone. Caught in the storm I guess. I sat down, rocking in Grandma's rocker until dawn.

As the storm passed, a large gathering of black crows

perched they selves on the roof of Coral's house. *How would she look to me now? She had to know. What to do? What to do?* I heard the lumber truck come to a stop across the road to pick up Melvin. I looked out, 'cause they was sounding they horn. Once, maybe three times, and no Melvin came out. I came out on the porch to see that, 'cause one thing for sure that boy never misses work. In fact, I remember he was saving what money he could to go on his own. One of the men knocks on the door. Still no answer, and come to think of it, the stand wasn't set up either. It was strange, but I wasn't going over there. I had not figured out how to look at that yellow heifer yet.

I went back in the house and began to iron Grace and Glory's half wet clothes, even they underpants. When I finished, it must have been about six thirty in the morning. I tiptoed upstairs and looked at them two angels sleeping, both sucking they thumbs with they arms locked together, and it was all I could do not to start that crying again. Well, we all know crying ain't never solved nothing. Lord, Jehovah, Yahweh, King David, and the Saints and anybody else in Grandma's Bible, I need you right now.

The truckload of men had pulled off, leaving two men standing off to the side of the house. One man was vomiting, and the other one was slowly shaking his head from side to side. My curiosity got the best of me. It certainly wasn't courage, 'cause my bladder was full as I cross the road, and I hadn't had a thing to drink since yesterday. As I get to the house, the vomiting man said, "Lady, you don't want to go in there."

"What's the matter? Where's Coral and them boys at?"

He opens his old nasty mouth and vomits again.

Oh hell. I'll never get to the bottom of this waiting on him to stop being sick. The other man looked like he was hiding. So I push open the screen door and step in. There laid Coral with an ax stuck in her head. She was split half into, right down the middle of her head. Blood was everywhere. In fact, I was standing in a big puddle of it. I couldn't scream but I hollered, chile, I hollered. The men grasped me out of there, and I heard them say that the other men had gone for the county sheriff. *You ever wished you was blind?* They was trying to calm me down but I couldn't calm down, not with them shoes on.

The sickly smell of death covered my shoes. Finally, about twenty minutes or so, my body stop trembling and I ask one of them men to git them shoes off me. I sat off to the side, barefooted, trying to collect myself. The stink of fresh blood in my nostrils rooted me. I heard Mama's voice say, "Still yourself. Go on home and rock a while and I'll be with you." She did not have to say it twice. *In the last twelve hours the world had empty it's sewer on them children...and let me witness it. Oh Mercy!*

Rocking in that chair always did sooth my nerves. At first, I rock so hard I near bout flipped over. Then, after a while, I push lightly and my thinking starts. It would at least be four hours before the sheriff came out here, 'cause if a black person was reported dead, them crackers figured if they dead now they would still be dead the next day, so it was never no hurry to git out here. The men waved away the school bus. Thank goodness. Them children was still sleep, probably the first peaceful uninterrupted night they had in a long time.

Grandma's voice spoke first, "Them your children now. You they auntie, but don't let them destroy the dolls." Grandma's always got a "but" with her. I wondered what she was talking about. Where was Melvin, Percy, and Malcolm? I mean I wanted the twins but they did have kin.

When the sheriff and his deputy did come, they found Melvin hacked in half in his top bunk, Percy's head cropped clean off in the lower bunk, and Malcolm was nowhere in the house. They found my shoes over there in the grass and came over to see if I knew anything. From they investigation and pictures in the house, Malcolm was wanted in two states for killing folks, so of course, he was thought to have done this too. The sheriff asked me had I seen the two youngest children, and I said yes they was my nieces and they was upstairs sleeping and didn't know nothing. He was glad he had someone to take care of them kids. If the state had to take them it would mean a lot of paperwork for him. I stood nervously, holding on to the door wondering how this man could move from talking about murder and death to he don't want to do paper work.

It took six men to carry Coral's body alone out of that house. They brought out Melvin and Percy last. I thought I didn't have anymore tears but I did. I went back to rocking. *How am I gonna tell them children they mama and brothers was dead? Lord, I'd called they mama a heifer just this morning. I didn't know what hell she must have been going through. Worst of all, I didn't see it.* A hard knocking scared me from my rocking. The sheriff came back saying; maybe I better lock-up the house tight till they find Malcolm. Right away I pulled all the shades down and lock every window and door to make us safe and to keep the children from seeing anything across the road.

Mama's voice came to me just then saying, "Sweetheart, you've seen enough. It's time to go. Take the girls and go!" Grandma was there too, fussing about leaving her house. In fact, Grandma had been flurrying through my mind the whole week.

When the twins got up I told them some of the truth, that last night they mama and brothers went on a trip to see a better life and left me in charge of them. Glory was pleased as punch and so was Grace, but I could tell she had some questions but not today. *Today I was going to teach them how to start a weaving loom.*

#‡#‡#‡#‡#‡#‡#‡#‡#

The sheriff only had one dog, but they caught Malcolm. He was about ten miles backwoods with clothes soaked full of blood. Sheriff said he yelled at them saying, "Nobody takes my pure pussy from me." He tried to run and the sheriff and his deputy shot him dead. "Nasty business, when families fight." The sheriff stood on my porch shaking his head. I just shook my head too cause he didn't know the half of it. I wanted him away from here so I changed the killing conversation.

"Sheriff I got my two nieces in the back weaving, and they don't need to see none of this. Can I send payment for cremation of the bodies to the county? I don't know how but I have to break the news to them kids, and I think a funeral would be too much for them."

"Ms. Almena, I understand and of course you can. In matters of murder we still have to conduct an investigation. So just send the payment to the County Medical Office with a note about your wishes. You take care of them little ones, you hear? The county holds ashes up to one year."

"Thank you, sir." I prayed he didn't come back.

I knew where Coral kept the vegetable stand money. She told me bout the false bottoms on the cleaning cans Percy had made just to hide our money. It was two days later before I got up the nerve to cross that road again. While the children took an afternoon nap I went for the money. Holding my breath and willing myself not to just drop; I tiptoed in the back door this time. I got what little clothes the girls had and the cans with the money in it. How I would have liked to have something of Coral's just to remember her by. But sometimes you have to hold onto what you have. Besides, I was afraid to go to the front part of that house. I walked with my head held high back across the road. I never looked in that front room, no sir, I didn't want no reruns. When I reached the porch of Grandma's house, I looked back across the road and wondered why this place do everything I come to love so bad. This town should be called Regretsville. Tears once again poured from my eyes.

This crying has got to stop, if I want to help them children.

From what I counted, we had about twenty-six thousand dollars between the stand money, Melvin savings, and what Grandma left. Most of it was from Grandma. Money smart is what they called my grandma. *I'm going to have Coral, Melvin and Percy put in pretty vases. Oh, I am so out of focus. Thoughts keep coming.....fast and twisted*

Later on, maybe I would tell the girls the real story but

not this day either, 'cause they was learning the cross-weave, a very tricky thing. You got to concentrate to learn that one.

I packed up my rugs and all our other almost precious stuff. We was leaving Elktown. It was time for me and my children to leave here. It took us only two days to organize ourselves. As I looked out the window I saw a flock of birds soaring high in the sky. They went sailing by. Then it came to me, that's what free look like.

Taking that old, worn book of maps out again, I called the girls. "Grace and Glory, I want you to help me out with something." They eyes was big with wonder. "Let's find a new home for us."

"Let me do it" Grace hollered. "I can pick a pretty place."

"Pretty or not, you better make sure Mama and them like it." Glory shook her head.

The mention of they mama made me take in a sharp breath. We studied over that map for hours. We pick on the map New Haven, Connecticut, mostly because of its name. We need a new haven. I rocked on it a while and got no fighting in my head. Oh, Grandma was there in my head but she said, "I always was hardheaded." That's her way of saying she don't know if my leaving was a good thing yet.

Bus tickets sold at the post office. I hated going in there. Taking the rocker, me on one side and the twins on the other, we caught the bus in town to face what was sure going to be a trying situation.

I had to go through Sadie to get the bus tickets and to send Grandma's rocker to New Haven. Walking up to the post office, I could see Sadie looking out the window at us like we was from the moon or something. Sadie lives in other people business. At least she wasn't busy right now. She took every opportunity to show off in front of people. I knew she was going to give us a hard time so I gave the twins a dollar.

"Y'all go on in the store next door and get us some treats for our bus ride." I smile down at them.

"Yea! I want some Mary Janes. They last long." Glory claps her hands together.

"Come on, Glory you know they stick to your teeth and you got a loose one," Grace said. I open the door to the post office and slid the rocker in. Sadie started sucking her teeth, putting her hands on her hips and patting her foot. She had been waiting for this opportunity like a fly trying to git to shit. "Well," she said, "don't scratch my floors with that chair. Now I know you upset and all but you can't sit in here. Only federal business in here and crazy ain't allowed."

"I want to send this chair general delivery to New Haven, Connecticut and I would like three bus tickets too." I said this nice and steady.

"You want three tickets to where?"

"New Haven, Connecticut," I said it again.

"Who you know way up north in Connecticut?" She asked and not getting nothing.

"What a friend I've always had in Jesus," I said to her and I felt my nostrils flaring.

"Now Almena," she huffs, "Don't be a smarty pants. I'm looking out for them children's benefits. Who told you to take care of them children? I might need to call somebody 'bout your mental health. You know you tried to out-run the world before and anyway since you got a chair, sit right down there and tell me all about the killings. It must have been horrible and unsettling to them children. Chile, why did they father kill his kin?"

"Lord, Sadie the mother of the children left them with me and why don't you just do what a person asks you and leave us be." I was mad enough to choke her but I needed the tickets.

"I'm not going to be responsible for sending them children off with a nut. If them kids is with you, they might wind up nutty, too. She bucked her eyes and rolled her fingers around the side of her head, making the crazy sign. Reaching down under her counter she pulled out the yellow pages. "Now let me see, what was the name of that mental hospital you was in?"

I stood there with my hands heavy waiting for the next words of hurt to come out of her mouth. I knew one more and I was going after her. *Calm yourself, I heard Mama say. She can't stop this.*

I was just about on my way to telling Sadie where she could go, when the door open, and the twins came bouncing in with the deputy who was at the house that morning. His name was Ray.

"Good morning Ms. Almena, I see the twins look happy and buying candies for a trip up North they tell me. Is there anything I can do for you?"

"Yes, if you could help me in getting our tickets without further delay and seeing to it that my grandma's rocker gets sent general delivery to New Haven, Connecticut, I would be so relieved. I'm having a little trouble explaining things to Sadie." My words tumbled out. I was mad and nervous.

"Of course I will." He turned and said, "Sadie," in his big important voice, "can you handle that or do you also need help?"

She looked like a deer caught in a headlight. "I'm doing it right now, sir" she said. "It wasn't going to be a problem at all. I'm just trying to be sure of some things. People can't just take charge of things. I'll check them out for myself later, I guess." She raised her left eye at me when she said this and kinda rolled her neck. In about fifteen minutes, we had our tickets and Grandma's rocker was tagged and ready to go.

My Grace spoke up and told Sadie as we was leaving, "We would take you, too but we are afraid people won't understand your ways." We laughed all four of us, the deputy, my twins and me. Tomorrow we going to catch the Trailways bus to New Haven, Conneticut. Grace had her mama's ways all right. She was an outspoken little thing and she knew people.

My head was elsewhere when we got home but I manage to get the stuff for sandwich making out of the icebox and on the table. I sat down and started softening the lemons for lemonade. Glory reached up on the table

"I'm going to make the sandwiches. My special one is bananas and baloney."

"Don't put any butter on mine, Glory. You make it too greasy," Grace frown her face up.

"How many you want, Auntie Almena?"

"Just one will do. I'm watching my weight," I replied. To tell the truth I had never heard of that kinda sandwich. I had so many things to learn about these children. So many things... My trembling started again.

Lord, let this be right, moving and all.

"That's what Mama always says, she watching her weight but Melvin says it ain't going nowhere." Glory and Grace laughed loudly at that. All this talk about Mama and Melvin made my stomach jump. It was like a death rattle in my ears. I push my chair back from the table and rushed to the bathroom to muster me up some courage. I caught a look at myself in the mirror. I didn't look no different, well maybe a little bug eyed but that's my look. I guess I figured with all the responsibility I was about to take on I would look like Mama. Not so much, although I saw some lines in my face I had never seen before. Kinda like when your shoes is too tight and you been wearing them all day.

Returning to the kitchen table and looking at they strange sandwiches, I pinched Glory cheek. "That's enough of this sandwich making. I need to get some fresh air." We put our sweaters back on and took a walk, not across the road, but backwoods to clear our heads, or at least mine. "Now before we leave here, I want to know what's on your mind and y'all ain't even told me what you want to be when you all grown up." *I've not only got to love these children but I've got to know these children.* Our steps in the woods sounded like soldiers marching in my ears. Twigs broke in a one, two, three order. Crickets and bees and bugs of all kind backed up the rhythm of the marchers.

"How Mama going to know where we at?" Grace asked.

"Sweetheart, she'll know because I'm going to leave our address with the deputy and your school, as soon as we get settle. We got that all worked out." *I'm becoming quite a liar, seem like if my mouth is open...I'm lying.*

"Goooood...Imma be a doctor," she announced.

Glory looked at me with a big grin on her face. I don't think anybody had ever ask her what she wants to be. Her chest rose up and she said in that deep voice of hers, "I want to be the best damn weaver there ever is."

Children can make your soul sing.

CHAPTER SIX
Traveling Mercy

The 6:30 a.m. bus was right on time, and since we had been waiting outside the post office for over an hour, it was a blessed sight. I figured if we set off in the morning, we could take advantage of the light and the sights. The bus was shiny and new inside, even had its own restroom and there wasn't but about five people on it. We took a four-seat section. I knew if the children wanted to stretch out for a nap, this would fit them. We struggled to put our basket of food above us and the bus driver had put our suitcases under the bus in the luggage compartment. Well, the bus was about five miles outside of Elktown and all three of us was sleeping.

We awoke to the stopping of the bus in Wilmington, Delaware. The bus driver, a thin black man with a comely smile announced that we would be there for a forty-minute break and if we wanted to, there was a cafeteria that would welcome our visit. We got out to get the girls some breakfast and to stretch our legs. They had oatmeal with fruit, and I notice that Grace's eating habits had slowed down. When we had the farm stand she was constantly eating something. Glory's shaking was down to a tic. I was the one nervous but it was on the inside. I kept my voice low and to an even cadence so as not to show my uncertainty.

This stop in Delaware was across from a waterside park and we walked over to share a roll with the ducks. As we fed the ducks, more came from everywhere. Glory asked, "Do they know they are ducks?"

"Well I guess so," I said. I knew right then I would need

to get a little more learning in how to answer them children's questions. They was always coming up with something I didn't know. This was an adventure for them and they wanted to know everything.

When the bus driver announced that we had crossed the border into New Jersey, Grace asked, "Where's the old Jersey?" By now, the bus had picked up more and more passengers at every stop. A man sitting across from us started laughing and before long, we was talking. He introduced hisself as Mr. James Grey. His voice had deep, rich tones, and he laughed often. His eyes was warm and alive. He reminded me of Johnny Mathis, the singer.

"How old are your children," he asked.

"They six years old, going on twenty-one," I said.

"It looks like they're a handful but never stop their curiosity. Some of their questions sound very sensible to me."

"I don't think they going to allow me to stop them. It can leave you breathless."

"How far are you going?"

"New Haven. Although we don't know anybody there, we're going to get a new start in life."

"Well," he laughed again. "You got a lot more questions to answer and a long way to go."

"I'll try to get ready for them. Do you know how much farther New Haven is?"

"About five to six hours. I used to live in New Haven. In fact my sister still does. If you want, I can call her next stop and find out if she knows of a good place for y'all to stay. I mean if you need a place, that is."

"You must be heaven sent. We was going to go to a hotel until we found good lodging but if she knows of a good place, we sure would appreciate it."

My angels are looking out for us. Just like he said, he phoned ahead to his sister and she would be waiting on us. He gave me her name, phone number and address.

I relaxed a little bit more. Not only did he give me an address to go to but he was nice looking. He had a sweet potato skin color, bright brown eyes and just a little bit of gray hair at the temples. Truth is, the man was so easy on the eyes. I was sorry when Atlantic City, New Jersey came, that was where he was headed. I wondered if he was a gambler, like Daddy used to be.

It was exciting to see all the tall hotels in Atlantic City. There was many people rushing in and out of the bus station. They walked right by the invisible ones; the ones camped out on the sides of the station begging for money, cigarettes, and food. The unfortunate ones, whose stench over-powered the smell of the ocean air. They was line up like unruly soldiers guarding they carts. These are the ones that Lady Luck had not smiled down on. It was a lesson I never wanted to learn. Seeing it was enough for me. I held my purse tightly and thought about the families many of them had left to be lucky. The twins was again asleep.

The bus pressed on northward with a full load of people. I found out this was a local bus and it would not use the turnpike. We went through touristy villages, some with big and little boats, some with beaches and all with antiques shops and lobster restaurants. Peaceful looking places with big, white, sea birds. *I hope New Haven is like this.*

The bus driver made another announcement, "Ladies and gentlemen in about fifteen minutes we will be entering the Lincoln Tunnel in route to New York City. Please remain seated while we are in the tunnel, no restroom usage. We will change drivers here, and the wait time will be one hour for continuing passengers."

Two heads shot up. The twins knew this was the Big Apple, 'cause I had told them that. "We're ready to go apple picking," Grace hollered back at the bus driver. That got a lot of laughter. The traffic tightened as we approached the tunnel and the inside lights of the bus came on. It was a little scary being in a tube. There was silence all the way through. Into the light we came and the mere size of New York made us catch our breath. The buildings seem to never end, they was so tall. People scurried around the streets like squirrels all going about they business. We pull into another tunnel. It was a part of the bus terminal.

The twins needed to stretch they legs so when the New York passengers got off, we followed them. Right away, a man wearing a bright blue shiny suit with a big golden chain and a big white hat grabbed my arm. He says to me "My beauty, have you ever thought about being on stage?" We was standing a few feet down from the bus. People seem to be running every which away. Both Glory and Grace was holding on to my coat. This here place is just too big for us.

"No sir," I said. "We don't know nothing about a stage."

"Well, sweetheart, I can teach you all you need to know. Is that really your hair?

"Yes it is. I know I should have had it done for the big city but..."

"Don't you worry about a thing. My agency likes talent with real hair. He reaches up and turns my head to the side. "Yes darling the audience will love that profile. His hands was soft and he had big rings covering his fingers. "Who's these little rug rats you got with you?"

"This is Glory and Grace. They six years old twins and sweet kids too."

"What you call me?" Grace almost spit at him; while Glory grinned shyly up at him.

"That's just a pet name little one. Here, let me see what I got for you. He reached in his pocket and drew out a big chunk of hundred dollar bills. *This here man was rich.* "Oops, wrong pocket," he said. And then he pulled two lollipops out of his other pocket and gave them to the kids. They took them but Grace was standing there with her other hand on her hip, giving him the evil eye. *Grace, poor baby, she must be tired.*

"We got parts available for kids, too. Listen my name is Magic and I am so excited 'cause when I saw you. I said to myself there goes my next star. Here's my card. Looking at you is like finding a pearl in a clam. You are perfect for the part I'm thinking of. What's your name sweetheart?"

"My name is Almena." Reading his card I broke out in a

smile. Can you believe this man is from the Broadway Stage Actors Company? We was going to be famous!

"The only thing we have to change is that name, otherwise you are perfect. By the way what size are you?" He was looking me over.

"I think I'm a size 12, but then it's been awhile since I sized myself."

"It really don't matter. Just looking at you I can see you got a decent figure. I can hardly hear myself talk in here, it so loud and busy. Come on sweetheart, let's discuss your future over lunch. There's a real nice place right across street. Bring the kids on. How come your husband let you travel alone?"

"I don't really have a husband and..."

"My Lord, you are fine, sweet and single. The money you can earn for you and them kids is fantastic, my darling. I met a lady last year, not near as pretty as you and now she's in Hollywood making movies. How does the name Misty Rose sound to you?"

"I love the name Rose. But, we was just going to the restroom and our bus leaves in an hour. So maybe...."

"They got a much nicer restroom across the street and I'll make sure you on your bus in plenty time. This is your first time in New York, ain't it? We take care of business quickly here, my princess. Damn, you got such an amazing smile." Mr. Magic was the perfect gentleman.

We began to walk toward the door. I had not noticed his teeth. They was gold on the sides. Oh, I felt so special.

Our bus driver saw us talking to Mr. Magic and came running over to us. "These ladies are with me and are not interested in the entertainment business," he told Mr. Magic.

"Man, you need to stay out of my business. You a bus driver, find a bus. That's what you do. Let me get your badge number anyway." Mr. Magic hissed hard at the bus driver

"Your bus is boarding, miss. Trust me," the driver said. Mr. Magic did kinda back off but he told me "Princess you got my number so you call me." He now leaned over close to my ear, “Listen,” he said. “Be careful. Some of these bus drivers can’t be trusted with women.” *Oh Mercy*! The driver took a hold of my arm. I thought they was going to fight. They began to stare mean-like at each other. Mr. Magic tipped his hat at me and strolled away. The bus driver reached for my hand and raised his brow at me.

“Glory, didn’t Mama tell us not to take candy from strangers?” Grace said loudly.

“It’s okay Grace. Calm down. I have Mr. Magic’s card right here. He’s not a stranger.”

The bus driver shook his head, laughed and ushered us back to the bus. We never did get to the New York City bathroom.

What a nice man that bus driver was. He took his time with us.

“Miss, don’t get off the bus until you reach your destination. It’s better for you.” He said, looking down at the ground.

On the other hand, Mr. Magic, he didn’t give a person a second to think. I was getting favor from everywhere. Maybe, if my weaving don’t work out too good, I’ll call Mr. Magic one day. *Imagine me on the stage....*

CHAPTER SEVEN
New Haven

Twelve hours after leaving Elktown, we arrived in New Haven, wide eyed and body tired. The City of New Haven looked like pages of a calendar, or a collection of winter garden-like postcards. The streets was clean and there was a mixture of old fashion and new style buildings. The people was not in a hurry like they was in New York. The air was different, tight, with a wind that hurt your ears and searched for openings in your clothes. Seem like the wind would eat your words. It smelled like rain, but there was not a cloud in the sky. I could hear proper accents of southern people. You know, the kind that no longer considers themselves countrified. I look around for a taxi after getting our luggage and told the driver to take us to 240 Dixwell Avenue.

It had now been almost two weeks since our lives took on such a sudden change. In three more weeks it would be Thanksgiving Day. Our thankfulness had already kicked in. The taxi made a left turn on to Dixwell Avenue off Whalley Street, and the calendar-like pages of New Haven got a lot darker. Five minutes or so later the taxi pulled over at the given address.

Along the front of the house was a white picket fence, broken by a gate in the middle. The fence turned at the corners and went partially down the long sides of the property. Small hedges line the property as well, but the coming winter had left the rest of the yard undressed. It was a real nice house, not at all like the ones in Elktown. This place looked roomy. We climbed the seven stairs and stood on the porch when suddenly, while I was getting up my nerve to knock, the doors open up. Before us stood a light brown woman, kinda skinny with short silver hair that was waved down to her head, framing it like a halo. She had high cheekbones and one of the worst coughs I'd heard in a while. Her black dress with its white collar had seen better days. I could tell it was made from high quality fabric. It didn't shine. Her black shoes, serviceable rather than pretty, was a reminder of Grandma's church shoes. Her eyes was watery and move over us completely and quickly. Standing there in the doorway she had a coughing spell. I had to put my hand over Grace's mouth as she blurted out, "What's wrong with her?"

"Hello, my name is Malinda Grey and I suppose you're the family that James called about," she said after she wiped her mouth with her hankie.

"Yes, ma'am" I answered. "I'm Almena and the kids names are Grace and Glory. They twins. We so happy to be here and kinda rest broken. It is true that you have a room we can rent, isn't it?" I was trying to sound proper with the isn't it business.

"I do have a kitchenette available now, but I don't usually rent to women with children. You didn't run off from some man did you?" She motion for us to come in, waving her hand toward the insides.

"No ma'am," I thought to myself if she only knew.

"I run a well kept and quiet residency. No company allowed in my house. What's your name again?" I told her and she looked us over again. "James did say you are very mannerly, but he neglected to tell me you was so country. What brings you to New Haven?"

I had to think fast for an answer to that one. "I heard from a friend it's a nice place to live and bring up children."

"It is. I just got rid of my roomers on the third floor. They was drinkers and disrespectful. I am fair with people if they fair with me, you follow me." She cut her eyes at me. "You don't drink a lot do you?"

"Oh no, I don't drink at all. I try to set a good example

for my girls. We respect ourselves and others as well."

"I can't stand a lot of noise." she said, "If them children make a lot of noise you'll be out of here, you understand?" I shook my head, and she continued. Her voice, when she wasn't coughing was light and proper talking; she stressed her Ts and Es.

"Now, that will be fifty dollars a week for rent in advance or two hundred dollars for the month. Speaking of rent, I don't take no excuses. If you don't pay, you can't stay."

I paid her for a month, even though I hadn't seen the room yet. She had stuck her hand out. I had to wait on Grandma's rocker. She led us up through the huge hallway and up a wide staircase to the second floor. At the top of the stairs was a large bathroom with a large claw-footed tub, and around to the right was two doors. We pass the first door and entered through the second door to a large living area with a connection to a sleeping room in the back. Actually, where we came from, it was large enough to be considered an apartment. Between the two rooms was a cooking area with a small low refrigerator and a sink. There was two double beds in the back room and even a television sitting on the dresser. Everything in the rooms was the color of burgundy, the wallpaper, the rugs, the curtains, and the bedspread, all burgundy. There was two bookcases and a sofa; of course they was burgundy too. Taking it all in it was a funeral parlor burgundy.

The twins ran to the television and turned it on, while deciding what bed they wanted. "It's a very nice room." I said.

Ms. Malinda smiled. "I really try to keep a clean place for my guest, just as long as they remember they are guest. We'll talk later about the house rules 'cause you do look tired." With that, she left us, breaking into a hacking cough all the way down the stairs.

I closed the door, and there was a full-length mirror on the back of it. I didn't know who that was staring at me. I flinched. Looking back at me was a weary soul. Her hair was in two nappy braids, going east and west, her coat was buttoned wrong, one side was hanging longer than the other and her eyes was big as ripe pineapples with bloodshot lines in them. Then it came to me, this was my own image. *Oh Mercy!*

Turning around, I let my mind and eyes roam around the room. This was it for now. While I was waiting on Grandma's rocker, I had to think on earthly things like where to get food, clothing and answers to some more of them questions Ms. Malinda had. I could tell she was going to have plenty more for me. Nothing was familiar.

Miss Malinda did keep it warm in the house, too warm in fact, but I thought maybe she's trying to get rid of that cough she got. The bathroom was at the end of the hallway, and we all went there together. Our first night there we ate tuna fish sandwiches and of course, my famous lemonade. I wasn't sure about that little hot plate stove or that child size refrigerator yet. Talk about fish out of water, we didn't know nobody and I was having trouble keeping my knees from shaking. A sure sign my courage was slipping. Glory took both my hands in her small ones and said, "I see good." Imagine that. Glory, at six years old, was steadying me.

Over the next few days, we got settled in and would take long walks to get familiar with the neighborhood. We walk the streets until our feet hurt. One of the first things we hunted for was the post office. We found it. I ask a really pretty young lady, "How can I change my address? I got a chair coming general delivery but I really need it brought to the house. I didn't know this city was so large."

She smiled and said, "Just fill out this white card with the name and address of the person to whom your package is to be delivered."

I put Ms. Malinda Grey's name and address down on the card and what I was expecting to come and gave the card back to her.

"That's fine. We'll notify the sending post office of the correct address and that's all there is to it. Your mail will now be forwarded to this New Haven address. Welcome to our city."

"Thanks," I answered her but my voice sorta of shook. I thought to myself 'bout Sadie and her meanness. A shiver ran like a black snake all the way down my spine. Our address could mean trouble from Sadie. I didn't know they would tell Elktown Post Office where to send mail. Well, it's already done now maybe she'll let it be.

Walking back, we came to a wide-open space called Green, across from the library and down from a famous college. We went to the library so I could get the girls some books. I figured since Grace was not in school, the books would help both her and Glory keep up with they studies. I got myself some books on heaven and how to talk to children about death. I thought I might fully explain why we was together before Christmas came.

I cleaned that kitchenette the way Grandma had taught me to clean, from the walls to the floors. I bought new bedspreads, light colors anything bright or shiny that wasn't burgundy. I hung nice lace curtains to let the sun in. After all we come to start anew, not to mourn.

The black women in New Haven was going through a culture awakening, that's what they called it. In this awakening, they hair was either braided or in a large wild looking mess called a puff. I admired the braids so that's how I wanted mine done at the African beauty shop. The shop was right across the street from the house. I could see the women going in and out of the shop from our second floor room window. I was hypnotized with all these things to study.

We'd been watching women come and go out of the braid shop for three days before I got the nerves to go in and ask if they could do my hair. Two Africans came out of the back room and started asking what I wanted done at the same time. I pointed to the style I wanted, 'cause they talk with an accent and so forceful. It was almost like being cussed out. They noses was turned up like they smell something. I was taking it all in, the colorful long tops, the dirty shop, the pieces of imitation hair on the floor, the air of "better than" and the falsehood of some blacks who thought that hair can say who you are. There was a sticker on many of they cars. It said, “It’s now and forever.” Sounded like they was mad to me and with nobody to tell me, I thought maybe I better stay clear of them before I got tricked again. I wanted to say, who are you trying to be? I knew I was going to weave this one day, and somehow, I knew it wasn’t all about the hair. It just couldn’t be that simple. I miss my rocker.

My braider’s name was Habibah. She was the color of nutmeg, large lips, sharp-like nose and a very slight built. That girl didn’t have no butt at all. I thought now that’s peculiar for an African. She wore shells around her neck and big silver-like bracelets that clang and jingle when she gripped my hair. She did my hair in about twenty cornrows with a small bun in the back. It was simple but beautiful. I ask Habibah where her home was. Her face lit up as she tried to make me see her home and how beautiful it was .She told us that she was from Zambia and how she longed for her family. There was something about Habibah that let you know that this young woman was educated, if not by school then by her own curiosity.

Grace and Glory wanted they hair done, but to tell you the truth, my head hurt. Oh, it was pretty like I said, but tight. It felt like I had stitches in my head. I explained to Grace and Glory they had fine textured hair so you could just wash it and twist it up and they was ready to go. Braids would not hold on they heads. Black hair can really be a job. Our clothing changed, too. We went from just anything to jeans and printed tops (African of course). We wanted the city folks to know we was awoke, too. They scarring was coming along good. I kept them in white heavy cotton underwear with plenty of salve. Now I knew that would not heal them inside but I needed some help with that problem. So many troubles, it was hard to stay upright. If only my rocker would come, then maybe my burdens would lighten.

We hadn’t seen Ms. Malinda for three whole days but could hear that coughing. Now, I was beginning to worry about her. *I think I’ll make her some soup and befriend her.*

Besides, I want her to know my grandma's rocker is coming.

CHAPTER EIGHT
Malinda

Rays of light flicker behind the heavy burgundy drapes at the windows. A stale Robitussin taste lingers in my mouth. My chest feels like a lion had just sat down to feast on me. Late last night the pain was so deep in my chest it made me dizzy. Everything in me wanted to just shut down. I had heard my new roomers as they climbed the stairs. The fifth step, which was on my list of repairs, gave out a severe scream as feet touched its tired boards. In pain, I almost cried out to my roomers.

"Today I will get up," I whisper to the cobwebs dangling from the ceiling in my master suite. *Christ, a woman with children living in the best whorehouse in New Haven. What was James thinking? My baby brother is too much!*

As I lay there, I think to myself of how fool-headed James had been coming up in the South as a child. Whatever could happen, James had always been on the starting end of it. A "wild child," that's what people had called him. I miss my baby brother. I turn facedown now and push myself up. It takes all my strength just to sit. *"Damn it, Malinda Yolanda Grey you're stronger than this,"* I say to myself. I wish the bathroom would come to me. Finally I pull myself up but the phone rang before I can relieve myself of three days of nothing but water and Robitussin.

"Yes," I manage to whisper into the phone.

James playfully answers, "Have you ever said no?"

I pull my shoulders back and laugh, "I'm going to kill you! Where you at and what are you doing? I was just thinking about you."I could tell James was smiling by the tone in his voice. He likes to catch you off guard.

"It's a jungle out here but a man's got to do what a man's got to do." That phrase has always been his slogan. "How is my sophisticated sister and her new family getting along?"

"I'm doing the best I can. I haven't seen my roomers for a couple days. Those little ones are so adorable. The mama is sweet too. But what I want to know is where the daddy is? The children must take after him 'cause I don't see none of the mama there."

"There you go, being nosey again. Before you ask, let me tell you straight out, I am not the daddy."

"When you coming to see me?"

"Not long now, had a few stops to make."

"You're making a lot of stops. I could use some company and some of your down home teasing."

"Well, Malinda, since you running a clean house now, maybe it will be sooner than you think,"

"Clean is right! Shit, I might even open a day-care center."

"Sis, the poker table is calling me. I just called to check up on you and your new roomers. Peace and wish me luck. Take care of yourself, big sis."

"Yeah, I am....peace. And you stay outta trouble!" I hung up the phone and wiped the sweat off my forehead. *That brother of mine is still a little boy. When will he grow up? James loved to fight and loved to gamble. Those was his two loves for sure. I guess I'm his third.*

A wave of nausea sweeps over me. This is no ordinary cold. I refuse to give in to this sickness I just ain't done yet. Perhaps tomorrow I'll go see my doctor.

A knock on the door brought me back to the right here and now. "Go away," I yell. Another wave of nausea rippled to the back of my throat. I sit sideways on the bed, not straightening up until I'm certain I will not up chuck on my duvet. The knocking continues. *Roomers are always trouble. Never have I ever seen one with a life of their own.*

"Miss Malinda?" Almena calls out.

"That is one country mama. God, why are you

punishing me?" I whimper lightly

"Miss Malinda! I made some soup for you!"

Managing to get to the door, I swung it open wide. The smell of kale, corn, and garlic floated up from a hand held crock pot. Her scent of coconut body oil mingled with the pot's content surrounds me like a cloud. Saliva gathers at the sides of my throat. It is all I can do to hold on to the doorknob, cover my nose with my other hand, and nod a thank you.

"That's so thoughtful," my head now laying on the frame of the door.

"This will certainly help that cold you've got, Ms. Malinda. I want you to know that I have a rocker coming in the mail and I hope it's not a problem."

"No, there's no problem with that." She stood there. I could tell she wanted to come in. I must look a sight.

"I'll just leave this here soup by the door. Call me if you need anything at all Ms Malinda. I'll stop back for my pot later. I hope you feel better soon."

"Thank you, dear." I manage to move the soup pot just inside the door with my foot.

Dragging myself back to the bed, I bumped my foot on the night stand. Another round of pain shook my body. Oh, this is getting ridiculous. Falling face first on the bed, I had to laugh. *Was that a countrified African I just saw or what? Lord, how many colors did she have on? The United nations don't have that many colors going on at one time.*

#‡#‡#‡#‡#‡#‡#‡#

Checking on Ms. Malinda again about three hours later I got no answer. I heard no coughing, but I did hear a mumbling sound. Earlier, I noticed that Ms. Malinda was tired looking. Sweat had gathered around the edges of her hair and her eye color was past beige. It ain't good manners but I got to see. I peeked in to find her on the floor in a vomit soaked bathrobe and unable to control her bowels. "Leave me be! I'm fine," she said, but it didn't sound like her normal voice.

I helped her to a long chair and she sat there with one

hand to her head and an address book open in her other hand. At the top of the page there was a number for Dr. Moss. I sat on Ms. Malinda's round bed and called him on her fancy phone until I reached him. Then I got up and told Ms. Malinda, "He said he would come out. I'm gonna give you a bath."

"I can take my own bath. I've never needed anyone to bathe me!" She moaned as she spoke. She stood to walk, but couldn't make it all the way to the bathroom without me helping her. I cleaned Ms. Malinda up as best I could. What a mess she was! Every time I wiped Ms. Malinda winced and moaned. When I was done, I helped her to the bed. Oh Lord, the room smelled like rotten fruit mixed with spoiling cabbage. After holding my breath until I was lightheaded, I let go. A mistake. It would take days of airing, and plenty cleaning to get rid of that smell.

Now I could see this room was twice the size of our upstairs kitchenette. It looked high fashion, like the rooms on television. I ain't never seen a round bed before or such a high headboard. On one side of the room was a giant sit-down dresser with a large round mirror, and on the top of the dresser was nail polishes, lipsticks, make-up potion and so many perfumes bottles. It was fancy. There was a fireplace on one wall with a tall mantle that held pictures of men and women dressed in stylish clothes. Some of the pictures had men stepping out of fancy cars. Some pictured women with fluffy fur coats. Two long French chairs sat on either side of the fireplace. *I knew they was French 'cause I seen them in Life magazine and that's what they called them.* The carpet on the floor was so soft your shoes sunk in as you stepped. The only thing that was disturbing was that it was all done in that color burgundy again. *Oh Mercy*!

When I went into the drawers to get clean bedclothes, my hand ran across some of the finest satin there was. It was like touching cool spring water. Fancy nightclothes and sheets too, so soft it was a shame to sleep on them.

Dr. Moss was a tall version of the man on the box of Uncle Ben's rice. Weathered creases of experience framed his forehead. But his smile was the kinda appreciation that only comes from having truly lived. Grandma would have called him handsome. He was only here for about thirty minutes, but before he left he told me that Ms. Malinda was suffering from a variety of things and was one step away from pneumonia. Ms. Malinda did not want to go to the hospital. She wailed, pouted, and called the hospital the “house of death.” As far as she was concerned, hell would freeze over before she would go to any hospital. I stood outside the room in the hallway and took all this in. Dr. Moss stuck his head out in the hallway and said, “Young woman, come on in please.” I went in. Ms. Malinda sat on the bed with a determined look on her face. “Malinda needs care and against my advice she doesn’t want to be hospitalized. Do you think you can administer her medicine and keep an eye on her until her relatives get here? I will leave a clear set of instructions.”

“I will be more than happy to help out I ain’t doing nothing. Besides I have always been a capable person when it comes to tending to the sick.” I smiled over at my Ms. Malinda.

“Don’t think you running my house now!” she said.

“Malinda, it’s either her or the hospital. Now take your pick.” He stood there closing his bag and looking over his glasses.

It was worked out that I would take care of Ms. Malinda. My job was giving her the right medicine and the right dosages. I was to keep her warm when she was cold, cool her down when she was hot and call the doctor if she got any worse. Dr. Moss wrote it all down for me and his last words was. “Let some light in this room and don’t worry, Malinda’s a tough lady but she knows the difference when something is best for her. Stand your ground and make sure she takes all her medications.”

A week went by and Ms. Malinda was up and about, slowly but much better than before. I was so proud of myself’ cause I just knew it was my soup that did it. The twins even helped with the caring of Ms. Malinda. They combed Ms. Malinda's hair, and watered her flowers, and Glory drew happy pictures to lift her feelings. Now Ms. Malinda didn't carry herself as a sentimental person but she was growing soft for these kids of mine. One day Glory asked, "Ms. Malinda can we call you auntie too."

Ms. Malinda teared up and manage to say, "It would be an honor to be your auntie."

With all the new things I had to do I had not even touched my weaving. Time was passing. Then five days before Thanksgiving, to my great pleasure, Grandma's rocker arrived. It was days early; it was like a visit from a long lost love one. I sat right down in it before I could take it upstairs to my room. The hugs that chair gave me, oh Lord. I imagined all my confusion about what to do next would soon be gone. Home! Well, not home but feeling like home. Lifting the chair over my head, I got it upstairs and into my room. Placing it right by the front window so I could tell Mama and Grandma all that had happen since we left Elktown.

I sat down to rock and I rocked. After about thirty minutes, no one come to me. My throat was closing, knees aching, and I was rubbing the arms of that chair with all my might. Still no one came to me. I pleaded down in my soul. *Please don't be gone to the everlasting yet.* The twins saw all of this. They didn't understand it. One day I would explain believing in spirits and self. So many things to explain to them. *Oh Mama, don't be gone always.*

"Grace! Glory!" I called them to me. "This is Auntie's thinking chair and I need to rock and consider things for a bit, so don't be afraid if I'm a little different. You see, I'm setting up things."

"When is Mama coming? She can help you out," Grace said.

"It won't be long, Grace. Now you and Glory just bear with me on this and play in the bedroom for a while."

Glory gave me a hug and off they went. They really did try to mind me. Every now and then they would peep out to see if Auntie Almena was doing better. It was two days later before Grandma came through, complaining 'bout being in a shut-up truck for days. Mama spoke out about how much she missed and loved me. Mama always was the one who was more affectionate. Even so, Grandma's complaining was music to my ears; I would take anything, just as long as they was talking to me.

I talked and rocked in my chair that night; telling all that I could remember, 'bout Sadie, the bus ride, Ms. Malinda's brother, and of course Ms. Malinda. I was damn near out of breathe with all that we have seen in New Haven. When I had finish with my story, Mama told me to weave my story not just tell it.

"Your rugs will tell more than you can say. There are some concerns I have but we'll touch on them later.... after Thanksgiving. Be still," Mama said. And with that she was gone.

"Chile, please! Throw that card with the magic man's number in the trash, fore you disappears." Grandma laughed real loud.

CHAPTER NINE
Thanksgiving Day Jazz

The next morning I ask Ms. Malinda if I could cook our Thanksgiving dinner in her kitchen and she said, "Yes, you'll find everything you need in there." She was feeling much better. She always had a smile, almost a laugh on her face when I came into her room. She's a nicer person now. Sickness makes some people mean, and others, it brings the best out in them.

My plan was to have a grand Thanksgiving Day dinner. The grocery store in this city is one of the biggest I have ever been in. Grace and Glory put everything they could get they little hands on in the cart. We was of course going to make my famous pies, and turkey with dressing, seven vegetables, baked breads and no dinner would be complete without cranberry sauce. Grace put a couple of big containers of ice cream in the cart. How I love the way she thought she was getting away with something. My warrior she was, she was going to try you. It's important for children to win sometimes. Hell it's important for every human to win sometimes, least that's what I think.

What with so much happening, Thanksgiving, getting awakened starting to weave again and nursing Ms. Malinda back to health, I had pushed back telling the twins that they mother and brothers was in heaven. It just wasn't the right time or, more than likely, I couldn't find the right words. They looked so happy, so full of innocence, and so peaceful. However, Grace couldn't be held off but so long. Whenever there was an unexpected knocking on the door or the doorbell would ring, Grace would jump toward it with anxious eyes.

My rugs had been under the bed all the time we been in New Haven. I wanted to show them at Thanksgiving, especially the family rug. I did not know if my rug of Coral and our lost ones would be too much for the twins. Looking at it, a person could see how happy I had made that family seem. I can hide misery in pretty pictures if I ain't seeing it. That rug might be pretty but it ain't the truth. Putting that rug back, I began to weave New Haven with fullness. Scenes of our present days move fast through my mind. My fingers was jumpy for the feel of fabrics.

The morning before Thanksgiving, there was a loud knocking on the front door. It wasn't six o'clock yet. Well, since Ms. Malinda still moves slower than Heinz ketchup in a bottle, I answered the door. There stood Ms. Malinda's brother, James. Bag and baggage. He was smiling and I forgot myself for a moment and hugged him. It was almost improper the way I swung off that man's neck. Ms. Malinda screamed with joy, too. She got James settled in a room off the kitchen. He looked a little tired but that bus ride can wear anybody out. Of course, Grace and Glory was pleased to see him. They bombarded him with a million and one questions.

The house was alive, everybody talking and laughing. I caught James looking at me longer than necessary. On my way out of the kitchen, I paused at the door to look back, and yes he was staring at me. I ain't slow when it come to that so I put a little sway in my walk. I wanted to look good to him.

The braid shop was very busy but Habibah took me in. She freshened up my braids. I believe she likes me, 'cause I was interested in her life. She even put gold thread in my hair. I was shining like a new car. Now if James wanted to look, I figured I would give him something to look at. I was getting me a circle of friends. Looks like this might be a fairytale but that's not how life is. Chile, it began to get complicated from this point on.

Thanksgiving Day, my dinner smelled so good. Real

down home aromas, I had seasoned the food perfect. We ate everything on our plates and had seconds, too. James told stories about his almost big win in Atlantic City. Ms. Malinda told stories about how she first came to New Haven and was so muddled about things here, but she was a fast learner. It wasn't until then that I knew she was originally from Sumter, South Carolina. They was embracing us in they lives.

Ms. Malinda's first husband was a railroad worker and much older than her. He died on his job and her second husband was what she called a slick bum. She hadn't seen him for the last fifteen years. I got the feeling she didn't miss him at all. The children was at the table so we didn't go into detail on such things. I had on a new African top and some kinda musk perfume Habibah told me about. My figure was still decent so you couldn't tell me James's mouth was watering only for the food. We made polite conversation. Our eyes and smiles said other things.

I was cleaning up the kitchen when he came in with that smile of his and said, "Have you seen much of the city since you been here?"

"It's so much to see. We have been to the library; a large park called the Green and the downtown shopping center. Even the post office here is big and it's all been friendly. When the weather breaks, the twins and me are going to see much more."

"If I got Malinda to watch them kids, would you let me take you to hear some good jazz? It's the least I can do after such an excellent dinner?"

"I don't leave the..."

"Come on, Miss Lady, let's do some grown people sightseeing."

"I don't really know a thing about jazz. I probably wouldn't understand it." I wanted to go. I turned my head and hid my grin from him as I was drying a pot.

"Not too many people do," he said. "They just pretend they do. Let me show you how to enjoy what you don't understand. You know, Almena, you don't have to understand or know it all."

I looked in his eyes. With them twinkling the way they was, who could say no to that. Of course I didn't want to say no anyway. I put my hand over my mouth and shook my head yes.

"See you shortly, Miss Lady, at the bottom of the steps." He turned and walked toward his room popping his fingers and swaying his head.

I was getting ready when Ms. Malinda called me down to her room.

"I have been meaning to discuss some things with you and now is the perfect time. Why don't we find something in here for you to wear out tonight?" She went over to her large closet and opened it up and there was some of the fanciest clothes I'd ever seen.

Standing there looking with my mouth open, she pulled out a beige dress with a chocolate jacket trimmed in fur. They was beautiful. That jacket felt like a cat laid across my shoulders. The softness hugged my neck. "Ms. Malinda, this feels too nice to go outside in."

"Nonsense, that's what it's made for," she giggled.

"Thanks so much for offering but I don't think I can fit in your dresses. They are beautiful." I seemed to be so much bigger than Ms. Malinda. In the last couple of years, after all the grieving and homemade wine; I had put a little weight on me. Standing in the middle of the room round all them pretty clothes made me shame.

"Hush girl, I got all sizes in here. I wasn't always this thin."

The dress slipped right over my hips like it was made for me. I look like some of them women in the magazine.

"Take off them clogs you got on," she said hard-like. "Here, try these on." She handed me a pair of suede heels. Well, I lost my footing. I couldn't walk in no heels so she got out a pair of patent leather flats. I felt like Cinderella. Then she looked at me real serious.

"What I want to say is this. You are new here and I know you want to fit in and some of them outfits you been wearing are really brave, but darling, some of them bright African tops ain't for you. People will like or connect with you for who you really are. Don't try to change for change sake until you sure it's better than what you are. Almena, you are caring, honest and yes naïve. Some people will take advantage of that. Be yourself and it will work out much better. Do you understand what I mean?"

I shook my head yes, but it almost sound like I had done something wrong again.

"Now," she went on, "let's try a little make-up. I wish I could take that gold stuff out of your hair. That's not so hot to me." She made a sad face at me.

"Habibah just put that in. What? You don't like it?"

"No, it looks like you trying to get attention, but maybe it's a new style I don't know about." She turned my head from side to side, frowning up her nose.

"James is going to use my car. Almena, don't let him drive you too fast. I mean that in more ways than one," she winked at me and then she went on, "I told James to watch out for you, but I also want you to watch out for James, 'cause he can be a handful. We'll discuss some of his shenanigans later. But tonight, I want you to have a good time, you deserve it."

#‡#‡#‡#‡#‡#‡#‡#‡#

When James came out of the back room, all I could do was stare at his dark blue suit. He wore a baby blue tie and a matching handkerchief in his pocket. His shoes was blue and made outta some kinda snake. Chile, he was dressed!

Going back upstairs to hustle the kids along I found Glory leaning over the stair rail peering down. I kissed her on the top of her head. She looked shook up, I didn't know whether she like my outfit or not. She stood there twisting her undershirt around her waist. Grace went into the bathroom and locked the door. Then it come to me, this was the first time they would be without me.

"I'll be with you soon," I yelled down the stairs. "I need to have a word with the kids."

I managed to get Grace out the bathroom by pretending I needed to use it. I grabbed her under her arms and swung her around and until she started laughing.

"Don't be mad at me. I'll only be gone about three hours and I need you and Glory to make sure Ms. Malinda takes her 10 o'clock medicine. For all that tending I'm a give you a big surprise."

"I don't want no surprise. You look different," Grace pouted.

I stuck my thumb in my mouth and walked knock kneed until they both started laughing. "Come on now, help me out, I can't leave you if I think you mad with me. Besides, I'm sure I'll have a lot to tell you when I git back." My silliness won them over and we all went down in Ms. Malinda's room.

James had warmed the car up for me, a burgundy Cadillac with white leather inside. I had butterflies in my stomach. "What's Love Got to Do With It" was playing on the radio.

"I love this tune," James hummed along. Tina sounded hurt to me but I didn't mention it. Her words are hard and warning like to me. I wished he liked "I Feel for You" by Chaka Khan.

We pulled up in front of this bar-lounge called the Sandman. Flashing lights greeted us. A doorman opened the door for us. The street had many bars with people staggering from bar to bar. No drunks was allowed in the Sandman. The doorman asked them to move on. James was the perfect man; he took my arm and led me into the club. It was almost like walking into midnight. Slowly, my eyes was catching the low lighting and images began to take shape; colors and shadows formed. This was like weaving from your mind, with darkness as your companion. Your hands take total control until what you think is what you see.

Frame by frame the room came together. There was a horseshoe shaped bar, surrounded with blue velvet stools, the walls held pictures of famous musicians playing they instruments. James told me the musicians was famous 'cause I didn't really know. But they did look wrapped up in what they was doing in them pictures. Off to the left was about thirty tables with light blue table cloths and little glasses with candles in them. James led me to a little table right up front. Folks in New Haven sure know how to enjoy themselves. I bet Mama had never been to a place like this. James raised his hand. A waitress appeared. “Bring me a Long Island Iced Tea and for my lady, a Shirley Temple.” James ordered. She smiled at me and I began to feel comfortable. She had on a blue and sand colored African robe and a big matching scarf wrapped around her head. It was beautiful. I fought the need to tell her I had a robe like hers.

“Coming right up, sir. Would you care for a light snack with your drinks?

“No thanks. We’ve already had a wonderful dinner.” He winked at me.

The band hadn’t started yet but the club was lively. People wasn’t dancing but they was moving in they seats to the recorded music and swinging they heads to the jazzy beat. All I could do was grin. I tried to stop grinning but I couldn’t. These city people sure know how to live. James explained to me that we was going to hear Mr. Earl Hines, who according to him, was one of the greatest jazz pianists of all time. James had plenty of friends in here. They kept coming over and speaking, laughing, and wanting to know who I was. Well, not all of them wondered about me. This one lady was very interested in who I was. She had on a white suit with a suede cape around her shoulders. She studied me from my braids to my shoes. I felt like she was stripping me naked right there in the bar. She saw something wrong ‘cause she kept laughing loudly. I realized for the first time just how much of an outsider I was. She act like it’s alright to be rude to me. That woman strolled over to the bar and sat on a stool right in the middle of a bunch of tipsy women and pointed at me. They found her conversation all too funny. James took hold of both my hands and gave them a kiss. “The sight of decency disturbs some folks. Pay their envy no attention.” He started looking at me as if I was a prize. Some things you just know, I could tell the troublemaker used to be a friend of his.

He rubbed my back and, then louder than they laughter, James says, "You definitely are the star here tonight. Heaven must be at a loss! Did you fall from heaven?" I didn't know shit about what he was talking about but that was the nicest thing anyone ever asked me. I was not used to that kinda talk, so instead of answering him, I sat there grinning.

Mr. Hines played that piano like his fingers was the keys. His drummer would brush the drums and tambourines. His beat made the whole room tremble. When he was finished, everyone knew that they had heard the best. I wanted Mr. Hines to play on forever. His music made me see a breeze as his fingers ran the keys. A tingling settled in my spirit yet I was nailed to my seat. I got lost in the music and so did all the back-up musicians. I can't explain it but it was almost better than loving. *Oh Mercy*!

James excused hisself to talk to some of his men friends so I decided to order another drink. Since that Shirley Temple was like drinking Kool-Aid, I figured I'd have some of that iced tea James was drinking. I grabbed that tall glass of tea and drank it down real fast, thinking I would order another one for him. Instantly I knew something wasn't right. It tasted like Grandma's nerve medicine. I felt dizzy and tried to steady myself by holding on to the table but the feeling wouldn't go away. By the time James came back, I was stretched out on the tablecloth, crying and slobbering all over the place.

I stood up but couldn't walk straight so James picked me up and took me out of there. What a mess. I was so shame of myself. James drove me around with the windows open trying to sober me up. I had ruined his night. I wouldn't call it a look of disgust on his face; it was more like he smelled something. He didn't say too much to me. Mama was right; I needs to be still.

Soon as I could, I took the dress to the dry cleaners. Maybe they could remove saliva stains from silk. When the twins or Ms. Malinda asked how my night was I just said, "Oh, it was nice." I stayed out of James's way. I was sneaking around that house like a thief, shame-like.

CHAPTER TEN
Second – Skin Confusion

My weaving started back up. Some days I would spend six hours getting my patterns just right. When things bothered me or I make a fool of myself I always run to my weaving. It ain't so judging.

Grace and Glory had use of the whole house now. Ms. Malinda had really taken a liking to them. Glory was weaving pretty well for her age. She makes pot holders on a little loom. We will sew them together to make a bath mat, her first rug. Grace loves to read her books and she plays house doctor with Ms. Malinda. They scarring was coming along too. *Now, if I just don't go make a fool out of myself again, we will be okay.* I rocked every night but Mama and Grandma have not returned. I figured they probably was angry with me getting drunk and all.

I was in the kitchen one evening when James caught up with me. "Are you ever going to speak to me again?" he asked.

"I was wondering the same thing about you, I'm so sorry. I had never had iced tea like that before."

He laughed, "Almena, you's a treasure for sure. Sit down and let me talk to you. I really like you, but is there something I ought to know?" He seemed to be real concern, which made me nervous.

"Well, what do you what to know?"

"I want to know all of it. All of it. Like why do the kids sometimes call you Auntie Almena? I thought on the bus you said you was their mama. Are you running to or from something? Do you have any other family and why ain't those children in school yet? I see you can't drink liquor so whatever it is, it can't be that bad. If you let me, I think my sister and me might be able to help you."

My breath caught in my chest. I shrugged my shoulders.

He could tell by the look on my face that I wasn't going to answer him. I was fear frozen. "Girl, you are not going to answer me, are you? When you ready to tell me, I'll be right here for you." He got up from the table and walked toward the kitchen door and said in passing, "I like your hair without that gold stuff in it."

I thought on what James had said, but didn't I come here for a new start? Why must I go through the past? He's nosey, if you ask me. I guess I shouldn't feel that way. I think he only wanted to help but I don't really know him or his sister well enough to tell them everything. Mercy! If they know 'bout how dirty our lives had been and the killings and all. They might change they minds about us. Somehow, being considered country didn't seem so bad at all. Life is hard and I'm just one of them people that rewinds it. I'm going to weave a while and loose my mind and keep my mouth shut.

Weaving the bus was not going to be a problem. I recall almost every detail and what I didn't remember, Glory was right here to help. But weaving in a different place takes time for your fingers to remember the flow of stitching. Sometimes everything in a room has to stop for me to start. Weaving is a place too. When I weave a person, I go to a room that puts me in mind of them. Grandma, I can weave her face in the kitchen in one day, winkles and all. For the bus I was going to need a good quality silver thread to do the body of it so we got ready to go shopping.

Downtown New Haven had everything you wanted. There was two fabric stores. Grace and Glory ran up and down the aisles in a total trance at all the fabrics and threads available. We brought more than we could ever use. We ate hot dogs with sour cabbage on it, a first for me and I might add my last. Grace asked if she could buy

Auntie Malinda some candy. Of course I knew who would eat most of it but I went along and said yes. Glory wanted a new coloring book and we all got new outfits. I knew we needed to have church clothes 'cause at Thanksgiving, our praying needed some work. Don't get me wrong. We was all thankful but seemed like we couldn't say it like our hearts felt it. I was going to find us a church this week.

I told James that I needed more time before I could reveal all our lives to him or Ms. Malinda, not that we was in any kinda trouble but I needed to get my senses together and know who my friends are. I explained I didn't like to rush into things.

He sighed deeply, "I thought I was your friend."

"Then if you are, you'll still be my friend when we have that talk you want to have." He nodded and we tried to smile at each other, 'cause there was nothing else to say.

That night as I rocked, Grandma and Mama came to me talking so fast and together that I had to ask them to slow down so I could understand what they was saying. Grandma said, "I'm glad you are getting ready to find a church 'cause it would take the Lord to guide you through this life. Listen to me now. Stay away from nightclubs no matter how good the music is. The drinks are lethal. Almena, you been spending a lot of money, too. Where you keeping it?"

"In my purse hidden under the bed." I whispered.

"Chile, you can do better than that. Find yourself a better hiding place. You got to make that money last you for at least a year or two; till you find a job and the children is settled in school. Did you sell my estate?"

"Of course not! We might go back home in the summers to enjoy the country." She was pleased with that.

"Never forget your roots, girl."

"It ain't time to go courting yet. There will be plenty time for that in the future," Mama said. "Your housemates," as she called them, "are good people but they done had some mess in they lives too and you never know when a rat might go back to his hole."

Mama softly added, “However, it is time to let them children know that their kin is gone forever. I know you don’t want them to hurt. You suffered and I saw that. But, see Almena, you doing better now, honey, it just takes time. Let them children know you love them and nobody, especially James, will take you away from them. Show them that family rug ‘cause, to me, everybody on it looks happy and should be remembered that way. Don’t be afraid of their questions; answer them as best you can. Let them cry now for their losses, and then love them into their future. Tell them you understand the loss of a family ‘cause you lost yours. Tell them they mama would be proud of the good little girls they are. Her wish for them is to grow into fine young ladies, and that they mama is always in their hearts. Talk often about her brothers too. As for their father, Malcolm, let them know he was sick and that’s what made him so evil. I’m glad you going to find a church, but be careful. Some of them can scare you. Let them little girls want to be good for goodness sake and because it’s the right thing, not because the devil will get you. Do good for their mother’s sake, their brother’s memory and for the sake of Jesus. All this will take time but stay on this course of action and you’ll never fail. Your housemates, as I said before, have past lives that ain’t too pleasant but we are all flawed and nobody on earth can judge. Just be yourself and never make a decision without thinking about it first. Time is something you got, use it. I wish I was there with you, but I didn’t take time to think about what I was doing. I love you, my chile, when you wrong and when you right.” And with that, she was gone.

Grandma hung around. She said, “Don’t be a hot ass for that James or Malinda. You hear me?”

“I hear you.” I had a lot of thinking to do and a lot of courage to pull from somewhere.

Waking early and thinking about what to do I rocked until I heard the twins whispering in they bed. “Get on up, you two! We going to the park and the library today!”My voice was breaking as I spoke. Grace bounced off the bed and into the front room.

"Did you sleep in that chair last night?" She asked

"No sweetheart I didn't. Come give me a hug." I reached for her and held on tight. My hug was too tight. She pulled back and look me dead in the eye and said, "Your eyes are red, no rocking for you tonight."

"Okay but, get dressed. I want to tell you something very important." Glory stood in the doorway, rubbing sleep out her eyes.

"Can we get some hot chocolate before we go?" Grace asked.

"Yes and first one dressed can get a large one." They raced to the bathroom.

The weather was brutal, colder now than we was accustomed to. We suited up with snowsuits, hat, gloves and boots. Images of that morning in Elktown and they mama's death ran through my head. Nothing was as cold as seeing that. Still, I was sweating like a pig. Telling is hard. I will never understand the language of death.

When we got to the park, I took them to the swings and I ask "How have you liked New Haven so far?"

"Oh, we like it here. It's very big and Auntie Malinda and Mr. James are nice. I like my new clothes too," Grace said.

"I'm glad you like it here, 'cause I'm thinking this may be our permanent home. You see, when we left Elktown we was not in a good place. Sometimes, bad things happen to wonderful people. Your mama, one of the sweetest women in the world, and your brothers was killed in that town and went on to Heaven. It was best for us to leave. It was what she would have wanted. I believe that's why she left you with me."

I felt like I had just swallowed a bunch of hot rocks.

"I know I told you that they would come to us one day, but they won't. I knew how frighten you would have been if you thought you was all alone. So I kept a secret from you for a while. I will always be here for you, just like I am now."

The tears flowed from they desperate eyes, and Glory's shaking returned. "We will always love them, your family, and they will always love us. Only they are in Heaven, which is a faraway place."

Grace found her voice. "My daddy hurt my mama, didn't he?"

"Yes, he did," I said. "Cause he was sick in his mind and sometimes sickness like he had makes you evil. I know you are sad now but in time we will figure out ways to make your mama and brothers so proud of us. I promise I will never leave you. You are my children when you wrong and when you right."

We hugged and moaned in pain. Tears ran from they eyes, as they realized what happened. They tears come so fast, I couldn't think. I had no words to sop up they pain so I joined them. We stood in that state until our sobs turned too painful for our throats. We was overcome by something I have no name for. They cried for they losses, for even as kids they knew they lost a mighty precious part. When I finally got myself together I felt like a thirty pound brick was off my neck. One I would pick up if I could bring they mama back. I wasn't relieved. I was just sore....all over sore.

"My darlings, if you ever have questions about what I'm telling you, please ask me. I will try to answer them or I will find someone who can."

Glory said, "So what do we call you now?"

"Still call me your auntie, 'cause that what I am. Just call me. I don't ever want to be without you. And if anyone ever asks about your mama, you could say she in heaven helping out. Come to think of it, we ain't completely lost. Nothing is ever lost as long as you know where it is, and we know where your mama is. This is our new start, you see. We're going to laugh again, because your mama wouldn't want it any other way. We have shared suffering, and now it's time to share love."

We left the park hand in hand and with one last promise, no more secrets. We didn't go to the library that day. We had learned enough. We went back to the house to our weaving and thinking. For days we sank pretty low. Our hearts was past heavy. We loved on each other and assured each other that we was super girls who would make it no matter what came our way. Glory started that holding on to my skirts again and Grace seemed to have an I'm-okay-attitude with a hint of bitterness to it. Her little face looked like she had just tasted a spoiled lemon. I knew just how she felt. I thought I was handling it all very well.

Like anything else time will tell.

CHAPTER ELEVEN
Searchings

Monday morning, I went about seven blocks up on Whalley Street and found a bank. The First Federal Savings and Loan, it was called. I put twenty-three thousand dollars in there. Them people treated us like royalty. The manager was showing me how to make withdrawals and all. Then a spark came up out of Grace's spirit as she said, "We rich, ain't we?" I laughed at that and said, "No sweetheart, but we'll be all right this year."

Looking for a church was going to be my next thing to do. There was so many around Dixwell Avenue. There was almost as many churches as there was liquor stores. Some had signs out front saying they would have Bible Study on Wednesday nights. I asked Ms. Malinda about church and where we should go and she said, "Upstairs on your knees 'cause there are more devils in church than in your room."

She had begun to look a little sickly again. Bags of flabby skin hung under her eyes and a white pastry crust stayed in the corners of her mouth. Her talk was sharp. I know she ain't at her best. *I'm going to make her some of my soup to pick her up.*

While weaving that night, I look out the window just in time to see James helping Habibah into the car. He was dressed-up and she was looking very nice too. I guessed he figured if one fish didn't work out, he could always catch another. Still I was bothered by it, even mad you might say. I should be glad I was not tricked that night I went out with him. *Oh Mercy!*

The First Emphatic Faith Church was a big gray and

white building that used to be some kinda warehouse. There was large dark curtains that stood high on the walls, and light purple carpet covered the floors. All the men, women, and children was dressed casual like, 'cause this was a mid-week Bible Study. Some people smiled at you but not many. Everybody was trying to get to his or her own special seat. The twins and I sat in the back waiting for the Emphatic Word. Them people started singing. The singing was good, but long. They must have sung over an hour and a half. When the pastor did get up to teach, the twins was sleep. The pastor's name was Joel Jones and he stood tall and at ease. He opened his large bible and in a smooth voice began to teach. "Turn to John 3:3, Verily, verily I say unto thee, Except a man be born again, he cannot see the kingdom of God. Brothers and sisters, this is the word of the Lord."

"Amen" the members said.

"Amen indeed, but what does that mean to you?" The pastor stepped away from his stand and it looked like he was looking right at me. "It simply means you must turn away from your sinful ways and follow the way of the Word, the ways so laid out before you in your Bible. This is your road map; this is the way no matter what life you've been in. This is the answer. Why? Because God loves you and no matter what you've done, God still loves you. Forgiveness and salvation are yours if you follow God's Word.

"Alright now!" An elderly lady began to dance up and down the aisles.

"There are promises in God's words that you wouldn't even dream to ask for and he is not a man that he should lie." The pastor paced. "If you're tired of coming up with the wrong answers, maybe it's because the wrong captain is controlling the ship. Give control of your situation to the One who never fails and trust Him to work it out for you. Oh, it might not be the way you would work it out, but your way is not working out too good and sometimes hardships may occur but nothing is too hard for God."

"Amen. Hallelujah. Hallelujah!" The members did a

jumping joy dance.

Now I never was lazy, but if the Lord would take over my problems that would sure enough give me some free time. Of course, I did want to teach the children not to go down some of the routes I went in. The church people had a lot of announcements about children church activities, usher meetings, things to buy, and coming events. As I listened, the "Born Again" messages struck me the most, if only I could go back with all my wits and do my life over. I know I could do it better. I couldn't wait for Sunday to come, 'cause I was going to find out some more about this being "Born Again." I couldn't bring my mind around that part yet.

The twins went up to bed as soon as I opened the front door. Them kids was tired. I decided to check on Ms. Malinda. I knocked lightly but there was no answer so I tapped a little louder and still no answer. I turned the knob and once again there she was on the floor helpless again. This time I called the police 'cause her breathing was hardly even noticeable. Her eyes was doing strange things, moving to the back of her head and all. They brought an ambulance with them and went right to work on her.

James came in while they was putting her on a stretcher. He went to the hospital with his sister and I sat up worrying. Hours later he returned. I ran down the steps to meet him to find out how Ms. Malinda was doing.

"She doing as well as she can." A dark look came over his face.

"What's that suppose to mean?" I ask. "Is that cold back again?"

He opened his mouth and then closed it. With a broken voice he said, "Is that what she says she got? Almena, my sister been battling cancer for years. I came because she called for me to come home. She will get stronger this time the doctor said, but she ain't got too long."

I sat down right there on the stairs folding my knees to my chest and hung my head down. I was afraid to move, afraid to speak, because everywhere I'd ever been seem like death just left or was on its way. James walked back to his room, sliding his hand along the wall as if he needed to be held up. It was hard to sleep that night, and I didn't want to rock at all.

We was spared this time. On the day Ms. Malinda came home the twins was peeping out the parlor window. As soon as James opened the door, the kids ran to her. Glory had her by the waist and Grace held her arm. They was squealing. James took her camel hair coat off and Grace yelled "Thank you Savior, in her best Holy Ghost voice.

"I been missing you," Glory's deep whining voice gave way to laughter in the hallway.

"You hungry? Have they been feeding you?" Glory was looking at a large bag of pills James held on to.

"Will you let her get to her room, please?" I quietly said. But really I just wanted to get my hug in, too.

"We made you some chicken noodle soup and we got hot biscuits, if you want, Ms. Malinda." She moved steady but she was thinner than ever.

"I got just what I need, some love from y'all. Now, get up here on this bed with me, Grace and Glory. Tell me all about what's been happening. Grace fell back on the bed and said, "You wouldn't believe where the devil lives." We all burst out laughing.

"Almena honey, no soup please, that's all them hospital people know. Can we please have some ribs this evening? Ms. Malinda winked at me. "And ice cream and apple pie and chocolate candy and just anything but soup."

"Coming right up." As I left the room my spirits rose as the sound of they good-time talking followed me to the kitchen.

I had the house smelling good with them ribs in no time. James came in about two hours later saying, "I know I'm in the right house now. I smell food cooking; damn, it smells good in here."

"This is one of my special dishes. The meat gonna fall right off the bone."

"I'm ready for that! By the way, country woman, how you like that church you going to?"

"I think I'm going to love it and the kids like Sunday School. Why you asking?"

"Did you know that Pastor Joel used to be a friend of mine? In fact, he still is a friend. We just went different ways," James boasted. "When we was young teenagers we was kinda wild. Chasing girls and racing cars and of course gambling, but he has always loved the church."

That's the most James and me had said to each other in a while. I was jealous of him and Habibah so I didn't have much to say.

"You know, they got a school at that church that teaches kids all the way to the eighth grade. Did you know that?"

"No, I didn't know that, but I'll ask what I need to do to get the kids in school."

"Just tell me that you want them to go and they are in. Me and Joel go way back. I'll get them kids in school just like that," he snapped his fingers.

"Now listen, James. I don't have no papers for them girls, you know. The twins' Mama was a friend of mine who has passed on and them kids is all I got, and they only got me. We don't want no trouble from them school people."

"What happen? Was she sick?" His voice got soft.

"I ain't ready to talk about that now." I turn away from him to hide my nervousness.

"Ok, I can understand the loss of a friend but all I know is there hasn't been such happiness in this house since...well, since never. I can get them in that school with no problem." He tapped his finger alongside his temple. "Now, let's see. We'll put them in the second grade, 'cause I heard them reading and they smart. Doctor Moss will give them whatever shots they need. Just leave it to me. Lady, you're their legal guardian as of right now. I know people and I can get things done." He had his chest stuck out.

"Yes...I know. I see how you got my hair braider done."

"Now, don't tell me you jealous. Are you?" he asked, now smiling that smile of his and rubbing his hands together.

I turned around and basted my ribs some more. James is a big tease. I hope he could do what he said he could.

We all ate in the dining room that evening. Along with the ribs, we had baked beans with maple syrup and corn on the cob with hot and cheesy corn bread. Lip-smacking good. I woulda bet Habibah couldn't fix that kinda meal. James and me cleaned up the kitchen. Thank goodness he didn't tease me no more.

The care of the household and Ms. Malinda was all mine these days. I cleaned every corner of that house. I never thought anyone would trust me enough to be they nurse and head housekeeper. I had not made one mistake and I was good at it. Ms. Malinda wouldn't hear of rent from me. I liked the responsibility.

About a week later, after my talk with James, I answered the door and there stood Pastor Joel smiling at me. "Oh, my goodness. Pastor Joel please come on in. Would you like to speak with Ms. Malinda? I'll let her know you are here." Pastor Joel's smile is catching I grinned with him.

"Good afternoon, sister Johnstone."

I closed the door and ushered him into the parlor and turn to leave the room to let Ms. Malinda know she had company.

When he said, "wait sister, I would like to speak with Malinda, but first I want to meet the new second graders that will be attending our school."

Happy does not express the feelings I had. I wanted to hug him but, him being a man of the Lord I managed to hold back.

"Pastor, wait right here. I'll go get them. You don't know but my prayers are answered. They schooling is so important to me." I held some tissue to my mouth to keep from shouting.

I ran up the stairs taking two at a time. Calling them and laughing at the same time. Thank goodness they was pretty much dressed decently in jeans with red and white African style tops. When we reached back downstairs Pastor Joel was standing in the parlor by the fireplace just like the saint he was. 'This is Grace." I put my hand to her head. And this shy one here is Glory." I beamed.

"There are no finer names, young ladies. I speak about your names often. I've come to invite you to be a part of our second grade class. Now, how would you like that?"

"Yeah," they both started jumping around.

"You must've heard how smart we are, didn't you? Grace asked, her eyes bright with excitement.

"Are we going to be in the same room?" Glory softly mumbled up at him while swinging onto my skirt.

"I certainly did hear how smart you are. Your Uncle James is highly impressed and I would not dream of separating two lovely little ones like you. You'll be in the same classroom and you'll begin school after this Sunday. So welcome to our school!"

"Thank you. Oh boy Grace! We going to be in the same room." Glory hollered as they ran back upstairs.

I stood there with my hands folded around my elbows. If he noticed Glory's tics he never showed any sign of it. James had come through for us. I think I'm going to cook him something special.

"Now, where is Malinda? Let me see my longtime friend."

I knocked on Ms. Malinda door. "Ms. Malinda you got company."

"Who is it?"

"It's Pastor Joel."

She yelled back, "Tell him I ain't dead yet so go sing 'Amazing Grace' somewhere else." I was so shame, but Pastor just said, "Let me handle this. Malinda, I'm coming in because I know you are not dead. Dead people scare me and I ain't never been scared of you. In fact, I was wondering when you coming to hear your old boyfriend preach?" He entered her room and you could hear the two of them laughing past 9 o'clock that night.

Rocking and weaving that night, Mama simply said,

"You did good."

My New Haven rug was coming along pretty good, too. I had to remove the ugly face I had stitched on Habibah, cause that girl wasn't ugly at all. I must of done that when my feelings was defeated about her and James. In fact, I liked her. Besides I needed my hair done for Sunday services at church. I was going to ask Ms. Malinda if she felt well enough to go with me, too. Maybe Habibah would do her hair here at the house. Little did I know that was an idea straight from the devil. Ms. Malinda did seem softer toward the church after her talk with Pastor Joel. She asked me how the people dress and if there was fainting. She even asked me how many times they took up collections. I think she wants to go, but something is holding her back.

Ms. Malinda started calling me at night to sit with her and talk. She looked fine. Just needed to say some things. "Almena," she said, "did you know that you live in the best whorehouse there ever was in New Haven?"

Well, I thought it was her medicine talking but she was serious and then she told her story. I know when to be quiet and the remark about a whorehouse had shut me right up.

"When I came here, I was a little younger than you with a husband that was thirty years older than me. Otis, that was his name, was good to me but I was in my twenties and he wasn't no fun. He just worked and came home all greasy and fell asleep on the couch. He would leave me with no one to talk to and no loving to speak of. When we did get affectionate it was over before I knew he was loving me. But he brought me this house, and sometimes he took me shopping. I bought the latest fashions, but I didn't have nowhere to wear them 'cause Otis believed a woman place was in her house. He didn't even trust church people. He used to say, 'All deacons is pimps.' I was so lonely but my mama couldn't understand that."

She'd say, "Girl you got a big house and nice clothes and a man who really loves you. Stop complaining."

"Where we from, Sumter, South Carolina, most of my friends was barely getting by and many had children by different men and no one to help take care of them. Every summer I would go down South and even if I was miserable, I was always thankful to come home. James, being the baby boy, sometimes I would bring him back here with me for the summer, just to give Mama a rest. Our father had gone missing about two years after James was born so it was just us three. Otis even sent money to Mama. The railroad paid good money to men like Otis who could fix engines. We never really wanted for nothing except I wanted excitement. What's the use in being in a city if you still live like you in the country? That's what I thought anyway. James, he kept hisself busy fighting city boys, or chasing fast girls, and he would gamble on a roach if it would move. He had fun here in New Haven in the summertime."

"Then, one day Otis was working on an engine and the cars had not been secured. He fell and the train car ran him over. "Gone just like that," she clapped her hands. "That's when I really found out what lonely means. Mama came for a while but she missed her gardens and house and friends so she went on home. James, he stayed on with me, I'm shame to tell now, but honey, we partied. The railroad had to pay me every month 'cause it was they fault I didn't have no husband. And me and James let the good times roll. We brought in bands and women of all shades to dance the night away. I am an excellent dancer. I could grind with the best of them." She popped her bony fingers. "And as time..."

I looked over at Ms. Malinda and she had fell asleep right in the middle of her good story. I covered her up and tiptoed upstairs. Oh, how I hoped she would finish that story. I couldn't imagine we was living in a whorehouse. *Oh Mercy! Now look what I done got us into.*

CHAPTER TWELVE
Faith

I made up my mind that I was going to join the church. After all, the girls would be attending school there and they liked the Sunday School. I don't quite understand much about the "Born Again" experience but people would shout and cry and then they seem like they felt better. This one man would take to running all around the church, arm waving and spit slipping from his mouth as he talked funny and fast. Some of them church people even looked better the next Sunday after being hit with what they called the spirit. So when Pastor Joel asked if any wanted to give they life to the Lord that particular service I walked up to the front and a big smile spread across his face. Tears ran down my face. I had held them all week. The Lord had answered my prayers and I wasn't even a part of the church yet. Things have never happen for me like that and it was choking me with tenderness. I was pleased, but I did secretly hope the Lord wouldn't want my life too soon 'cause I had seen and been around enough death.

In order to become a member of the church, I had to take lessons on what it meant to be a Born Again and what the mission of the church was. Thank goodness 'cause I was still confused. The classes was good, they help me a lot and I knew for certain that I wanted to be a member of this church. They explained forgiveness, salvation, holiness, and how to live right. Told me that your sisters and brothers in the church would love you no matter what, just like the Lord does. Can you imagine that? Right here on earth somebody would always see about you and lead you on the right path. I felt like I had hit the numbers. No wonder them people in church was dancing and falling out. Soon as I could, I was going to fall out, too.

Now, I had been wearing clothes Ms. Malinda picked out of her closet for me, so I was the best dressed. I had to join a group within the church to do my duty as a member. Since I didn't know nobody, I joined the greeters. That way I could get to know everybody who came into the church.

Well time passed. The children went to school, and Ms. Malinda had good days and some bad. None that she needed to be in the hospital for. I prayed for her loud and often in that church.

James was keeping to hisself a lot. Him and Habibah was still going out every now and again. He was drinking more than necessary. He walked in one evening and I could smell him coming. He put his liquored up breath in my face saying, "You saved yet?"

I covered my nose when I answered, "Yes and you ought to get a hold of yourself, too."

"I'm waiting to see what saving do for you." He was standing there swaying and picking lint off his coat. It seems like James ain't fit to think 'cause he takes long pauses between talking.

James was beginning to make me mad lately with the way he was making fun at everything I did at church, but I was determined he was not going to stop me 'cause for the first time in a long time I was peaceful and he was sinful and I knew that much.

The sisters in my group was pleasant and invited me to all they functions but I couldn't really attend, 'cause I was still taking care of Ms. Malinda. And of course, I still had the children to see about.

A sister name Mavis was very friendly. She asks me my address to send me event notices and when I gave it, her mouth flew open. "You mean the big white house on the corner."

"Yes," I said proudly.

She took the number down and moved away from me quickly. The rest of the service I caught them sisters whispering and pointing in my directions. The news of my address went around the church like bees to a honey comb. Them folks was buzzing. Something was up and it wasn't just Jesus. It seem like our address was off-limits to them church people. Some of the sisters started acting just plain evil with me. I wanted to go to the pastor and ask him what I had done wrong but it sounded like such a small thing. I mean we had people in the church that was sick, no jobs, no homes or about to lose they marriages and here I was going to bother him with a why-don't-they-like-me problem. I said to myself I'll wait till these other problems git fix and maybe if I tried to be more friendly, they'll be more loving to me.

Coming home one Wednesday night after Bible Study, I saw the ambulance at the house. I released the twin's hands and ran as fast as I could. "No more death! No more! Please, no more!" I muttered just above a whisper. James had called for help for his sister. Two ambulance attendants was working on Ms. Malinda. They took her in the ambulance with an oxygen mask on and I went with them. I yelled at Grace and Glory to stay in the house and we'll be right back. James seemed a little rocky to me. Torn down as usual. Things didn't look good that night. Oxygen mask means breathing trouble to me. The doctor at the hospital, her last name was Angel, told me that Ms. Malinda needed surgery to remove a tumor that was hampering her breathing. It would be about a three-hour procedure, and afterwards Ms. Malinda would be able to breathe better and go home in a few days. That doctor seemed sure everything would be well. I was so uneasy but with a last name like Angel I began to believe every word she said. Especially when she said, "I've seen things like this happen and the patient survives longer after the surgery is done." James was looking lost so I stayed at the hospital with Ms. Malinda and sent him home to be with the twins. James is good with the kids and I knew he wouldn't leave them. We had already been gone about two hours.

The first three hours went by uneventful. In the sixth hour of waiting my throat began to get tight, and by the eighth hour I was making frequent trips to the ladies room to relieve myself of nervousness. On the tenth hour, I approached the doors leading to the operating room and waited for someone, anyone, to come out. I cried out to whoever came out "Can you please go back and ask them what is going on with Ms. Malinda Grey. She should have been out at least six hours ago!" They came back with the old stand-by answer. "Her surgeon is finishing up now and will be out to speak with you shortly." Finally the doctor came out, she looked at me like a cat that had swallow a fur ball and said, "We ran into some problems, your aunt's spleen started bleeding and we had to remove it. She's now in the recovery room and you can see her in a few minutes. She's had a rough time but she's a strong woman. It will be a while before she'll heal."

There was a scream in my head. I ran to the recovery room. My heart began thrumming like the wings of a caged wild bird. Heat passed across my forehead, yet when I got closer to the glass door marked recovery room, I froze. One peep in brought the scream I had been holding back. It burst forth with full force. From what I could see there was tubes everywhere coming out of Ms. Malinda's body. Two attendants push me back to a waiting room. One said, "We're doing all we can. Maybe you shouldn't be here alone. Please let us work on her and you can come back later." One of the attendants then gave me a cup of water, some tissues, and excused herself.

I don't remember the cab ride home. Sleep came only 'cause I was worn out. If Ms. Malinda didn't survive, once again it would be the twins and me fending against this world alone. Silently I pleaded. *Not now, I just need a little more time. God, I just got saved, I love you. Why now? I never knew hurt could repeat so often. Lord, this can't be your will for us. Lord, I know you did not bring us out of the country for this. Lord, have mercy. We're still broken from the killings we ran away from. Have mercy. We need a healing against all odds. Lord, you know that our lives have been littered with pain. Not now. Ms. Malinda looked liked she had been attacked with a hacksaw. Couldn't she go softly in the night?*

As the sun move over the house, I sat rocking. When the girls came into the front room declaring that they ain't going to school, I didn't push them. To tell the truth I was getting what they called depressed by all this possibility of death and pushing against the scents of life as, Grandma used to say.

About noon the following day, I returned to the hospital. To my surprise Ms. Malinda had been moved to a room. I stood in the room looking at wires, IVs and a small TV drawing mountain and valleys on a screen. I thought this was a good sign; at least she was in a room so maybe she was going to recover. Her face was ash like; the lines on her forehead was so deep they look like a field of corn. A jerky move of her eyelids almost cause me to upchuck. I lean down and said, "Ms. Malinda, I'm here."

She grimaced around that tube that went down her throat and then suddenly the television blinked and the lines on it stop climbing and a loud humming surrounded us.

"Fight! Ms. Malinda, fight for your life. Don't let nothing take your life!"

I ran out of the room and pleaded with the nurse to call the doctors because my aunt was dying. She called for help. I stood over Ms. Malinda still commanding her to fight for her life. "Fight for our little family, for without you our sanity is at stake. We need you to be here in our new start. Please Ms. Malinda you are a big part of our dream." The screen lines jumped a couple of times yet continued to loudly hum. Finally, the team of doctors from the ICU was running along side of her bed making every effort to save her. That same nurse once again came and walked me away from the area. "Come on, miss. Let them work. I'll come get you when things are better." The hardest thing in the world at a time like this is to wait. A large bright light over the nurses' station was beating down on my nerves and made my head bob as I tried to wait and breath steady. It may have been minutes but it seemed like hours when she came and told me that Ms. Malinda was stable.

"What is stable?" I said with tears in my voice.

"It means she is fighting and holding on to life and that's a good sign."

Six days later, Ms. Malinda was sitting up in bed. She had lost a lot of weight but she was talking about going home. I was so grateful to be able to tell Grace and Glory she was so much better. I gave them a hug, "You'll go on back to school and make-up your work cause our dream is still alive and well. We going to make it this time. Ain't nobody going to die or stop us now."

Then I started thinking about that church I was going to. Not one of them greeters came to help us, watched the children, or offered any kinda assistance, not even a ride to the hospital. This was a church that spoke of love and oneness. I found out the hard way, that oneness could mean you are on your own. My church sisters knew I was going through hell. Not one of them was by my side. I knew they couldn't heal Ms. Malinda but it seemed like since they was so full of love, they could have stood with me to aid me in whatever way they could. I may not have been the quickest but I wasn't stupid. Pastor Joel didn't even come to pray with me. I had to get in my rocking chair to figure this one out.

When Ms. Malinda came home, we celebrated Christmas. A couple of weeks late but it was a great day for everyone. For Grace and Glory, I found twin Cabbage Patch dolls. Only one had eye glasses on and the other had a nipple in her mouth.

Glory squealed as she grabbed the one with the glasses on. Grace took her doll and said with a laugh "We got to break you from all this nipple sucking."

They jumped around, pretending to be real mamas. When they found out the dolls had birth certificates, they set right down to fill them out. They was acting like real mamas taking care of they babies.

I had knitted a camel scarf with dark brown trim for Ms. Malinda. She modeled it for me. I had to laugh 'cause she had her mouth pouted out like she was cute but her hair was scary. It stood on her head in a point. James presented each one of us with a box of candy and them kids went right to eating. A large box sat on the parlor coffee table. James says, "Almena close your eyes." I did and when I open them, Glory and Grace stood on each side of a trophy with the words "World's Best Auntie" on it. James had taken them to the awards store one day when I was at the hospital. I was so touched my eyes filled up with water. Happy tears. I had never won a trophy before or felt so loved.

I told everybody I had a surprise for them. I went to the hall closet and presented them with my family rug. "Chile....this is beautiful." Ms. Malinda ran her hands over it.

"The people look real. Girl, you need to open up a shop," James added. "Look at the lights in the people's eyes." But what gave me the most pleasure was Grace and Glory, through tears, smiled and said, "That's our first family. That's my mama, my brothers, and us." They kept touching and saying, "How did you get Mama's hair so right or Melvin's eyes just so?" They even laughed at Percy's hair.

"Thank you, Auntie," Grace said and gave me a big kiss. "Now I know we will never be without them. It looks like they watching us."

I thought it might bring sadness but it didn't. It seem like it was healing for the girls. They had a rug full of people who loved them and room full of people who loved them. How blessed can you get? It has been a happy and exciting day for all and when I looked over at Ms. Malinda she had fell asleep.

James help me put her to bed and out the door he went. James is always running somewhere lately. He don't even keep hisself up like he used to. I figured between his sister's illnesses and running after Habibah, his appearance wasn't on his mind. I know, I need to stop seeing so much, but I've accepted that I was made this way.

Time passed and Ms. Malinda looked good except for that hair of hers. I did the best I could with it but it still was a mess. I went over to the braid shop and ask Habibah if she could come to the house and braid Ms Malinda hair and of course she said she would be there as soon as she could. Now with all I had to do around the house, I forgot to tell Ms. Malinda that Habibah was coming to do her hair.

When Habibah came later that evening, I tapped lightly on the door and we went right in. Ms. Malinda looked up from the television and bucked her eyes while grabbing her hand mirror. She held that mirror up high like she was going to whip on us. "Ms. Malinda, this is Habibah. She's come to do your hair. I forgot to tell you it was going to be today."

With anger in her voice, she raised up. "I know you did forget 'cause if you did I would have told you I don't want no strong smelling African touching my hair. Get her out of here. She's funking up the whole room." Ms. Malinda was puffing bull-like.

"Ms. Malinda you don't mean that." Habibah push toward the bed, her eyes drawn tight like a cat's.

"What did she say? Oh no, I will not take insults from a person who cannot clean her own ass. I was brought up to respect elders but I do not discriminate when it comes to rudeness. You will always remember me if you live to tell it." Anger boiled up and poured from her lips with a hard accent. I stood in front on Habibah and lightly push her towards the door.

"Shhh, shhh now. Don't get your feelings hurt. Ms. Malinda isn't well and maybe we could do it another time." I could see Habibah was really mad and ready to whip on Ms Malinda if I hadn't been there. I had to get Habibah out of there fast. She wasn't about to be talked to like that. I pushed her again, closed the door and pleaded with Habibah to leave. She left but she called Ms. Malinda a "Sheila toppie." I don't really know what she meant but she thought it fit Ms. Malinda.

Getting Ms. Malinda back and comforted in the bed was hard, I ran a cool wash cloth across her face, lotioned her back and held her in a hug until her breathing returned to normal.

"Ms. Malinda, why you so mad at Africans or is it just James's friend Habibah?" With moist eyes she continued her story she started before she went into the hospital. Her words fell like heavy dust in the room.

"I told you 'bout my first husband dying and all and how me and James partied every week. Well it turned, Almena, from just partying to a business. The women was prostitutes James and his friend, Good Doing Dog, brought in from New York. Overnight, this house was full of men and when they wasn't downstairs in the basement gambling, they was upstairs renting rooms out to be with the women. I know it was awful but the money was good. First money trickled in, and then it became a waterfall. My life was a big ol' party. I was wearing pretty clothes. And since I wasn't sleeping with the men, I excused all my wrongs. I was keeping them girls off the street. I made sure they was clean and all. I made up all kinds of excuses for running a whorehouse. You can justify anything if you try hard enough. Did you know that?"

"Yes, Ms. Malinda. I know, but sometimes your reasoning is good, ain't it?"

"No, unless you're a child, it's not good. And me and James was well past childhood."

"Suppose you was tricked, Ms. Malinda."

"Listen now, all tricks get old, and you suppose to have enough sense to not touch things that ain't right. Anyway what's so hard about saying, I don't know about that or let me think about it? It's easy if you ain't greedy, looking for something for nothing or just plain crazy. I want you to stop leaning on I've been tricked and stop looking like a dog waiting for a treat after a trick."

CHAPTER THIRTEEN
Sabua

Ms. Malinda got her legs caught up in the bed covers and I heard something crack. I jumped. She was getting serious about owning up to her faults and I thought maybe I better calm her down. "Ms. Malinda, let's say a nice prayer and you have a blessed evening," I suggested.

"What's the matter? Did I hit home with my talk about learning from being tricked?" Her eyes was bucked wide open. "Don't stop an old bitty when she trying to testify. You need to hear this. Go get me a glass of water and let me finish."

I went to the kitchen. *This is what I get for being nosey; Malinda Grey was almost shouting like a deacon, Oh Mercy!*

When I came back, Ms. Malinda took several long sips and continued on with her story. "The party house went on for about two maybe three years with no trouble until, and I never will forget this, the blackest man I ever did see come to the house with Good Doing Dog. He was the color of coal. He had this funny accent and bright white teeth. He was from South Africa, he claimed. His name was Sabua. His arms was muscular, his body slim. He didn't talk to none of the girls and didn't gamble either. He was dress in a fine burgundy silk suit tailor-made just for him. His shirt and tie was matching and even his socks was burgundy. But the thing that really laid me out was he had on burgundy alligator shoes. This darkie was clean or as the kids say, he was sterilized. I was impressed, chile.

He sat, charming me all night. He stood when I entered the room, lit my cigarettes, and commented on my hair, my dress, even my feet. Ooh chile, my shit didn't stink to him or so I thought. He started taking me out of the house to restaurants and all. We went to plays in New York, and after about three months he brought me a big diamond ring and asked me to be his wife. Now, me being love struck, I never did ask him where he got the money to do all them things and I don't think I much cared. His attention had just swept my senses away.

"I have to return to Africa on business, but I will be back in about a month. When I return will you marry me?" He asked on his knees while holding my hand.

"Oh Yes!" I told him. "A month was fast but...." Ms. Malinda had drifted off again, just at the good part. I was almost tempted to wake her. But I needed to check on the twins and get some sleep myself. I went to turn out the lights in the front hallway and make sure the doors was locked, and there, laid out drunk was James, his body sprawled out between the two doors. Now I said to myself, *I didn't sign up for all of this.* He's testing my limits, so I kicked at him. "James, James get up. James!" My voice was sharp but not loud. "Get yourself to bed before the kids come down here and see you like this."

It was a struggle for him. He sat up blinking his bloodshot eyes at me. I grasped his arm and pulled him to his feet and lead him down the hall toward his room. With slobber slipping out of his mouth he whispered in my ear "Damn, Baby, I know you want me but we ain't got to run, do we?" I shoved him in his room, closed his door and shook my head. *Oh Mercy*!

That night I rocked hard but again I didn't hear from Mama or Grandma. I couldn't help thinking the worst. *Maybe they gone to the everlasting. Now, ain't that just like them not to say goodbye.*

The next day around about noon, I sat with Ms.

Malinda at lunchtime and even if it was her soaps time, I wanted to get to the end of her story. About twenty minutes into the usual arguments of Victor and Vicky on the television, I couldn't hold myself no longer.

"Ms. Malinda, your stories are way better than these. Tell me what happen when Sabua came back."

She laughed. "Yes, I suppose my life is more interesting. Now where was I? Oh yes, when Sabua came back he brought his three sisters with him. They were dressed in fancy African clothing, bright yellow and greens but kinda hard to understand because they didn't really speak English. They had beautiful names I couldn't pronounce and I could never remember who was who. I thought the plan was for them to be here for our wedding. Almena, within days they were working with the other girls, giving a humping kinda dance before the men. Their dancing drove the men crazy but I didn't say a thing. Money makes you be quiet sometimes. About two weeks later Sabua and I were married, right here in the parlor."

"That man loved the color burgundy. He told me that burgundy was the color of wealth and power in his country. He wanted to do the whole house in that color. I didn't mind at all. I was still in the worship stage of my marriage. A couple of months went by and his sisters were still with us. I was beginning to wonder when they were going home. When I asked Sabua, he told me that they had six-month visas. Okay, I could do another four months. That didn't seem that long to me, but these women were getting kinda nerve racking. I explained to him one night that he was upstairs with them a lot and I was getting a jealous feeling. He laughed and held me close saying American women are spoiled and that he was mine."

"One day I was on my way to check the rooms and when I passed theirs, I overheard them talking. They had picked up English much better now. One of them said, "That number four wife is just an old lady who could never really satisfy Sabua." I went in there and demanded to know what they were saying about my husband. One of them, I think it was the one called Elmai spoke up. 'We ain't talking about your husband. We talking about *our* husband.' I could not believe my ears. I was beyond understanding. It seems that I was number four wife and they was number one, two, and three. Now, Sabua was away on one of his business trips to New York and I hollered, cried and torn-up things. I just went crazy. I called a phone number he had left here in case of emergencies. Almena, it was to a diner in Brooklyn, New York. Some clown got on the phone and said Sabua is busy right now. I cussed him out too. I must have called that number twenty times if I called it once, and Sabua never came to the phone. That night I shut the house down. It wasn't going to be nothing happening here until them lying Africans got the hell out of my house."

"James and Dog came over when they heard I closed shop. Them low-down Negroes, tried to console me by saying, "'Malinda, you the only wife recognized in this country and when their visas expire, they all have to leave. My brother already knew! Well, it wasn't soon enough for me. Chile, I put them out that night. James, my brother, kept telling me, 'Now, Malinda don't blow this.' My own brother. Can you imagine that? I put him out too. Sabua came home about two days later and tried to get indignant. He had the nerve to say, 'You will not disgrace me! You are my wife and you will do as I say.' As it turns out, it was the custom in his country to have many wives. The problem was that son-of-a-bitch never told me that. He lied and said these were his sisters. Trouble was they all wasn't in his country anymore; they were all here in America. But before I got a chance to say any of that, Sabua went up side my head. Now I ain't never had much strength against a man, but I've always had strong teeth. I bit him across his cheek like I was a vicious mama bear. We wrestled for about twenty minutes; destroying a lot of my beautiful statues. It was like the furniture took wings in my parlor. Oh, it was awful. That was the first time I ever called the police to my house. But I told them if they didn't take him out of here, I was going to kill him. Love can turn to hate instantly, especially when a person has been made a fool of."

"In those days a woman could be beaten up, bleeding and broken in pieces and the law wouldn't do a thing. The police would only tell the man to leave the home and go cool off until the wife and he could figure things out later. But Sabua, oh he would hit a woman, but when he saw the police; it was like he wanted to shit on hisself. Honey, the look on that man face when he saw them at the door in their uniforms was priceless. Sabua ran out here like he had been set free from flaming gasoline. After a week, he sent James by here asking me, 'Did I miss my husband?' James always was crazy, so I told him, 'Hell no!'"

"Then he told me I should at least listen to Sabua side of the story. We went round and round with this discussion, 'cause I felt like James should be somewhere kicking Sabua's ass for putting his hand on his sister. Finally, I told James that Sabua could come get the rest of his clothes and whatever else his whore-wives left here. He must have been around the corner he was here so fast. He was dressed and trying to be charming, but all I could see was that fist he had thrown at me. Then he had the nerve to offer me money to remain his wife until his citizenship papers were in order. I felt like the biggest fool in the world. I did boo-hoo then. I wanted to bite him just one more time. But instead, I cussed his mother. Now I know that was wrong but at the time it seemed more than appropriate. He looked like he was going to pull out a can of ass whipping on me again. Then he placed his hands on my shoulders looked me directly in my eyes and said, 'Woman, you don't know what you doing! If I leave, who will take care of your brother? Think about that!'"

"'James is a grown man. He can take care of himself.' I said. He laughed, a big nasty laugh and said, 'Mindless one, James is a heroin addict and he can't take care of nothing. He needs me more than I will *ever* need you.'"

"Now, you know I was mad at Sabua, lying on my brother like that. I insisted if he didn't get his clothes and get out of my house in the next ten minutes I would call the police again. All the while that man was gathering his things, he kept calling me a mentally disturb old bitch, but he left."

"I couldn't get over what that no count husband of mine said about James. I asked myself, *could this be true?* I had been so wrapped up in my own life. *Did I miss something?* I decided me and James was going to have a sit-down soon as he came back. I could always tell when James was lying. He looks down at his feet or checks his watch when he's lying."

"James didn't show up for over a month. He was a sight. Clothes dirty, odors coming from everywhere, eyes red and swollen, and about twenty pounds lighter. Then I knew that the one truth Sabua did tell was about James. I should have known when you hang around dogs you're going to catch fleas, ticks, and any other demons they got."

"Doctor Moss, my oldest and dearest friend, came to our rescue. Bless his heart, that's who I should have married. He had heard of a place in Arizona and suggested that he might be able to get James some help there, because, as he explained, you just can't stop taking drugs on your own."

"James and I had our little sit down and it took all day for him to give me the real story of his addiction and Sabua. Long story short, Sabua and his sister-wives were drug smugglers James had met through Dog. My brother was addicted to some of the strongest heroin there was. Sabua gave James all he wanted because our marriage would make him a citizen and it would be easier to travel back and forth. James cried for using me but he was sick. This was a lot for me to take in. I was hurt to the core. Doctor Moss helped me a lot, not only with the addiction center but also with understanding how much the sickness claims of a person's life. It would've destroyed mine too if I couldn't forgive my own brother."

"First James went to a drying out center and came back home with me until it was time to go to Arizona. That boy was in misery. Looking at him in those days was like watching a caged panther. There wasn't a thing I could do but hug him as he suffered."

"I went to Arizona with James and got him settled in. He was like a little boy going to first grade. He was afraid. He wanted to get well but he felt sure he would fail. I stayed there in Arizona about two-weeks but James was there a whole year. His letters from that place was so pitiful at first, begging for my forgiveness and saying he would never do anything to hurt me. And of course he was cured, mind you, it had only been a month and he said he wasn't no hard-core dope fiend like some of the people there. That's what he said. I was smart enough to show those letters to Dr. Moss. 'The time has come, Malinda,' Dr. Moss told me, 'to stop being a big sister and let James be a man.'"

"I knew James needed to finish the program so I decided under no circumstances was I going to give in to his pleading and send him money to come home. I didn't open anymore letters, well except for one, which made me cry. It said that they, the counselors, made him say he was addicted and would always be an addict, which hurt. I did not see the sense in that. We sent him there to not be an addict and here they were making him own it for life. I just knew James's addiction would be the death of me. I felt like a bee was stinging me whenever I saw a young man about the same age of James. Oh, what a horrible way to view your life. James stayed and when it was time for him to come home we both agreed that New Haven was not the place for him. He went back down south. He had learned to be a barber while in Arizona and he earned his living like that for many years. Of course, he's still a womanizer but he was so much better than before. At least I think so. I don't have anything but hard memories of Africans. It's been hard for me to forget what Sabua did. It's not that girl, whatever her name is, that stinks. It's me. I'm an old woman and I still have a bad taste left in my mouth. I think all Africans are always after something."

"Will you tell her to come over here? I mean after she settles down." She cupped her hand around her mouth to hide a smile. "I'm going to apologize to her. Now, let me ask you a question or two, Almena."

Just then the door bell rang. It was the twins home from school. I was saved again by the children, 'cause I just know Ms. Malinda was going to ask about James and me. What happened? Why we ain't eyeing each other no more? *Oh Mercy! What am I going to tell her?* "I'll be back later when I git the children straight and see about they school work," I quickly said.

I never thought I would think this about James, but he's a drunk. Or is it back to that drug problem that Ms. Malinda thought was gone? I couldn't tell her either one of them things in her condition. I needed to rock on this a while.

CHAPTER FOURTEEN
James

James usually came in and out at late hours. I decided to wait up for the sound of moving around. About three thirty in the morning, I heard stumbling in the hall downstairs. I went down to talk to him, 'cause if you want to know something, ain't nothing like asking a drunk; they will tell you the straight out truth. James looked greasy and tired. *Lord, he looked like he had run through a garbage heap.* I started in anyway, "James, what is the matter with you?" He was standing in the hallway holding on to the coat rack and licking his lips at me.

"Nothing that a little country love won't take care of. Come here, girl!" He reached out and grabbed my shoulder. Even though he looked tired, his eyes was darting up and down my body. His head kinda drooped and every so often he would rub his face with his free hand.

I pushed him away. "James, you smell like a country mule. Ms. Malinda is wondering if you alright or not. Fix yourself up!"

"I will do just that! Now if you will excuse me. I'm going to take off my clothes and get in my bed." He waved me away like I was a fly or something.

"Why are you trying to get rid of me?" I moved close back to him and held on to his hands. If he moved one way, I moved with him. There just so much room in the hallway.

"Girl, get your ass out of my way and let a man be."

"Don't talk to me like that! And stop drinking so much!

What's the matter with your eyes? You look scared."

"Almena," he said nasty-like, "Mind your business. At least my head ain't down on no table. What you need is a man so you don't have no time to mess with other folks business." His words sizzled like they had been dipped in hot grease.

I stood right there between his doorway and the hallway, not moving, just watching him. He knew that remark about my head being down on the table would feel like a slap in the face. He didn't seem to like me at all here lately.

"James, get a grip on yourself and I'll fix us some coffee. Then maybe we can talk."

"Girl, I don't have nothing to say to you. You asking for a good cussing out. That country side of you ain't working on me. You just a nosey-ass bitch!"

He look like he wouldn't have no problem cussing me out either. Lord, where is that lovely man I met on the bus?

"I just want to know are you using drugs again."

He looked like he was caught. Three wrinkles creased his forehead and his eyes narrowed down. His Adam's apple move sharply as he swallowed. "Do you know who you talking to? A grown man, not them children, and what I do is my business. Woman, don't make me crazy in here. What? You and Malinda been discussing my past, is that it? Tell my sister I'll talk to her in the morning and you ain't the one to tell me how to run my life. Now let me get some sleep. I'm not going to ask you again!"

I backed away and hauled my ass back upstairs. At the top of the stairs I felt my body sway a little and my head didn't really seem to belong to me. I felt as if the floor was tilting under my feet. Our argument had warped the possibility of sleep.

James was using. I didn't know what, but he was using. In the little time I been in New Haven I been called country, a drunk, a nosey bitch and I think Ms. Malinda done called me a dog. *I hope I can be still. It's getting hard up here on Dixhill Avenue. I want our new start to work. Me and my children must never turn around. We've got to make it!*

All my life I had temporary homes, just stops. Oh, the house in Elktown was just that, a house which you run back to 'cause life had whipped you. I did not belong there, never had. *I want a home, a feel good place for me and now my children. One of them like you see in Life magazine.* A connection to the good in life. Not a place that was proof that you failed again. Not a place where you was hurt just being there. How could we stay in a place where across the road they mother was murdered and a town where I was thought of as the town retard? What kinda mother would I be to them when all I could think on was the raping and faults I had on me. It would be like living in a dark pit. *This has got to work out for us until I can figure out our path. I got to be still! We've got to move on past the past. My head is swarmed with worries. No wonder I feel light-headed with all these thoughts going in and out of my head. I'm going to take me a packet of Stanback Headache Powder.*

A couple days later, he did stop in to see his sister. I was sitting with her, weaving as I usually do. James had cleaned up good. Except for a little sweating on his upper lip, he looked like his old self. Leaning in to Ms. Malinda, he asked, "How's the only love of my life?" He was grunting and sucking on a yellow lollipop.

"No use complaining." Ms. Malinda sighed as she said it.

"Life ain't treating me right either, but I'm on top of it." *He was looking at me sideways and cross-eyed behind Ms. Malinda's back.* "Malinda," he said, "I been looking at a nice little shop right off Whalley Street as a possible site for my barbering business. I just need the funds to make it happen. I really need to keep busy and get my hustle on and this spot has enough room for four chairs."

"James, are you licensed to cut hair in New Haven?"

"That's no problem. I can just switch-up my South Carolina license and pay the fees." *He was sucking hard on that lollipop now.*

"I'll see what I can do, James." She had closed her eyes and began to rotate her neck." How much we talking about?"

"Oh no, sweetheart, I'm just mentioning it. I don't need you worrying over it. I'm going to come up with five thousand dollars from somewhere. Barbershop or not, you can count on me. I'll be here until you get well." He leaned in again to kiss Ms. Malinda.

"Gotta go and see if anything fell in my traps I laid last night." He chuckled at his own lie. I swirled my strand of wool tight for at this time I was braiding to the edges of the rug I was working on. The thread popped; I had clenched it so tight. *I knew what fell in his trap and it was nothing nice.* I looked up and James gave me one last roll of his eyes, as if to say, you better not be talking bad about me. The whole time he was talking, he looked at his feet. He going to hell sometime soon, I betcha!

When he left, Ms. Malinda sighed and said, "Almena turn the television off and put the record player on." It was on the bottom shelf of the nightstand. "I think I want to hear some Etta James," she said just above a whisper. "I'm tired so would you please turn out my lights too, but let the music play itself out." A look of sadness come across her eyes as though they was standing in her grave. She turned on her side and went low in the bed. I put it on and as I climbed the stairs, I could hear Etta's smooth vocals of "This Bitter Earth."

Speaking of bitter, that's what it is up here in New Haven. Bitter cold. I turned the furnace gauge up at the top of the stairs. The heat kicked on instantly; still I think I better ask Ms Malinda where I can get wood for the parlor fireplace. *There are so many things to remember around here.*

Sitting in Grandma's rocker and looking out our second floor window, the first big snow of the season began. It was beautiful, like one of those scenes you see in a glass globe. Trees accepted the snow on they bare limbs like a long lost friend. In a matter of minutes the whole street was white, fresh looking but hard for me to capture in my weaving mind for without color I couldn't tell a story except that it was cold. I wish I was like them trees. They able to accept and they prove it every spring with new limbs, and new leaves, and new reachings.

Grace and Glory was sent home early from school because of the weather. After watching the snow for a while, I decided that we would play a little game they had called Go Fish. It's a card game; I never was any good at it. Grace always won at this. We sat down in the middle of the front room. She shuffled the cards. Then she dropped a card in front of me and asked,

"What's a whore?" Grace had raised up on her knees.

"A whore is not a nice lady," I said. "Where you getting that kinda of talk?"

"At school, that's what they call Auntie Malinda, and I'm going to beat the snot out of some of them kids if they say it again."

"How long has this been going on?" I asked.

"All week."

"Well, we know that it is not the truth and fighting never solved nothing. Do you think that the good Lord would want you to beat the snot out of somebody?"

"No," Grace said, "but it sure would make me feel good."

I knew I had to git down to that school and see if anything could be done, 'cause like I said, Grace had slimmed down a little but she still was one hefty second grader.

"Grace, don't you be mean to anybody. I'm going to speak with Pastor about kids that used that kinda language and I'm certain he will put a stop to it. In the meantime remember stick and stones may hurt your bones but words can't." Even as I said it, I know the power of words.

Hurtful words can linger long after wounds heal. They'd get in your mind, store themselves just out of sight, and then pop out whenever you're the least bit unsure of yourself. Someone called me broken one time and I've been trying to find the right tool to fix me every since. It's even worse when you don't know what the broken part is or the part can't be touched by hand, like your spirit. Many a time, I wanted to turn myself inside out and just let all the bad things inside me float away, like the dust beaten gently from a beautiful rug.

"Fish!" I hollered. I finally won a game. Glory laughed at how overjoyed I was to win.

"Glory, you doing alright down at that school?"

"Oh yes," Glory said. "If some of them bother me I just start shaking and they run away 'cause they think the Holy Ghost is on me."

We all laughed, but now for sure I had to git to that school.

It snowed so hard that day and night that school was closed for the next two days. We kept busy, cooking, weaving, caring for Ms. Malinda and having one giant snowball fight. Of course Grace won. That child would line up her snowballs and fire them at you till you pleaded for mercy. Glory studied things. She brought a snowball inside and she watched it melt. Her eyes fixed on it like a picture-taking person, and she studied that thing with a smile on her face. That's when I knew she had it all. A smile crept up the sides of her lips and her cheeks became round and her eyes twinkled. She had what she needed, the done-of-it. Weavers see things as if they were done. They change things. It was time to teach Glory and Grace the beginnings of weaving what you feel.

James hadn't been home for three nights and not one of us asked about him. I best be thankful for that, I suppose.

CHAPTER FIFTEEN
Busted

Looking through bleary eyes from the backseat of the police car, I stared through the wire cage at the revolving lights of what appeared to be ten police cars surrounding Habibah's apartment building. What a messed up high this was. I didn't want to blow my high but the feel of steel cuffs around my wrists quickly brought me down to reality. I was busted. The door to Habibah's apartment fell in so fast I still had the needle pumping when they opened the bathroom door. I heard her crying, "James! James! The police have come!" I felt myself slumping. *Ain't no use in wasting a good nod.*

After being processed and charged with possession of drugs, my high was of little importance. The following day my sickness kicked in and I vomited into the stainless steel toilet, which would become my hugging partner. In the cell with me were two other men withdrawing from drugs or alcohol. We took turns with diarrhea, vomiting, chills and sweats. Every bone in my body ached and my legs had a mind of their own, moving and thrashing uncontrollably.

It took two days before I saw the judge. "Mr. Grey," he said, "since you have no prior offenses and because we are informed that you are not violent, we will release you to a treatment facility, but only if a responsible person from the community will sign for you. Do you have anyone you can call?"

"I do." I said, trying as best I could to stand up straight.

"Once that is done, you are to report to drug counseling immediately. Mr. Grey, the court often gives second chances to violators who are addicted, but should you ever appear in front of me again, you will be shown no leniency and will be prosecuted to the fullest extent of the law. Do you understand?"

"Yes sir," I said. I knew I didn't want to call my sister, her being sick. Besides I really didn't want her to know that I had fucked-up again. On the way back to my cell I got to use the phone. I called our old family friend, Dr. Moss. "Hey Doc, this is James, Malinda's brother."

He answered quickly, "Yes, James. Is your sister having problems?"

"No, but man you will never guess what happened. I'm sitting over a friend's house and the police come busting in. Now they got me for possession of drugs and Doc, you know I been clean. Man, I was at the wrong place at the wrong time. Can you please come get me out of this hell hole?"

I could hear Dr. Moss clearing his throat and then he said, "James let's try the truth. Are you fighting those same demons from your past?" He clearly did not want to hear my tall tales. "Doc, can you help me? I'll do whatever you think is best." I was whimpering. "Doc, I've got to be around for Malinda."

"Okay James." He paused and then added, "I'll be down there this afternoon. I suppose Malinda knows nothing about this, right?"

"No, she don't," I whispered. "If possible, considering her condition, please don't let her know. I would really appreciate it. Doc, man, we both really need you this time."

"I will be down later," he said and we hung up.

It was two days later before the cell door swung open for me. Doc stood in the hall waiting. "Man, I thank you, I promise—"

Before I could say anymore, he said, "James, don't start with the promises. Until you make up your mind to beat this addiction, I'd rather you didn't speak and just listened. I have been thinking for the past day on whether or not I should even sign you out. I have always considered Malinda and you family but there are limits even where family is concerned."

"This is it, Doc. I have been shocked, demoralized and desperate like never before. You will never get a call like that from me or about me again." For some reason, an urge to burst into tears took hold of me but I nailed it down in my throat.

Doc shook his head and then spoke, "Man, do you know how many people could be devastated by your actions? I've had a friend of mine look into these charges. That young woman, Habibah, is in a great deal of trouble. She is being held for immigration and will be deported, all because you were followed to her house after leaving a drug house that was being watched by the police. Now, the police think *she* is a trafficker. This thing is not all about you. That girl has two small kids in Africa who are counting on her to make a way for them to come here for a better life. She's going to need help from somebody who don't need the kind of help you need. James, you can't keep using women. This arrest may cost her not only her dreams but the dreams of kids you haven't even met."

I pressed my hands to my head. *Could it get any worse?* All I could do was stare at the floor.

"James, you got three hours to get to the rehab center." Doc said, wrinkling his forehead at me.

Discharge papers laid out the conditions of my release. I was to do fourteen days in-patient and six months outpatient counseling. I couldn't see Habibah if I wanted to. Immigration only allowed visits from lawyers, family members or sponsors. I was trying to look manly but I felt like a piece of crap.

Doc drove me to the house to clean up, change clothes and tell Malinda I was going out of town for a couple of weeks. Now, if I could just sneak in without Almena seeing me. I could not take all them questions today. Easing into the door, I made it to the shower without anyone seeing me. I showered, shaved, changed my clothes and was on my way to talk to Malinda when here come Almena down the steps.

"Hey, James," she said.

"Hey, country woman. How's my sister?"

"She's just fine. Have you seen Habibah? I need my hair done."

"No," I replied and slipped in Malinda's room. My sister looked smaller than before. I could have broken down right then but I knew I had to keep it together.

"Hey, big sis what's up? Listen, I have to go check out some business out of town for a couple of weeks. Are you going to be okay?" I was talking fast and looking at the floor. I hope she didn't notice.

She looked up at me and said, "Of course I am. You still need that money?"

"No, it can wait until I get back." Now that was hard to say, cause the taste of addiction is excited by money.

Malinda smiled. "Take care of your business, brother. I'll be here when you get back." Something in her eyes told me she still had hope for me.

Doc came back to take me to the center. I was standing on the porch with a small duffle bag, willing myself to control my shakes. As I struggled to get into the front seat, he gave me a hard look "James, that girl has a hearing in about sixty days," he said.

"Doc, I don't know what I'm going to do right now, but I will do all I can to help her out of this mess I started."

"I'm glad to hear that, James. Now show me!" We rode in silence for the next fifteen minutes and I put my hand over my eyes to shield the light of day. It was mid-morning. Damn, I needed a hit. I shifted my body around in the seat as a wave of chills took over and hoped that Doc didn't see just how bad-off I was.

We pulled up in front of a brown three-story building, there were no signs out front, a non-descript brown building, maybe once used as a small school. I was buzzed in and signed in. Doc gave me a hug and said, "Try harder than ever before, son. I still believe you can beat this thing. And James, ask your counselor for something to ease those withdrawal symptoms you're having."

Once inside with Doc gone, I handed over my paperwork to a tall black man behind a counter just inside the office door. He looked at the papers and, with lips poked out said, "Have a seat, brother. Someone will be with you shortly." I staggered to a long wooden bench in the hallway. After about forty-five minutes of sheer agony on that bench, my name was called and my rehab was about to begin. I was shown up to the second floor by a short white man whose shirt had a name tag with the word "Staff" on it. "Room 203, this will be your room," Staff said. It was an open room with four bunk beds, and four lockers with combination locks. It reminded me of a small army barracks. Dull green walls and gray cement floors. Navy blankets covered the bunks and the two windows at the end of the room was painted black. "Your counselor will be in to speak with you in a few minutes," Staff mumbled.

I sat on one of the lower bunks and wondered how the hell I got here. In less than two months, I had gone from a suit wearing, clean and sober brother coming to care for his sister to a broke down and busted dope fiend.

About ten minutes later a young black man, about twenty-four, walked in with a clipboard in hand. "Good afternoon, Mr. Grey, my name is Kevin." He was dressed in a white sweater, tan pants and white sneakers. He could have been my son, but he was my house counselor and after a number of questions, he looked up and said, "You can take that bunk you're sitting on and locker number two will be yours."

"Okay, I'm in no shape to be climbing up top." He went right back to the rules and regulations. "Mr. Grey, we use first names here. You don't mind if I call you James, do you?"

"Naw, James is fine."

"Let me go over some expectations we have here. There's no drinking, no fighting, no leaving the building without permission, no opposite sex members in your room and of course, there are no drugs allowed unless disbursed by the facility doctor. Also, James you must attend your meetings. Don't blow off a meeting. They're very important for you and this program. If you are sick, see me and I'll get you help. Dining is as follows, breakfast served between 6:30 and 8:30 am. Lunch is 12:00 to 2:00 pm and dinner between 5:00 and 6:30 pm. I'm going to give you this handbook and you can read it. For now, sign this form saying I went over the rules with you. The bathrooms are located at the end of each hallway to the right and your meetings will be held on your floor." Walking to the door and pointing to the left, Kevin added, "That large room to your left is your meeting room unless changed by the staff." He spat all this out like it was a sales pitch.

I signed some papers saying I understood the rules.

"Okay, that does it for now. You really don't have much time to settle in 'cause your first meeting is in about fifteen minutes, my man." He waited for me to protest but I was silent.

Turning to leave he said, "James, I read your case and I know you've been to counseling before. All I ask is that you don't bullshit me. I may be young to you but I can see through bullshit. If you don't want help, do your two weeks and return to your hell, but if you want this cycle to stop, we can show you how and that begins with being real. Most of our residents are younger than you. You can be a good example of what not to do, it's up to you. Every morning I'll stop in to give you your schedule. Let us help you." Kevin had softened his tone; now he sounded like a friendly waiter. Again turning to leave he spotted my luggage and whispered, "Shit, your bag should have been searched and tagged downstairs. I'll have to confiscate this and bring it back after group. Rules are that we search for contraband. I'm sorry about this but the guy who escorted you up here is new."

"No problem I play by the rules."

"So does everybody in here, James." He shot back at me with arched eyebrows. He left swinging my bag over his shoulders.

I wasn't thrilled about going to a meeting right away but I didn't have a choice, I only hoped it wasn't one of them twelve step meetings that everybody lied about. Running both my hands around my head and down my neck to massage my shoulders I thought about being an example. *Of what? Shit, I don't know how to end my own nightmare; I thought that was his job.*

The meeting room was about the size of a small classroom with twelve white folding chairs place in a circle. As I peeped in, five residents (that's what they called us) were drinking coffee and picking over a tray of brownies. They stood there looking back at me. To describe them would be like viewing a late night television commercial of *Save the Starving.*

I took a seat near the arc of the circle of chairs and once again stared at the floor. I wondered what the hell these young people and I could possibly have in common. Still in denial, of course, that I was their future. The woman that was standing with the young men, her hair was matted with several bald spots and hanging from her left ear was a walnut-sized growth. A down-right scary sight she was. One of the young men had tattoos in the shape of tombstones running down his face, while another had on shower shoes and a drab green cotton jumpsuit signifying he was straight out of jail or the county hospital. He had two or three large abscesses running up his right arm and his hands were the size of catcher's mitts. The fourth one wore tan pants and a white tee, like Kevin, but I knew he wasn't a counselor; he was agitated more than me. Sweat rolled down his neck, a sure sign he liked his drugs main-lined. Nobody spoke, just a nod of the head by the main-liner.

In walks the group counselor, a white woman with

blonde hair. She was dressed young but she was already beginning to crack because the lines around her mouth and eyes gave her away. Her miniskirt and knee high socks couldn't hide the wrinkles. She walked in with a cocky I'm-in-Charge stroll and a box of Kleenex. Right away I got the feeling she was studying for a higher degree, and we were her lab rats. Now, how a forty-two year old black man like me was going to relate to her? I didn't know. Tagging along with her were three other residents, all so thin you could almost see through them. As I surveyed the whole bunch of them, I knew everyone was here, court ordered, made to come to escape a jail sentence. But who was I to judge? That's the alternative I took, too. Drifting off in my thoughts, shame weighed down on me. My expectation of this counseling session was nothing I hadn't heard before.

I thought about Habibah. It wasn't that I loved her; she was just exciting to be with and very accepting. Her accent added to the excitement. The girl could moan. I would be nodding my ass off and she would say, "Oh, James you're so tired come on let's lay down awhile." *I must get this girl back on the streets. Damn I feel so guilty.*

The meeting counselor's name was Ellen. She began the meeting by defining cognitive-behavioral intervention, in other words how to change your behavior. I sat there in a stupor until suddenly the lights went out and the front wall became a white frame. We were shown a film on behaviors of addicts. *Bullshit!* On the screen was a teaspoon holding the holy mother lode of heroin and a match coming closer to dissolve its contents into glorious relief. That one scene made me start craving like an animal in heat. *I don't need this shit. Behaviors my ass; everybody in here knows how we act, we live it. Right now I'd give my left pinkie for that spoon.* I close my eyes, lace my fingers together and place them between my legs.

Finally the lights came on as I opened my eyes. Ellen had been watching me and had a victory smile on her face. I looked around for cameras to see if I had been taped. Call it paranoia but I got the feeling she was out to get the old man. For a second our eyes met. "Did that make anyone uncomfortable?" Ellen asked.

I'm not going to admit nothing to her, besides, the smile let me know she knows I'm near panic. *I'm dreading the next fourteen days of my life.* Two residents fled the bathroom while the rest of us sat there as if we were at a wake.

Ellen, eyeing me, reached for a little blue book under her seat. I know the book. "Why don't we get to know each other, starting with our newest resident?" Nodding in my direction. I stood after a few minutes. *I might as well get this over with. Counselors love it when you spill your guts. Maybe this will be the last time I'll have to speak. My tongue was plastered to the roof of my mouth but finally it moved.*

My name is James Grey and I am forty-two years old. I am addicted to heroin, the rush of it and the carefree feelings. I inject it; it's like a love affair with a monster that won't be ignored. I've been a lover of heroin since my twenties and I'm sick right now. The only thing that keeps me from being sick on the outside is rushing to get it at light speed. It's the first mission of the day for me. Prior to this bust, I had been clean for more than ten years. No matter how long I been without it, the need is still there. I'm tired of relapses like this. I was your age when I first went to rehab; what I need to be is tired of heroin."

My voice was raspy, almost croaking at times but they all seemed to lean in to hear my tale. One by one they introduced themselves and what their drug of choice was. Up until now I hadn't noticed the strong sting of disinfectant in the room and I teared up. I wanted to reach for Ellen's Kleenex but I didn't. I took a deep breath and wiped my eyes with back of my hands. My hands were trembling.

Ellen seemed pleased that six people were participating and her notebook would be now full with observations. Most of my fellow residents were cocaine users.

Fourteen days of being subjected to this! Maybe jail would have been better.

My little admission had opened up a tell-all meeting. The others tell one sob story after another, the young baldheaded women cries rape as a child, the guy with the tattoos is lost without his friends who were killed in a gang fight, the green jumpsuit wearing youngster was at the wrong place at the wrong time and the main-liner needs cash 24/7. He was as crazy as they came. He kept laughing between farting and snorting. With each story they told, they are tried to trump the other. They could write scripts for *Tales from the Crypt*. They clearly manufactured false alibis. They blamed innocent family members and they try to lie on police in a pitiful effort to rewrite their history. I am sitting here watching as they give each other high fives and right on signs. They are proud of their problems. I wonder what would happen if I held up a bag of dope right now. Who would jump me first? At this point, after thinking about it, I would probably beat myself up for a hit. *This is bad and this ain't helping.*

The super-thin members of the group were too busy stuffing their mouths with brownies to talk; they ate them brownies like they hadn't eaten for months. For the second time in my life, I felt lost. I couldn't even write or call my sister to complain. My Arizona stay was a country club compared to this place.

After that enlightening meeting, Ellen announced we had all made progress. *Progress?* I felt like saying, *we're all here so we don't have to go to jail and everyone here will have a different story tomorrow.* But I didn't. Mainliner tried to slap hands with me. I kept mines in my pocket.

I went straight to my room. This was not going to help me and I knew it. I pulled the rough navy blue blanket over my head and began to count the hours in the thirteen days I had to go. Kevin stopped in carrying my bag, "How's it going, James?"

"My bones are killing me and I need to be left alone."

He slapped his hand on his pant leg and said, "We've got something for that. Have you ever tried methadone?"

Ain't that a bitch? Another drug. "No thanks, sleep will

work." I mumbled after catching my breath.

"Okay, my man, I'll leave you with this schedule of your meetings. He left satisfied that he had done his job.

Ten days went by quickly, full of stories, promises and even boasting about how much dope or how much dope money the group got a day. Daily it got worse. They perpetrated like none I had ever seen. *Calm down these are only young people who think they can beat the system and drugs whenever they want to. Just dry out and get out. Malinda and Habibah need you now, so keep what you're thinking to yourself. Work on your shit.*

Three more days to go; at the evening meeting we were to have a guest speaker. Along with Ellen, in walks Pastor Joel. I wanted to crawl under a rock but finding one in here was like trying to hide behind one of my stick thin cocaine head associates. He looked mildly surprised, eyebrows arched he let out a little cough as if something was stuck in his throat. "This evening we are lucky to have with us a member of the community that really cares about your survival, meet Pastor Joel Jones," Ellen announced. *This is so awkward.* Neither one of us acknowledged the other.

"Yes, I do care," Pastor Joel said. "I had been thinking about what I was going to say to you. It's more than important to me. It's personal." He walked in my direction never letting on that he knew me and then he began to speak. "Brothers and sisters it is my sincere hope that you overcome the demonic illness you have. From what I understand it is a formidable sickness to defeat. It's going to take a lot of work, a lot of time, and a lot of honesty. You must detoxify not only your body but also your mind. It will take not only will power, but also strength pulled from learning your weaknesses, from learning your triggers and from loving yourself and your family enough to fight with everything you have to be the kind of person you want to be. I find that not everyone is up to the task. Not everyone has the tolerance to endure the hard work it takes to beat his or her addiction but trust me; it is worth it."

Tears ran down my face and saturated my lap. Mainliner bit hangnails off his fingers. I was sobbing now. Joel handed me a Kleenex and continued. *Damn, I'm a punk!*

"That's where the church comes into this. I believe we can help you love yourself enough to not destroy yourself and your love ones. You do understand that your illness is like an infectious disease. Everyone who comes in contact with you is at risk of some emotional or physical scars."

"Our church is one in the city of New Haven that cares. We have an outpatients meeting group two nights a week. We have mentors and problem solvers who can help you walk upright again. These mentors have sat in the same seats you're sitting in. I'm not here to preach God just yet, but if you ever need a life raft, we're here for you. Come to our meetings when you leave here and let's fight this devil together. We also have at this time two part-time janitorial positions. We would love to offer you a job. Finding a job can be almost impossible when you have no references. I promise there is a new way to get high and the elation comes from living a Godly life."

I had never heard Joel speak with such feeling, when he and I had talked before it was on an old friendship level, like everyday talk. *Do something for me for old-time sake.* Standing there it was as if he was different, speaking from somewhere he was convinced was the answer to everything. He had changed from the street thug I once knew to a strong black man who was committed to living a life of well-being. I didn't see that when I ask about the kids getting in school. I saw an old friend doing a favor. It was right then that I stood up and said, "I know you, and you know me and it would be an honor to apply for one of those jobs and find out if I can change my life."

We hugged, and of course I heard some in the room say, "Man, I ain't got no time to be a janitor or go to no more meetings." Well, that was fine with me, 'cause I didn't have no more time to be a junkie. I was trading these alligator shoes in for some Rockports and a broom.

Don't get me wrong I knew it wasn't going to be easy but with a support system that went way back to my young days, and two very important reasons to succeed: Malinda and Habibah. I felt like a weight was slowly being lifted off me. For once I could do something for somebody else and benefit myself as well. I was going to stick close to this man, sweep, mop floors, wash windows, look in on my sister more, get Habibah out of trouble and through all of this I would still be doing it for my life, a life free from drugs. It sounds like a fairy tale. But a good fairytale usually ends with "and they lived happily ever after." *I'll take that!*

In seventy-two hours I was released from the center. I jumped out of the cab before it stopped in front of my sister's house. I had the key out and in I went. Like a kid, I sat my bag down and went running to Malinda's room. She was sitting propped up reading the newspaper. She looked good, I don't know what Almena was feeding her but she looked wholesome to me. We both screamed with pleasure and held each other like I had been gone for years. I started singing "You Light Up My Life." Malinda laughed so hard. I was so off key. In fact I never could sing. Why is it when you think you are going to lose someone that's the time you show your love? Well, from now on I was not going to waste a minute.

"James," Malinda said, "you looking good."

"We both looking good," I replied.

"Let's catch up, baby boy. Whatcha been doing and where you been and was your trip successful?"

"It was all good, sis, all good. Seeing you looking so well has really made my trip successful. Where are Almena and the twins? I have got to thank them for taking such good care of my big sister."

"You're going to make me cry if you keep talking like that, James. I do feel so much better. I think Almena went down to the school to talk to the twins' teacher. Oh uh, James... If you could have been here last week, when Grace demonstrated how she was going to whip them children's asses. You would have fell down laughing. I don't know what the problem is but Grace was going ass whipping today if the matter wasn't handled and she told us so. Little Grace was going to get her some satisfaction. She made me laugh until I had to go to the bathroom. She reminds me a little of you as a child, fearless. She will tell you she's going to tear-up somebody before and after she does it. We've been having a good time in this house, little Glory been sewing with a passion. She's going to be very good one day. They'll be back in here shortly with all the news of the day."

"Well, I can't miss the blow-by-blow details. I'm glad they came to live here. Give me the sports section of that paper so I can see how sorry my Boston basketball team been doing."

We sat there reading the paper with underlying smiles, I was happy to be home, right next to my one and only sister. Tomorrow I would begin to work on Habibah's problem but just for today my sister and I was going to have a great day.

Malinda wrote me a check for $5,000 the next day and I went straight to Doc Moss to see what we could do. He cancelled his patients and called a lawyer who had connections and for $2,000, we had Habibah back on the street that evening. She had to return for a hearing in two months, but at least she was out for now. She rushed into my arms. It was so good to see her. More than good, but I wasn't what this woman needed. We hurried to Habibah's apartment 'cause she did look like a refugee. Her hair, skin, and clothes smelled stale. I wondered if she knew that I wasn't the man she needed during her time in the holding pen. I had a monster to deal with, one that is an undercover agent who might raise his head at any given opportunity.

I gave Habibah some money to pay her rent and send some money home to her kids. I got me a little loving. I'm a man. How could I refuse? My next stop was the church. Joel welcomed me with open arms. We joked around, like old times. You see, Joel always did have a crush on Malinda, but he was too young. She would have him pick up Sabua dry cleaning and he would do it. Talk about sprung he was sprung. We laugh at how our lives had changed. “Listen Joel, I’m here about the job. I’ve got to be occupied.”

“It’s yours, so long as you attend the meetings.”

“No problem,” I said.

“You know, James, I’m a man just like you with faults and problems and needs, but in this house there is one who handles them for me. If you stay here long enough, you’ll meet him.”

I thought, *Okay, here comes the sermon.* Joel turned and said, “Respect yourself, the brothers and sisters in this house and above all for your life don’t mess with my God.” He then showed me to an office in the basement where an elderly man named Mr. Morrison would show me the duties of the part-time janitor. I felt like I was George Jefferson. Yes sir, I’m moving on up.

CHAPTER SIXTEEN
School Days

I was a daydreamer when I was in school. Teachers would be calling on me. "Almena," they would say. "Almena Johnstone! Where is your mind? Please pay attention." I just had a lot to think about. To them, I was trouble and hard to teach. Some of the notes they wrote about me made me feel headless. They didn't see what I saw or live like I lived. There was times when I would sit and stare at the patterns on the teacher's clothes. It seemed like I could tell what they lives was like by the stitches in the outfits they wore. Sweater knits meant they like hugs, light see through patterns suggested they had nothing to hide. It's funny now, but I think I knew way more than they did, 'cause I saw more life than them and I didn't pass judgment on it. I just weave it out in my rugs. Tomorrow it would be my turn to ask the teacher some questions.

I walked the twins to school early the next morning, so I could speak with Grace's teacher. Her name was Miss Nelson. She was a black lady, nice enough, but a little out of touch. I say that because she wore a bright red mini skirt showing off her old swollen knees. She stood in the hallway just outside the classroom counting the children as they entered the room. "Miss Nelson," I said, "How's my girls doing?" She blinked and began to twist a tissue she held in her hand. I had met her the first day they came to school. I also had greeted her many times in church but she was acting like she didn't recognize me this morning for some reason.

"Oh, Ms. Johnstone, excuse me," she blinked

suddenly.

"I was concentrating on my class. Your twins are just fine, no need to worry. They're so intelligent and mannerly, too." Ms. Nelson's gray-blue wig moved up and down as she spoke. I was studying her. Her wig didn't fit on the sides. *Oh mercy*! I never saw that before. I could see her edges and wasn't a thing about them blue.

"Well, that's good." I said, pulling my eyes away from her busy wig. "Cause I think we might have a little problem with some other children that don't have manners." I rocked back on my heels. Grandma always did that when she knew she was right.

"I don't follow you Ms. Johnstone. The children are fine." The tissue was in pieces now.

"I know mine is but some kids are calling out terrible names and my kids are taking it to heart. They seem to be calling members of our family whores and the like."

"Oh heavens!" She put her hand to her mouth. "Well, I'll speak to the children and let them know this is a Christian school, and we won't put up with that at all." Ms. Nelson's blinking had become faster now. She went on to say, "I'm sure there has been some mistake. I will speak to them about our rules."

"You do that Ms. Nelson, 'cause I'm worried about how my girls will do if it happens again."

"I promise I will take care of it. Now excuse me, but I must get back to the children. It's so nice of you to bring this to my attention." All the color had gone out of her face; not that she had much to begin with. She was ashy.

I nodded and walked away but, what she said didn't seem strong enough for me. *That statement bout there must be a mistake, there wasn't no mistake. My kids don't lie.* So I went marching to the Pastor Joel's office. Brenda, the church secretary, took one look at me, and saw I was breathing kinda hard. She calmly said, "Good morning, sister dear. It's good to see you this morning. Pastor always has an open door for members of our family. Would you like to see him?"

I calmed right down. "I sure would, Sister Brenda." By

this time my armpits was wet. You see, it bothers me when people don't take what I say serious. Ms. Nelson answers had made me mad. Like I didn't know what I was talking about.

"He will be with you shortly," Brenda said.

Pastor's office door opened and he waved me in, smiling brightly. "Good morning to you. What can I do for you today, sister Almena?"

"Good morning, Pastor. You've already done so much for us and we thank you from the bottom of our hearts. I'm sorry to have yet another need."

"Don't be. That's what I'm here for, to help in any way I can. What's the problem?"

I just right out told him my girls been through some things, and for better or worse, they have learned some lessons that some folks should never encounter. "We from a small country town, Pastor, and making fun and calling us names hurts us more, 'cause we know we ain't quite like city folks. Now, some of the children are calling Ms. Malinda a whore. She's precious to my children. I wouldn't want what has happened to us in the past to show up on some of them children's behinds. So, would you take a couple of minutes to strengthen the rules about calling people out of they names?" *Grace might beat the Malcolm out of one of them kids, if you know what I mean.* I also told him about the changes in hospitality I was receiving from some of his flock and ask him what he thought I should do. Pastor Joel looked at me so kindly and said, "I don't permit that kind of behavior anywhere in this school or the church. We are about love and acceptance. I will put a stop to it right away. And don't worry, it will be stopped. By the way Malinda is precious to me, too."

I found out he's a very easy person to talk to. He was on his way to that classroom before I could get off the church steps.

When I got back to the house, James had returned. His homecoming was like seeing him on the bus again. He looked rested and his attitude was upbeat. Whatever the business he had been to see about had made the shine come back in his eyes. I don't need an excuse to cook but I used James's return to make homemade corned beef and cabbage with, of course, bacon bit cornbread.

That evening, when Grace and Glory got home they told him all about they adventures at school. I had warned them never to repeat the name calling, 'cause we didn't want to upset Ms. Malinda. Ms. Malinda was strong enough to walk into the dining room and enjoy the food with us. She'd just laugh at about everything that comes out of them children's mouth. I think she would have been a good mother if she had been given a chance.

Speaking of chance, I never did get the chance to tell everybody what happen when I went to the braid shop the other day. I walked in and ask for Habibah and them African people started clucking they tongues at me and told me to get out of they shop. I mean I had to move fast, I didn't know what that was about. I figured I'd have to keep on wearing my scarf, 'cause my braids was as fuzzy as a sheep's ass. Habibah must've done something to them people. They was real upset! I have to find me somebody to do my hair, people I don't have to run from. Ms. Malinda said they was all disturbed. Maybe she is right.

Right after dinner when the kids were upstairs, James walked in the kitchen. "Almena please forgive me for the way I talked and acted with you. That's not who I am."

"Of course I forgive you and I know who I met on the bus and that's who you will always be to me. Nothing will change that, James." He looked surprised and relieved when I said that. He smelled good, kinda fruity-like.

Time passed and things was going along fine. The Pastor spoke to the children about they name-calling, and he also gave a sermon about not judging people. Not all people got the message that he was talking about them but I did.

I tried hard to be friendlier and not take things to heart. James was full of surprises. He started working at the church part-time. He and Pastor Joel was becoming close like they was when they was young. James's barbershop was set to open in the summer. Ms. Malinda was getting stronger and the twins was fitting right in with the kids from New Haven. I hadn't heard from Mama or Grandma in a couple of weeks so I decided to rock long that night. Just so they could tell me how good I was doing.

It was past midnight before Grandma came roaring in my head about the dolls. Where had I put the dolls? She was asking. *Mercy*! Every so often she'd ask about them dolls. It was like she was in her second childhood. It wasn't like they was new fashion dolls. The clothes they had on was way past old, in fact I don't believe people ever wore them outfits. The dolls was in my closet, put back in they boxes and nobody was going to play with them, I told her.

"Now can you tell me how you doing, Grandma?" I ask.

"I'm fine, been lost a little, but I'm an old woman .What do you expect? Your Mama found me and keeps pulling on me. Soon as I get a good shot, I'm going to pop her one. This trip we on is getting near the end 'cause the road we on getting mighty empty. You been doing good I see. You know, Almena, I never thought you was slow. You was just my grandbaby and I thought you had a lot to learn; that's what I always thought. You was a promising child." I felt a tear creeping up in the corner of my eye but I was not going to cry. My grandmother loved me. This was good news!

"She was headed right to the pits of hell," Mama said, "I had to pull her back. Something tells me she going anyway still wanting to fight at her age. She done lost her false teeth. I'm telling you I don't know what to do with her. I got to hold on to her arms at all times. She just wanders off in a second. You are doing better than good, Almena. Now, when summer comes, I want you to get yourself a house of your own. Sell the house and land in the country. You can do it."

Grandma cut in, "See that's why I'm going to pop her. She always telling you to sell my stuff. She ain't never had a pot to piss in and she wants you to sell mine."

"Stop fussing you two," I joined in. "I'm still depending on you to guide me. Be nice. Stay still, Grandma. And Mama, have a little more patience. I'll always need your advice. Now, good-bye and I love you both."

It come to me after a while, here I was telling them what to do. Maybe I done caught my mind. Knowing what to do or not to do, that's a dream I've had for a long time. Balanced, that's what I wanted to be. I'm going to make a plan tomorrow, just like I plan my rugs. Oh brother, I dropped about six rows of stitches in my rug thinking about all this stuff. I guess I ain't good enough to do two things at one time, so right now I'm gonna be a damn good weaver.

After about a week of peaceful weaving and comfortable home life, there was a knock on the door, a rather urgent knocking. Habibah stood there looking kinda worried. I was glad to see her. "Come on in here, girl." I could tell she was scared. She pulled back a little. So I said, "Don't worry Ms. Malinda has had a change of heart. She's very sorry for her actions, and anyhow we really need our hair done. Let me tell her you are here."

Habibah stopped me, "Almena, have you seen James?" She has a cute accent. It's like cotton to your ears, real soft.

"Of course," I told her. "He working down at the church. He'll be home shortly. Now git in here, girl, and talk to Ms. Malinda."

She came in tipping and shy like. I left her in the hallway and went in and told Ms. Malinda that Habibah was here and ask her would she like her hair done. Ms. Malinda kinda rolled her eyes but she said, "Tell her to come on in." After a couple of deep breaths, Ms. Malinda said, "Young lady I owe you an apology. I'm so sorry for acting up like I did. I have some things that I need to work on and I'm sure that you are a clean and decent person. Can you bring yourself to forgive my behavior?"

"Yes ma'am, we all have bad days."

"Thank you for understanding," Ms. Malinda said, smiling. "But don't call me ma'am or we're back to where we was."

Habibah just needed to be needed. Her spirits picked right up and she said, "Okay, now let me make you a queen and do that head of yours."

We got Ms. Malinda to the bathroom to wash and freshen up her hair. It took some doing but Ms. Malinda's hair looked so good after it was cleaned and braided. She looked ten years younger and I know she felt better. We fixed lunch and settled Ms. Malinda down for her soaps.

I was next. My hair was a mess. But you know what? It had grown at least two inches. While she worked on me, I remarked to Habibah, "Chile, you look kinda sad. Is there anything I could help you with?"

The floodgates of heaven broke loose. She was crying, snot flying all about and sniffling. This here woman could wail. It seem like she was in some kinda trouble and James hadn't been to see her in weeks. I thought to myself men ain't never forever. She been tricked but it wasn't the time to tell her this. Of course now how did I know that for sure? But that's what I thought.

She kept saying, "I can't go home, I can't go home." I thought she meant where she was living. Now, I knew Ms. Malinda was sorry for her actions before but I knew Ms. Malinda wasn't going to take in no more roomers. James was going to have to find this woman some other place to live. "I don't want to go back to Africa just yet." She said.

"But I thought you loved it there."

That's when she explained, between sniffles, "It is beautiful and my family is there, but there is no way to earn a living." Her family depends on her to help them and she had somehow disgrace them. It was hard for me to keep up with her. Them Africans can talk fast when they upset and all. Some of the sounds coming out of her I had never heard before. It was screeching sound that climbed the walls. So I shut my mouth and made a hush sound "Wait on James, baby. He probably got some answers." I wished I hadn't ask her nothing. *Oh Mercy!*

Habibah calmed down after a brief hiccupping spell and helped me with the laundry. We mopped the stairs down and before long we was singing, “I Got A New Attitude.”

The twins came in about three, hungry as usual, and the first thing Grace asks Habibah was, “Why ain’t you working over at that braid shop? They don’t like you?” If that child didn’t become a doctor, she’d make a good lawyer, ‘cause she’d come right out and ask what happen and what’s wrong.

“It just didn’t work out,” Habibah quietly said.

Glory gave Habibah a pat on the back, shaking her Holy Ghost head. “A lot of things don’t work out. But you’ll be alright.”

I made them eat they snack and go up to do they homework.”We waiting on James for some grown people conversation, so git.”

Grace hollered down, “Well, you going to be waiting, ‘cause he taking my music teacher home first.”

Oh Mercy! A sob slips from Habibah’s lips. I could see the hurt lump in her throat. “Don’t pay them kids no mind. It’s probably is just a ride,” I said, trying to sound like I believed this.

“Why don’t you come see my rug I’m working on? I’m a weaver you know.” I was guiding Habibah up the steps. *The Lord knows, I’m going to have a talk with Grace about telling things without thinking or being asked. That’s my child, but she can test your nerves.*

James came home about an hour later, whistling as he entered the second door. As he had been doing lately, he went right in to greet his sister. I told Habibah to wait upstairs and freshen up a bit, until I let James know she was here. Running down the steps at full speed I could hear him as he greeted his sister. “Hey beautiful,” he said loudly to her.

And of course Ms. Malinda ate that compliment up. She asked him, “How you like my hair? Did you ever think I’d be wearing African braids?”

“No, but they are becoming. Let me know when you want to go to the motherland,” he teased her.

“Your friend Habibah did them for me. She ain’t such a

bad girl. She is very gentle with a person." I was standing in back of James now and when he turned around and saw me his face looked like he was sucker punched.

"Stop sneaking up on people, Almena. I'm going to get to you." He smiled and licked his lips.

"Hush, James. I never sneak." I raised a finger pointing to upstairs, but he wasn't getting what I was saying at all.

Turning back around he blew Ms. Malinda a kiss and said, "I've got to go back to the church to lock up after a meeting this evening. This part-time gig is turning into overtime work. Sis, you want me to bring you some ice cream tonight?"

Ms. Malinda laughed, "No thank you. It looks like you might be busy tonight. That girl, whatever her name is, is upstairs waiting on you, lover man." About that time, Habibah was coming down the steps. The look on James's face was like a caught up rat. He looked constipated. "Hey lady," he tried to recover. "How's my favorite girl?"

"She ain't well at all." I sang out, "Mr. Grey." I stepped around him and in between him and the now staring at him Habibah.

He took Habibah's hand and said, "Let's talk about it. My room is in the back." As they reached the doorway of his room I heard him tell her he had to go back to work in about an hour. *Ain't that just like a man when things ain't going so good? Now he got a time limit for discussions.*

CHAPTER SEVENTEEN
Pain

Closing the door to my room, I stood in front of her, arms outstretched and pinning her against the door, thinking what can I say to this woman. The darkness of the meager room fit in with the look on Habibah's face. Her face was so full of desperation and confusion. It choked me, like swallowing a pea that went down the wrong way. I took her in my arms and held her close.

"I'm working on it, girl. Believe me, I'm thinking of how I can make your situation better and how you can stay here in New Haven."

She moved away and waited for me to continue. I was mute. What could I say? She sat down on my burgundy covered bed. The springs of the mattress groaned with the weight of her world. "James, is that all you think I came here for?"

I remained silent. I didn't want to guess wrong. I lay down on top of her, putting my lips close to her ear. "Girl, you smell good," I whispered.

"James, don't!" Habibah twisted away from me. "It is important for me to stay here, but what I want to know first is what do we have? Why have I not heard from you these last weeks? I did not think you would leave me to face this problem alone. You said you would be there for me." Her eyebrows were arched high, her lips quivered and turned down. Habibah spoke with indignation in her tone. The cadence of her words was not loud but sharp. "James where you at?"

"You are not alone, baby. I have spoken to the lawyer twice and he says he is trying to call in some favors so that the case against you is dropped."

Her face tightened even more. "I repeat, where you at with us?"

"Baby, listen I have a problem, drugs. Right now I'm clean. I'm going to my meetings, working part-time and trying to be a man, a man worthy of a woman like you. I have not for one minute stopped caring about you, but you don't deserve a work in progress. I've always used women as a release and then moved on. That is not the case with you. If ever there was a woman that I would commit to, it would be a woman like you." *Gently I was trying to get to the truth.* Running my hands over her braids and along the back of her neck, I asked, "Do you really want a dope fiend for a man? How do you think I feel knowing that one more slip and you would be sent packing? Sweetie, I have my sister who is very ill and knows nothing about this latest mess. Every day, when I come into this house I see hope in her eyes, that I'm alright, that at the end of her life her brother is a decent man who has overcome drugs. I want that for her. I want that for us, too." *How could I tell Habibah, that sometimes a man just wants to have sex?*

"Don't take this wrong, but I never told you that I loved you, but I do feel responsible for you." I tried again to pin my weight against her, 'cause if I were her I would have slapped the shit out of me. She rolled away fast and stood with her back to me and arms folded just under her breast. I could see her reflection in the mirror on the back of my door. She saw right through my flip-flop explanations.

"Sweetheart, I have not been to see you at the house, because it's a danger for your freedom, not to mention the drugs I got came from the area you live in. It's a temptation I just don't need." Looking into the mirror, I saw tears flow down her face. I felt like a piece of dirty toilet paper. "I can't handle a relationship while I'm in treatment. Habibah, I just can't give you what you want right now. But I can guarantee you this: you will not be alone in that courtroom. We're going to work this out. The lawyer also told me if he can't get it dropped right away he could get a postponement so just hold on. I want you to call him right now, while I'm here with you to hear what he is saying."

She took tissue out of her bra and wiped her regal face, while I dialed the lawyer's number. The lawyer told her exactly what I told her; in fact he told her he had already had the case adjourned until the end of June. I could tell that made her feel a little better by the way her breathing eased up and she nodded. When she hung up, she turned her eyes on me again as if she could look right through me. Not crying now, her face had a worn out sadness on it. Nervously, I asked, "Baby do you need any money?"

"No, I'm working over at....What difference does it make?"

"Habibah, can you ever forgive me?"

"Forgive you? That's too much to ask of me right now. I know you say I shouldn't want you but I chose you. You didn't choose me. And right now, I hate being so wrong."

I reached to hug her. She was stiff so I held on to her hands. No words was spoken, no promises lent, but during that silence we both said the most meaningful things. No more. This wasn't the way grown people with any feelings should treat each other. I knew this was game, set and match and I lost.

She turned and was out the door before I could think of anything else to say. Almena was yelling something down the stairs as Habibah ran for the front door. I don't think either of us heard or cared what it was. I watched her dash down the steps and walk with her head slightly down up Dixwell Avenue. That's a strong woman walking there. She had come across the world with a dream, met up with the likes of me and still she charged only herself.

#‡#‡#‡#‡#‡#‡#‡#‡#

While Habibah was in the room with James, I went to

sit awhile with Ms. Malinda. I couldn't hear what was going on in the back room. Ms. Malinda looked up from her game show and said, "Almena, never chase a man. Before you know it you'll be the one who's caught."

Now, I don't think Ms. Malinda was a man-hater. She just understood the low-down type. Since our hair was done, we decided to do our nails the best we could and to my surprise they turn out pretty good.

"I'll be having a gentleman caller myself tomorrow," she said while blowing her nails dry. I looked at her. *Mercy*! Now she was better but a good loving would kill her for sure. When she saw the look on my face, she burst out laughing, "Not that kind of visit. It's a business meeting I've been putting off."

"Well thank you saints!"

She laughed again, "The business meeting will be around 11:00. Could you prepare a light snack?"

"No problem, I'm glad you feeling well enough to have a guest."

I went back upstairs to my busybody children to see what they might want for dinner. Grace was finished her homework and Glory was just about finished with her arithmetic. Her only problem was she was running out of fingers, so I loaned her some of mine to finish counting on. They wanted grilled cheese sandwiches and tomato soup, Glory's favorite and the easiest for me to put together. I didn't want to go to the kitchen too soon because James and Habibah was still talking, and his room was just off the kitchen. *Boy, would I like to be a fly on the wall and hear that conversation. There's a story there in that room. It was painful or full of lies or maybe it was full of forgiveness. I'm thinking too much again, but my seeing is coming back.* One look at Habibah's face had made my mind race.

Upstairs we played a couple games of Candyland until I heard walking in the hallway downstairs. James was walking Habibah out and I called down to them. "Habibah, can you come back next week and do our hair? Wait for me! I'll come down to pay you!"

She yelled up, "I'll get it next week," and ran out the doors.

James stood there rubbing his head; there's a spot right at the top of his head that was missing some hair. *Serves him right if he lost all his hair 'cause I know he done hurt that girl's feelings.*

"James, now what? Did you do something to hurt that girl?" I started in on him and he cut me off.

"Almena, not now, I don't need this now," he barked. He stood there rubbing his temples with both his hands.

He turned and went back to his room. As I heard the door close, I felt sorry for both of them, James and Habibah. The air in that hallway was heavy with pain, almost like smoke that couldn't be fanned away.

I made our quick and easy dinner, looked in on Ms. Malinda and tried to return to a peaceful night of weaving. This New Haven rug was going to be a big one. It took a lot of concentration to show all the situations and feelings going on around here. Only months ago, I needed a subject to weave. Now the subject was big and winding. *That's it! I'll make a big, winding road of emotions on my rug with sad bumps and happy humps!*

My weaving continued into the night, as I tried different ways to make sad bumps. Memories of Coral and the boys burst forth in my head. How would our lives be now if they was still with us? Would all my bumps be happy ones? What caused Malcolm to kill everything that breathed in that house? Right after the murders I had to push all these questions out of my head because of the children. I couldn't go forward trying to hold on to that ugly past. But at night, when it was just me and my stitches, I'd wonder. Was Coral running to the front door to try to get away and across the road to us? Was Melvin and Percy asleep in they beds and killed first and why? It was times like these that made me weave lies for the answers I didn't know. Sometimes the night wasn't right no matter how bright the day had been. The last few nights I felt something pulling me backward. A gripping feeling on my heart like the shadow of an intruder was biting at my mind.

I put aside my weaving. No need to stitch when yesterday's dried up pain comes calling. Walking as lightly as I could, I peeped in the children's room. I shuddered as light from a night light fell across Grace's face. She was a miniature Coral, and, aside from me being a weaver, my job was to make sure her mountains was mole hills. Warm tears gathered in my eyes but I felt my back straighten up and my shoulders square for I knew that I would throw myself in front of a speeding bus before I would fail them kids.

Tipping back into the front room of our kitchenette, I reached behind the sofa and pulled out the family rug, the one with Coral and the kids all smiling. I wrapped it around my shoulders. I sat back down in Grandma's rocker with my hand to my head. Glory must have heard my feelings. She came into the room and pulled the rug from around me, and climbed up into my lap. She laid her head right near my heart and we rocked until both of us fell asleep.

CHAPTER EIGHTEEN
Curtis

After the twins left for school the next morning I got busy making a small feast for Ms. Malinda and her guest. I made a crab dip, a creamy crab soup, deviled eggs and a fresh garden salad all surrounded with them small fancy crackers. I had hot ginger tea steeping in the teapot, too. A gassy morning brunch, but I didn't have such a good night.

Promptly at 11:00, the doorbell rang. It kinda caught me off guard I was so used to hard knocking. At the door, there stood a well-dressed egg yolk man with a fancy briefcase in one hand and a pleasing smile under a red mustache. "Good morning young lady, I'm Mr. Gibbs," he said, touching his hat. "I believe that Ms. Grey is expecting me."

He had the manners of a butler without the white gloves, of course. He was a portly man about five feet four inches tall and about four feet wide, with red chin hairs. I was studying him, as I do everybody, and he winked at me. *Oh Mercy*! "Come on in, sir." I took his coat and hat to hang on the coat rack. That coat was as soft as a cotton ball. Cashmere. It said so on the tag. I had never worked with cashmere before in my rugs but I had always imagined what it might feel like.

"She's been expecting you, Mr. Gibbs. If you can wait here in the parlor I'll let her know you are here," I said, but I was thinking. *He really do have eye problems, moving his eyebrows up and down and looking at me like he's some hog butcher.* I was scared to turn away from him, so I backed out of the parlor.

Tapping on Ms. Malinda's door and then entering, I found her fully dressed. All made up and sitting across one of them French chairs she had in her room. She had on a light blue velvet dressing gown with light blue slippers. Her eyes was even covered with light blue coloring and her lips was a shiny bright red. It's a wonder how her lashes had grown overnight too. *Maybe she is trying to court.*

"Set the lunch up in this room, Almena," she said, and then she called out to him, "Curtis! Bring your fine self in here and stop scaring my niece."

"I'm at your command, my lady. As for your niece, fear not my delicate one; I am harmless."

"Curtis meet Almena, she's come to help me out for a while."

"Pleased and charmed, Ms. Almena," he bowed.

I nodded and covered my mouth because he could hardly bend and it was funny. *Oh Mercy*! Half a bend and he was out of breath. *Now he's a whopper if ever I saw one.*

I served them the soup and placed the salad and dips on a teacart within easy reach of Ms. Malinda's chair. When I poured him a cup of tea, he called it "lovely just lovely." Then he smacked his lips and said, "Everything is just scrumptious."

I sure hope he felt that way about an hour from now. I don't know what's wrong with me. Grandma had once told me that strong ginger tea is better than Drano. They might be in a terrible way shortly.

They talked a while about the good old days and then he pulled out some papers from his case. Ms. Malinda told me to close her door and she would call me when she needed me again. She also told me on the way out, "Curtis ain't married, Almena, you know." Ms. Malinda could sure make me nervous with that kinda talk. She was always, when she wasn't sickly, matching folks up.

I had wanted to change those burgundy curtains in the kitchen and this was the perfect time. I would be close enough to hear them if they called me. I had purchased some white curtains, nothing fancy, but they might bring light into the kitchen. After hanging the curtains and taking the trash out—'cause crabmeat is tasty but kinda smelly—I heard Ms. Malinda calling "Almena! Curtis has some papers we want you to sign."

So I washed my hands and smooth my braids and went in there. I was trying to look like I knew what this was. I didn't have no idea Mr. Curtis Gibbs was Ms. Malinda's lawyer and they wanted me to witness Ms. Malinda's will. I thought to myself. *Here we go talkin' bout death again.* It didn't take much to make my mind go right to the grave. So I told them, "I don't want to witness no death statement."

"Oh, no, no, no, my darling sister. This is not a death statement, although I can see the confusion. Sit, my lovely, while I enlighten you to just what's happening here." Mr. Gibbs pranced to the middle of the room as he talked.

I sat down on the edge of the chair to the left of Ms. Malinda bed. Ms. Malinda looked over at him with a twinkle in her eye, like she was about to see a good television show. She brushed crumbs from her spread and covered her mouth with her hand.

He took a fresh hankie out of his back pocket and patted his face. "These documents," he said loudly, "Are living statements of wishes and desires of persons who see fit to give or shall we say bequeath things to others after they depart this world as we know it. The dead cannot do that, precious." He rubbed his hands together as if they was cold. "We all must depart and if we are wise and informed we are allowed by law to say how we, not being able to speak for ourselves, want our valuables to be distributed. So you see, you're not signing a death statement, you're witnessing a living wish of your lovely, living aunt who we shall pray will be with us a long time. Long enough to see you happily living a wonderful life, with a man who can make all things clear and concise to you."

He had moved in close up to my chair and I pushed back in my chair as I felt his hand tap my left shoulder. "Everyone needs to have these documents drawn up, it speaks for them. Do you follow?"

Looking up at him, I nodded, yes, but seem like he had danced around the dead part. Swallowing the lump in my throat that all them big words had caused, I said, "Well since she going to be around a long time, I better think this here signing thing over."

Ms. Malinda laughed and clapped her hands on the bed. She was laughing but tears was coming out of her eyes. She grabbed a hold of my hand and said, "Almena, do me a favor and sign these papers before Curtis does another round of his legal bullshit. Just sign dear, for me. She handed me a pen.

"You sure, Ms. Malinda? I don't want—"

"Girl, sign that thing so I can get back to bed and watch *As the World Turns*." I can't say no to her, not ever.

I signed maybe five or six pages as the witness to this will and with that, Mr. Curtis Gibbs handed me his card and said, "If you want to draw up one for yourself and your kids just give me a call."

I felt better then.

I was showing Mr. Curtis Gibbs to the door and on the way, he leaned into me, placed a sweaty hand on my arm and asked me, "Do you ever go to the movies?" *Mercy!*

I told him, "I'm saved and I don't sit in no dark room looking at nothing."

He snickered and said, "I beg your pardon, sister?"

I let him out and went to clean up they mess. I told Ms. Malinda what he asked me and she thought it was the funniest thing. I helped her back in bed and went back to my kitchen duties. She was still laughing at Mr. Curtis Gibbs. I like hearing her laugh and seeing her smile. Even some days when I knew she was struggling with pain, she's been able to laugh.

CHAPTER NINETEEN
Turning Times

It was warming up a little outside. The snow had melted and all there was to contend with was the cold air still determined to hang around. The cold made it hard to relax my muscles. Detail weaving cannot be done during the cold of winter. It ain't natural.

Glory and Grace was assigned a project for Valentine's Day. Glory was excited. "I'm going to make the biggest heart ever," she said.

Grace moped, pouting as she fumbled with her scissors and her poster paper.

"Whatcha going to make Grace? I asked, holding my scissors up to show her how to cut a heart

She frowned more. "Nothing. I don't like hearts."

"That's not like you. You like our hearts, don't you?" I rubbed her shoulders.

"Yes," she whined. "But not Henry Munson! He picks boogers all day and he already gave me a valentine."

I hid my smile by coughing into my hands. "Well, sweetheart, you don't have to be his valentine. Tell Henry you already have a valentine and it's your entire family."

"Okay but if he puts one of them boogers on me, I'm gon' git him." She balled up her fist and swung it around with the force of a boxer."

"Come on, my little fighter, none of that. Let's go to the art store and get what you need to make the best project ever. Since we had not been to the library in weeks, maybe we could stop in there, too." The girls had this Valentine's Day project due soon, so I was setting Grace up. I figure

Grace could do the writing part, and Glory could do the artwork.

I called us a cab. We bundled up and off we went to get what they might need. Glory got glue and red paper and shiny things, while Grace helped select the size of the poster they was going to make. We took a cab back to the library and, by now, the ladies who worked there knew us on sight. They was helpful and showed us where we could find out all the information on Valentine's Day. Some information was interesting but too much for second graders to really understand, so after a while I thought maybe Grace could write her own poem. The light came up in her eyes. She was on board now. She checked out some children's books on poems. "Now I'm gonna have something to say about this Valentine's Day stuff for sure."

My Gracie always had to have her say.

When we was leaving, I noticed a sign posted wanting part-time help in the library on Tuesday and Thursday from the hours of ten to two. I wished I could get that job. It was just shelving books but I loved books and being in the library was so peaceful. I took the application and one of the ladies said, "Ms. Johnstone, if you put in that application, I'll put in a good word for you. We miss you when you and those kids don't come in."

She knew my name from my library card. I was so tickled. You never know who is paying attention to you. That's why Mama always said, "Act like you got some sense." The librarian introduced herself as Doris Lambert. I thanked her but I still needed to see if Ms. Malinda would need me during those hours.

"We will see."

Ms. Lambert was a heavy-set white woman with small features. Her hands looked too tiny for her fatty arms and her lips disappeared into her round cheeks when she smiled. She had a light laugh, very pleasant. Grace was even more excited than me. "If my auntie works here, do we get to keep these books?"

"No," Ms. Lambert smiled down at Grace. "But you can

sure get all the books you want to read and she can return them when she comes to work."

"Oh, well den, how much you gon' pay her for all that book carrying?"

Mercy! That child had seen too much of *Let's Make a Deal.* I laughed and grabbed Grace's arm. "That's enough investigation for today." I left with my artist and my agent running along side of me.

James met us at the door. He had on his work khakis and the church keys in his hands. He patted the girls on the head, "How's my little women?"

"We good," they said in unison.

Licking his lips toward me and smiling he said, "I'm good too. I'm glad you're back."

Holding my hand over Grace's mouth, I stopped her before she could give the details of the day. "Y'all go head in outta this cold." James's hair was freshly cut and he smelled like talc powder and Old Spice.

"James, I been meaning to ask you if you would like to attend church this Sunday."

"I'll think about it, Almena." He jabbered and bounced down the porch steps.

We peeped in Ms. Malinda's room and she was not there. I thought maybe she was in the bathroom so the children and I headed toward the stairs. And then I heard a noise in the kitchen, like running water. Ms. Malinda stood in the center of the kitchen dressed in a nice peach colored sweatsuit and matching slippers. She had cut up onions, celery, carrots and green peppers and had the turkey wings ready for baking in the oven. Rice and string beans, each in they own stewing pots, surrounded the chopped vegetables.

"Now, close your mouth, Almena. I'm tired of that bed and that television. Come on in here and help me finish cooking. I had hoped dinner would be well on its way before you got back but you so fast with your errands. There'll be no soup and sandwiches tonight."

The children ran to her "I'm glad you outta that bed," Glory gushed.

"This is a good day, ain't it, Auntie?" Grace boasted. "We got a surprise for you too."

"Now Grace, let's wait awhile for surprises. Let's all help in the kitchen." I scooted the kids upstairs to take off their coats and wash their hands. It is wonderful to see her up and about. I'm taken aback daily at how much strength she seems to be gaining. Ms. Malinda was full of surprises. I didn't even know that Ms. Malinda could cook.

She sat down at the kitchen window and peered out, "I'm feeling stronger, Almena. I know I'm not going to get completely well, but why waste this day in the bed."

"Well," I said. "She got a new at-ti-tuuddeee." And I sang, in my best Patti voice.

She jumped in, shaking as much as her sick body would allow, "We got a new attituuuudddeee." After that, we almost fell down laughing.

Grace covered her ears as we continued, but Glory sang along as best she could using her own words in place for the ones she didn't know.

Ms. Malinda smiled hard, but there was a bit of sadness in her eyes as she stared at the curtains. "Thank you, Almena."

"For what? My off-key singing?" I laughed harder.

She shook her head. "Umph, umph sugar. For those pretty curtains, I like them." She looked at something on the floor. I didn't see anything there. "I know I should have took all this burgundy out of my life a long time ago." She turned and looked me in my face."On my next good day, maybe we could go shopping."

"One day at a time," I told her. "Burgundy ain't so bad."

"Yes it is." Ms. Malinda said rolling her neck. We pause for about a second and did we laugh then.

Grace made the lemonade and I showed Glory how to snap the string beans. I looked around this kitchen, seeing everybody working and being a family. I was so grateful we was where we was and somehow we was being allowed to still be ourselves. This here was better than good.

I basted the turkey wings in cream of mushroom sauce adding more finger licking goodness to it. We set up dinner right there in the kitchen. Of course, between sucking on a tip of them wings, Grace brought up the library job. "Surprise!" Grace boomed excitedly. "Guess who got a job at the big old library?"

"I don't know," Ms. Malinda said, "but I'll give some butter cake I been hiding if you tell me."

"Auntie, that's who and she can bring home all the books she wants."

"Yes." Glory added "They like us real good."

"Now hold on. I got to apply first and anyway I'm fine here helping out and I like that. I swear you two will make a mention into a sure enough thing. I need to be right here to help out."

"What a wonderful opportunity, Almena. You could sharpen up your speaking skills and learn about this area at the same time. How much is the pay?" Ms. Malinda asked.

"I'm not sure. I'm good right here with you."

"Stop worrying about me. I'll be fine with James. Now what's the pay?" She said again.

"Not so fast now. I ain't got the job yet and I'm going to have to rock on my decision to even apply for it first."

Ms. Malinda fish-eyed me and said, "Almena, will you tell me, what's to rock on? It's a job for four hours! It ain't brain surgery!" She didn't know how much trouble I could get in if I didn't think about things first.

"Well, I'll see." I took a picture of this setting in my mind. Weaving this into my New Haven rug would take some doing. Maybe I'll make more than one rug and if I did, this one would simply be called *Women.*

Ms. Malinda had worn herself out after dinner. We walked to her room and helped her get settled in bed. She looked at us and smiled, "You and the kids sure make a difference in my life."

James came back just in time to mess up my kitchen. He stood in the refrigerator door picking at food I had just put away.

"Here, stop that. Let me fix you a plate." I smacked at his hands. He was doing so much better. He wasn't drinking. He was working and he was taking an interest in our lives again. I really didn't mind him messing around in the kitchen.

Grace whispered loudly to him, "I bet you know a lot about Valentine's Day, don't you?"

"No I don't," he told her. "I usually disappear the week before it comes around."

"And the truth shall set you free," I said, hitting him with the wet dishrag.

He laughed. Today was a good day.

I rocked in Grandma's rocker about two hours and come up with nothing. The long days was catching up with me. I'm going to fill out the application and wait a day or so and see if I get any resistance from Mama and Grandma. Taking care of the children, Ms. Malinda, and my weaving, all that took up a good part of my time already. I don't want to be over-took. I fell asleep in that chair.

Sunday was my day to greet the members and visitors at the church. I was dressed in all white and feeling very blessed for this week's happenings. Grace and Glory went downstairs to Sunday school. I had them dressed in all white too with green ribbons around their pony tails. They looked so cute and so innocent and so eager for life.

The church was filling up. I looked toward the door as I passed out the programs for the service and there stood James. He had on his black suit and a light gray shirt and tie. Well, we all know he could clean up good. I gave him a hug and a program and directed him to an usher to be seated.

The choir had sung for at least an hour. When Pastor Joel finally stood up to preach, he seemed to look right at James and said, "Nothing is too hard for God." He may have been talking to James but something inside me leaped. I knew I could take the job at the library if it was offered. I knew it was a sign that if I had gone this far in our new start, it wasn't on my own. I still had two angels looking out for me. Even if I failed, which I knew how to do, I also knew how to get up and stand still until I figured out the right path. I decided I was telling Ms. Malinda that night that I was putting in that application.

James's showing up at church caused a stir among the greeters. Almost all of the single women, and if you ask me the married ones, too, wanted to know all about him. Sisters who had never spoken to me was greeting me and wanting my phone number. My seeing started up and let me know a mess was coming. I had to head this off or I wouldn't get no sleep, rocking all night. When he come back by the door after service I said, "James, don't wait for us I'll meet you at the house."

James always caught on too fast. Right in front of some of them sisters, he said, "No I'm going to walk my family home." Then he teasingly smiled. *Mercy!*

I could have killed him right inside the church. Standing there waiting for Grace and Glory, I lean into him and said, "James you always have to go too far." Nothing but a stinky mess was going to come out of James's statement 'cause I had already told them sisters I was not married. Then here come Glory and Grace running up the stairs, "Hey, Uncle James," they yelled. There wasn't a thing I could do but go on home like a family.

"Oh stop pretending, Almena, you know you want me," James heckled. "Save me from them men-hungry sisters."

He was prancing like a rooster. Lawd, I couldn't git in the house fast enough. I almost tore the heel off my shoe stumbling down the street.

Glory told James, "I'll save you, 'cause I'm a Holy Ghost-filled-child and them men-hungry sisters can't escape my powers. I'll shake them right away from you."

"Sometimes you can be so irritating," Grace told James. He let out a big old laugh when Grace said that. Ms. Malinda and James had fun with me all day about that.

"Now James, when you go next week with your family, you got to act dignified. You hear me, James," Ms.

Malinda teased. "Next week you sit your ass down and breathe easy around them sisters and stop lusting." They like to fell double over laughing at the whole situation. *Oh Mercy*!

James makes me unstable sometimes. Of course that didn't take much. I still liked him more than I should. That is disturbing to me, knowing his past and all. Now, I need to ask Mama why women, like Habibah and me, like messy men. Men who will take your mind and your loving for a promise and that promise never happens. It ain't right.

Later in the evening, Ms. Malinda asked to see how my New Haven rug was coming along and I showed her. This rug was a hook rug, so the threads stood high from the background. Hook weaving takes a steady hand. I had finished Sadie, the bus scene, the house, her, and Habibah. She quietly looked at it and then I noticed a softness come to her face. "It's beautiful, Almena! You should be in a museum! Your work is so detailed! You have made me look like I did twenty years ago."

"No, Ms. Malinda. That is how I see you today. I know the lines of life and I'm a damn good weaver."

The very next day, I bundled myself up and returned to the library with my application in hand. I gave it to Ms. Lambert, and she said she would see if I could be interviewed right away. They sure had a lot of rules for this shelving job. I waited about fifteen minutes, pumping my legs up and down. She came back saying I was to follow her and speak with her boss, Mr. Panchenko. I followed Ms. Lambert to a back office past bookshelves that reached almost to the ceiling. We turned left and entered into a large, messy, office. Papers was everywhere. Mr. Panchenko sat behind his brown desk never looking up. Both his hands covered his mouth and he was leaning forward on his elbows.

"This is Ms. Johnstone," Ms. Lambert said and walked away, smiling.

"Good morning, Ms. Johnstone. Let me look over your application," he said. Mr. Panchenko looked up and said,

"Please have a seat," before he began looking at the application again.

"Good morning. Thanks for seeing me." I sat on the edge of the chair nervously, 'cause I had not put down much on that application. I wish he would look up. All I could see was a white man with big black glasses on and dirty brown colored hair. He sat with his shoulders hunched over and shirtsleeves rolled up. Head still down.

"We're looking for someone who is most of all dependable. I see you are from Maryland. I love that area." He was reading that off my application and had still not made eye contact with me. "Doris tells me you're a frequent user of the library. Are you familiar with the Dewey Decimal System," he mumbled.

Well, I spoke right up and said, "I never met Dewey but I get along with people real good so I'm sure it wouldn't be a problem."

He looked up then and shook with laughter. "Ms. Johnstone, I'll be in touch within the next week or two to let you know if I think you are a good fit for the job." He shook my hand and nodded. As I walked out, he chuckled some more.

At least he's pleasant, I thought. It must've helped to have a good spirit. He had a port wine birthmark splitting down half his white lips, chin and neck. I knew life had been difficult for him. He was spotted. You never can tell what kind of afflictions you can just run into. I know I was saved, but I knew I was taking one of Ms. Malinda cocktails when I got back at the house. This here job searching ain't for the faint of heart.

Back at the house, Ms. Malinda told me that I had two calls since I was out. One call was from a sister of the church and another from Sadie from Elktown.

"From Sadie?" I had been holding my coat in my hand, getting ready to take it upstairs. It fell from my nerveless hands. "I wonder how she got our phone number." My voice shook. I sat down on the arm of the nearest chair to steady myself. The way Ms. Malinda drawled out Sadie's name on her tongue and rolled her eyes upward, I knew that she had an unpleasant talk with her.

"What happened with Sadie?" I asked. It seemed like when Ms. Malinda answered the phone Sadie went right into her questioning ways, like she worked for *Dick Tracy.*

"I don't know how you put up with her. That woman asked me who I was and what relationship did I have with you. I told her in no uncertain words that it was none of her business who and what I was. The party she is calling for isn't in and if she wanted to leave a number for you I would see to it that you'd get it. Her tone and phone manner are very demanding. Here's what I think; since she works for the post office, perhaps she should write a letter next time. That's what I told her, too. I rarely let myself get to this level of frustration. It has been a long time since I bit somebody but she will do just fine and I don't even know her."

We was silent for a minute then she burst out laughing. I joined in on the laughing 'cause it was catchy. She stood there swaying and laughing. But just like a hiccup I knew Sadie was trouble. I could just picture Sadie being properly bit by the lady from New Haven. Whatever Sadie wanted I wasn't going to call her now. Life was too good. I pushed myself to my feet, picked up my coat, and slowly climbed the steps to our kitchenette. My calf muscles began to cramp.

While Ms. Malinda settled again to watch her soaps, I brought my weaving down to start working on James. I had not thought of how I would stitch him. Maybe as the handsome man on the bus, or the man laying inside the doors of the house, or the teasing well-meaning object of women's affections. I had to figure out if I was going to just use one of those aspects or combine them in one. Up to this point, the rug had been light in feelings except for those bumps. I rarely do portraits and to me that's what it was now. James would be one of the seeds of my story although he wasn't the main concern. I wanted a person to travel with me and the children, looking at this rug, through our new start and know just what happen. Capturing our times and our personal feelings is important. Weaving is a complicated thing. I love doing it, seeing it and having others be moved by it. I'm going to work it out and that's for sure 'cause I'm a damn good weaver.

The phone rang and I prayed it wasn't Sadie again. Ms. Malinda was talking business like and then she said, "Of course you can. She's right here." As she handed me the phone, I got ready for Sadie but it wasn't her.

"Good afternoon Almena," he said.

My face got hot and I look down at the floor. "Hello, Mr. Gibbs." I thought, now he was getting too friendly.

"I was wondering what church you attended and would you care if I joined you for service this week," he said, all in his butler-talking manner.

I could have pissed myself but prayed instead. *Lord help me get this right.* "Mr. Gibbs, I go to First Emphatic Faith and you're welcome at any time to come and sit in the house of the Lord, to be taught His ways. I promise you, you will be blessed. It is the Lord's house and there is no darkness permitted. We love visitors who come for the right reasons. I will give your number to members of the evangelist ministry and they will be more than happy to meet you and pray with you about your spiritual needs. I hope to see you in church on Sunday. You have a good day, Mr. Gibbs." I dropped the phone down like a hot potato.

Ms. Malinda had pulled up the covers over her head. She was laughing so hard and when I hung up, she whooped and hollered. "You got them lining up like grease on a goose." I did not see the fun in all this attention. The thought of showing up with another man on Sunday made me start itching. Seeing me scratching at myself, Ms. Malinda said, "A salt bath is good for that, Almena." And then she laughed so much, tears was streaming down her face. *Oh Mercy!*

#‡#‡#‡#‡#‡#‡#‡#

Pastor Joel had asked James to come in earlier on Mondays and Thursdays. The church needed a good vacuuming after packed Sunday and Wednesday night services. After what had happened last service I worry about him. Brenda, the church secretary, was truly on the hunt for a good man. She had befriended me and asked several questions about James. I ducked them questions as much as I could but something was up with her and I could tell. She wore more lipstick than usual and her walk and talk became bluesy whenever James was in our company. She even bended over a lot around James, hinting at her breasts. Brenda had a cute round face but suffered from bad knees. Her cute face wore signs of pain when she walked around the church. Hip-itis, that what Mama called it. Brenda's hips was larger than a hog going to market. There was gossip among the greeters that Brenda's first husband ran off with the organ player. Now I don't know how true it was but it ain't nothing like church gossip. Some of them sisters would swear on their souls that it was the truth.

Not wanting to be accused of being jealous. I kept my thoughts to myself. Besides, James a grown man. He should know trouble when he sees it coming. *I hope she don't get him. He does have that wonderful smile.*

Church people, I wonder what they would say if they knew about James and my past. I bet the whole church would have a seizure.

CHAPTER TWENTY
Sadie

The week before Valentine's Day is a busy one for me. For the last eighteen years I had seen many foolish people come through my post office. Some of them will come in here the day before a holiday and want me to get their fifty cent card to a person that same day! I tell 'em, "Sadie Wilson don't move like that and neither do the US Post Office." Folks act like it's a holy day around Elktown. Well, at least I could tell who is courting who. This kind of information could come in handy should a person become confused about their affairs. I have seen enough half dead roses to last me a lifetime. Still it ain't no delivery service going on in Elktown. Folks here had to pick this stuff up. What a waste of money! My mind is too gifted for this foolishness. I have been considering applying for a transfer from this position but somebody has to watch out for this town. The sheriff is busy with other details and Deputy Ray, that redneck, ain't nothing but a messenger.

When the long black limousine pulled up in front of my post office, I knew it was somebody important. However, this is not the direction station but I'll tolerate whoever it is because of the size of that car. My goodness, the car was as long as one side of an Elktown street. A tall dark man in a black suit got out and opened up the back door for his passenger to get out and entered into my post office. In front of me stood a very smartly dressed, pale as butter, man who came straight to the point. "Hello, My name is CeCe Baldwin. Are you Miss Sadie?"

"Yes, I am. How can I help you?"

"I am a consultant from the Boston area and need your assistance. Would you know where I could locate a Ms. Almena Johnstone? I have been to her given address and found that no one is living there. Would you happen to have a forwarding address on Ms. Johnstone. It is most important that I speak with her."

Wonder what he wants with that nit-wit. "Let me see. It seems that I have an old Almena address somewhere, but most of the time she calls me and tells me where she's at and how she's doing. What do you want with Almena? She is a very private person. In fact, she has asked me to see to her affairs."

"I see," said Mr. Baldwin. "Well I need to speak only with Ms. Johnstone. Perhaps you can see to it that she gets my card." He reached into his jacket pocket and pulled out a business card, handing it to me. I took it and flipped it over and ran my fingers over it, this here card was made from expensive paper. Its lettering was printed in gold.

"Ms. Johnstone can reach me at that number. Of course, here's a little something for all your help," he said, handing me a crisp one hundred dollar bill. I know my ears was standing up. I sure could use me some money. He had my full attention when he went on to say, "I will make it worth your while to help me speak with her as soon as possible. This is a cozy little town you have here, a gem of an area indeed. I look forward to hearing from Ms Johnstone soon."

"I certainly will try to help you out Mr. Baldwin," I said. *Shit, for this kind of money I'll drag Almena back here.* "You have a nice day and we'll be calling you."

"Good day, Miss Sadie."

Soon as that car pulled away, I looked up the change of address card sent from the post office in New Haven. On the card, that rocker was sent in care of Ms. Malinda Grey at 240 Dixwell Ave. One phone call to information and I had the number. I called the number to the Grey's residence. "Hello?" a coarse voice said.

"Uh, hello, can I speak with Almena?

"Almena's not here. May I have her return your call?

"Where's she at? This is Sadie from the post office in Elktown and I need to talk to her right now."

"She is not available. If you leave your number, I'll have her call you when she returns."

"Who is this I'm speaking with? I'm a government officer and this is business. What relations are you to Almena? Are them kids with her?"

"I know you didn't ask who I was...'cause that is of no concern of yours. In fact, I don't care for your manner. Since you say you work for the mail service: why don't you just write the next time you need to touch base with Almena. I'm sure your number is listed if you work for the government. I will tell Almena to call you. I'm never questioned by rude people, government or not. I have no patience for vulgar behavior." Click!

She had hung up on me. Maybe I was sharp but I was in no mood for chatting. I kept thinking. *I want to speak to Almena, well at least I'm sure of where she's at. City folks, I dislike their uppity ways. I got a business card and a one hundred dollar bill. Whoever answered that phone, don't realize who she messing with. If Almena don't call me back soon, I'll just call again. The woman on the phone probably just as crazy as Almena.*

Four hours later, I'm still waiting for Almena to call. City people are always so busy. They sound like they ain't got time to tell you nothing about a thing. I would call again but now that I think about it, I still need to check some things out. If an important person wanted to find Almena and wanted to give me a monetary gift for information on her whereabouts, it was my duty as a government employee to find out what the matter is. *I am, after all, concerned about them children.*

Reading the card, I wondered what the National American Society of Fine Appraisers is and what could they want with Almena? I put the money in my pocketbook and tacked the card on my bulletin board. There was a potential for some more gratefulness from Mr.

CeCe Baldwin and I will not be denied. Important people valued my skills; I know that for sure. This might be a delicate thing and they take time. I can wait a little while, or maybe I will call back enquiring about them children....Maybe.

Little did I know but across town, back at the house Grandma had left Almena, Buck Willis the county manger was out there in the backwoods. The County Land Development Department crew was marking off stretches of land it would need to widen the road. Since nobody was out there living, not a soul had come to tell me nothing. That's how they do it around here. They sneaky, Buck Willis come in to the post office about four o'clock that same day and he said to me, "How you doing, Miss Sadie?"

"I'm doing just fine, Mr. Willis." He don't never call me Miss Sadie or ask how I'm doing unless he wants something and that's for sure. He's a redneck like his father was and like his granddaddy was. He don't even pretend to care for colored folks.

"I'm glad to hear that. Listen, Sadie, between me and you, I'm trying to get a hold some folks who done up and left their property. Where you sending Almena Johnston mail at? That piece of land she got out there is going to ruins and it's an eye sore when people pass by there on the way to our town."

That's a lie if ever I heard one 'cause people don't come to town that way and since when he cared about how them backwoods looked. I turned my back to him and made like I was looking through some papers to find the address. "Mr. Willis, come to think of it Almena didn't leave no address. She ain't settled yet. What she does is call me and I tell her what mail she got. What you want me to tell her, she usually calls me once a week."

"You tell that gal I said to call me at the county building. I need to know her intentions. It's a pity and a shame 'bout that place. It's a fire hazard. I wish people was responsible like you, Miss Sadie. It sure would make my job a lot easier." Just then Deputy Ray comes in.

"Hey now Buck! How y'all doing with the clearing?" The

deputy said, while slapping Mr. Willis on the shoulder.

"We doing just fine, Ray," he cut his eyes and cocked his head toward me. "I ain't seen you in awhile, Ray. Let me buy you a beer." He kinda rushed Deputy Ray out the door.

Right after work, I made it my business to drive by Almena's old house and that's when I seen all the road markings and bulldozers and a sign saying County Development. They had knock down all those old tracts houses. I come right back in town and found out that word was, a connection to the interstate was coming through this way. Folks who own land back there had money coming.

I shook my head. *Uhmp uhmp uhmp! I knew it! Them people are building something. Deputy Ray will tell it sooner or later, but in the meantime, I need to talk to Almena.*

CHAPTER TWENTY-ONE
Visions

Glory had worked hard on her school project, gluing and plastering hearts and ribbons with sparkles on the poster. Grace on the other hand would not let her poem be seen. It would be placed in the center of the poster. She was almost finished.

"I just need to find some good words," she said. She had been going around rhyming words and bringing smiles to everyone in the house. She labored with her poem 'cause writing was very important to her. This week my Grace was a poet.

I had not heard a thing from the library and it had been longer than a week. Seem like they would let a person know if they was still under what they called considerations. In the back of my mind was the call from Sadie. I was gathering up the sheets off Ms. Malinda bed when she said, "What's preoccupying your mind, you been like you in a daze."

"I'm just thinking what Sadie want." *I wish I had never filled out that change of address card at the post office. But that rocker is the only thing I really wanted from down home.*

"Let Sadie be. She don't fit," Ms. Malinda barked. "I can tell it ain't nothing but something upsetting. Don't let trouble in. If she took the trouble to check the change of address and then call information for my phone number, she's way more than nosey. She's going to make known what she wants. She already got you walking around here moving like Glory."

“Am I that nervous?”

“Yeah, I watch you sometimes when you think I’m watching my soaps. I’ve learned from you and this is what I think.” She patted the cushion next to her. “Sit. This won’t take long.”

I sat down like a child in wonder at what possibly Ms. Malinda could have learned from me.

“Life is like a layout of one of your rugs. When you begin, you use your vision of what it’s going to be. You lay all the materials and threads on the table and you determine if you have what you need just to start with. Of course you may need some things that are not there yet. Your vision may change. But first, you gather the pieces you can start with, like the backing and the cords for the borders. This gives you a frame into which to make your vision become a rug. Background colors are so important to you; they bring forth the emotions you want people to feel. I can tell. And then you put those feelings and experiences in just the right places, in just the right colors until there is no mistake as to what this image is, and what is happening. Girl, sometimes you concentrate so hard. I can see the wheels turning in your head. Now, sometimes you leave a hidden mystery for others to fill in. But for sure, whoever is really studying your rugs will figure it out and the answer somehow touches them. Stitch by stitch, your rug pulls at a life experience that we all can relate to. Do your life like the rugs, and leave it up to the onlooker, what’s most important about your work or life to them. The details, the story, the colors, the mystery or the knowledge that someone of substance occupied their lives for the time it took to create the rug. Sometimes I see you leave the complicated emotions till last. They may change or they might be too much for a certain type of onlooker. I know it can be tricky. As you stay focused on putting your rug or life together, you will eventually put it all in harmony. Sometimes you will try to place people or emotions where they don’t belong. Then you have to go back to the vision and reevaluate it and place it somewhere else or leave it out all together. That’s why it is so important to do your own rugs and live your own life. Leave other people's visions alone. Their visions may not fit in your frame and when you see it doesn't, stop the invasion. Trust yourself to recognize what's yours. But whatever you do, don't get caught up with other people's visions. Use your own. Some masterpieces and also some miraculous lives are mysteries to everyone but the artist or the liver of that life. Live your life like your vision. You know all this. You're a weaver, the best piecework you can get. Sadie don't fit."

I loved the way Ms. Malinda made sense of things. She had found her way through my rugs. I sat there in silence, trying to find the words to thank her for letting me know that I had reached her with my weaving. I had taught her my weaving feelings and I wondered if I would ever be able to say it how she did it. My eyes flooded with tears. I gave her a hug and swallowed my lumps of pride. "Ms. Malinda, do you ever think I could say things like you say things?"

"All you got to do is put the same mindset into your voice. You've come a long way since that first day I heard you speak. Start studying how to say things. You go to the library more than anybody I know. Study your speech while you in there. They got a room just for that. I know, 'cause I once was kinda slow talking. You got time and as long as you got that, you can do anything you want."

We heard James whistling before he could come through the door. "Angels, my fabulous sister and my wife. Now, what could a man ask for in the middle of the day?" *He was in a good mood today.* "Almena," he called out, "if you only knew what I turned down to come have lunch with you! Girl, you would fix me a steak!"

"How about I fix you some chicken and dumplings hot off the stove? Then, will you tell me?"

"No can do. But trust me. The spirit is with me, though." He was grinning.

"James, you got competition. Curtis Gibbs wants to attend church with Almena." Ms. Malinda kept the teasing up.

"I'm not worried about Curtis. I'll sic Glory on him if he

goes anywhere near my woman." We all started laughing.

Glory's shaking had eased off. If she was excited a person might notice it, but it had come a long way since we left Elktown.

CHAPTER TWENTY-TWO
Valentine

The evening before Valentine's Day, Grace and Glory announced that it was time to show off their Valentine project. They hauled it downstairs with silver flakes raining down as they came. The white glue humped in some areas but everything on it was in place. The poster was decorated beautifully with black butterflies, silver sparkles, and Grace's poem in the center in big red letters:

It is fun being with someone like you.
I like doing all that we do.
You make me feel warm inside.
And you look just like I do.
I smile big because it is hard to hide.
We are sisters, and forever Valentines!

Ms. Malinda and me clapped our hands and told them how we thought it was the best Valentine we had ever seen or heard. Glory stood there grinning and then gave her sister a hug.

As we got ready for bed that night Glory said, "We wanted you to be our Valentine, but we couldn't come up with a name to match yours."

I laughed, "I know you love me and it is a hard name. As long as you have the feelings, I'm happy."

"Are you James's Valentine?" Glory asked.

"No, I think James and me are more like best friends."

Then Glory whined, "Why he keeps calling you his wife then?"

"He's just playing around. Does it bother you?"

Grace spoke up loudly, "Yes! We don't want no more pushing. We don't like boys!"

We had not discussed their scars in months. They was so young I guess I thought it would just go away, but it hadn't. It was still on their minds and somehow I would have to deal with their fears. "That's not going to happen again, sweetheart. We're done with that. Now rest good. You safe here."

That night, because of my nighttime worries, I found myself up waiting for the sun. Helping the children to school that morning with their lunches, book bags, and of course their precious project, I was still thinking on our conversation about the pushing. I wasn't going to discuss this with Ms. Malinda. She was a part of our family but when it came to things like this I knew I needed to use discretion. *I learned that word at the library.* I got to rock until Mama or Grandma tell me what to do.

Coming back to the house after dropping off my two artists, I stepped up on the porch. There stood a messenger 'bout to ring the bell. "Can I help you?"

"If you are Almena Johnstone you can, I have a telegram for her."

"I'm her."

"Good, could you just sign right here." I signed a paper and took the message and stuck it in my pocket.

A telegram was bad news and it was too early for bad news. There's really no good time for bad news so I decide to read it later. Going upstairs to make the beds and gather the weekend laundry, the telegram was weighing me down, yet I am determined not to read it until something good happen that day.

When I went in Ms. Malinda's room to strip her sheets, I could tell she wasn't herself. She was moving very slow and only grunted a good morning. Her voice was rough as she cleared her throat. For the first time since I met her, she looked elderly. Her face likened a woman's who'd been passed by when life was handing out luck. I turned on the radio while she sat brooding about something. News was on all the stations and it was too early for her soaps. I wanted to know what the matter was, but with Ms. Malinda I knew I had to just let it come out on its own. She took her medicine and sat back in one of those French chairs in a dazed state. She tipped her head back against the chair so that the tears that filled her eyes would not spill. Not thinking, I pulled the heavy burgundy drapery back to let some light in the room. She snapped, "Close those drapes. There is no need for light today."

"But it's Valentine's Day!"

"This is also the anniversary of my marriage to Sabua, a sad, sad day." She held a handful of her robe to her chest.

"Not today, Ms. Malinda. This is a beautiful day that lets you know that you got over such a terrible time in your life."

Through waxy eyes, she said, "If you say so, but let me see it my way right now."

It never occurred to me that Ms. Malinda really loved Sabua. It's strange to me for her to be in so much mind pain. She usually bragged on how she got rid of him. But come to think of it, she had to love him. Twenty years later, she's still weepy. Real love. That was something I'd always dreamed about but never had. It didn't look so interesting today. I wondered if a person can really fall out of love. It seems lengthy and sad to me.

I tried to make small talk with her but she said little to nothing. And then I remembered the telegram in my pocket. It was eating a hole through it. But right now, Ms. Malinda's situation was all that mattered. So I asked her, "Have you ever thought about what happen to Sabua and where he is now?"

She was silent for a moment before her eyes tear up again. When she lifted her head, the tears ran down her face. I put my arms around her.

"No need for that. It's in the past," I said, handing her a tissue.

"Yes, it is the past! And if hell had a telephone number, I'd call him up and cuss his ass out!" After a two second pause, we laughed… hard.

"Thank you, Almena. I'm not going to waste this day, even though it brings memories of hurt. Reach into my bottom drawer and pass me my red sweat suit, my red slippers, and turn on that television to *The Price is Right*. Let Sabua's black-ass burn in hell."

The rest of the day moved slower than a snail. James came home for lunch, tip-toeing into his sister's room, arms overflowing with bunches of roses. She had fallen asleep. All her morning energy spent on sadness. I put the flowers in a large vase and went to the kitchen to fix James a tuna-stuffed tomato with chips and lemonade. James was making it his business to stand real close to me here. As I reached on top of the refrigerator, he came up behind me and blew his hot breath down the side of my neck. I push him away gently. His grinning at me made me drop the chips. I was acting silly, like a young girl.

"Are we on for dinner?" James spoke directly into my ear and leaned down and kissed my shoulder.

I took a couple steps back from him, "If Ms. Malinda sleeps most of the afternoon, I'm sure she'll have the strength to go out for dinner." My voice was cracking.

"Good," he said. "I'll take all my girls somewhere nice."

"James," I softly said. "Can you do me a favor?"

"Of course I can. I have been wanting to do you a favor for a long time, girl. You just name it," he said, giving me that sweet grin of his.

"Can you stop calling me 'Wifey' around the twins? You see, they don't understand and they think you might take me away from them."

"I'll do just that, but could you do me a favor? Explain to them that I'm a good guy and I would never take you away from them. I know that it's a package deal with you. Those little girls have won my heart. I'll ask their permission before I get me some of your honey bun."

"James, this is not funny!"

"Okay, okay. I'll behave but you know you got the hots for me. I can't understand how you've been able to hold out this long."

If James only knew. Lately I felt my body trying to get the best of me. "It's easy, James. You talk too much."

"In that case, can I use sign language?" He pointed to my chest and made sucking sounds with his mouth. I put him out the kitchen and told him to go back to his job at that church and pray for his own soul.

I went upstairs to weave a little bit and as soon as I sat down in my rocker, Grandma came roaring into my head from the celestial sidelines (*another word from the library, I'm getting smart).* "Girl, open that telegram you got! It's important, so you stop hiding from your responsibilities."

Mama came through with, "Almena you take all the time you need. You been doing good and this is something you can handle if you get the right help."

"How you two doing?" I said

Grandma said, "Been good some days, but tired."

"I'm tired too," Mama claimed. "Oh, how I miss your father."

"I know why she missed him. He was on the express line to the pit. I seen him. He was sitting in the front seat." Grandma laughed as she said this. I thought to myself that's the same thing Ms. Malinda had said about Sabua. I wonder if when you get older you speak the same way. "Now do what I tell you and open that telegram." Grandma broke into my thoughts. "It ain't so bad. Besides, I want to see it for myself."

"Grandma," I whined. "Can I open it after dinner tonight? I don't want to be thinking about disturbing things today of all days."

"Do what you please, but open it before night's end. You hear me!"

"I will," I promised. "I need your advice on something that's making me scared. The twins hate boys and think boys push and hurt you. I know it's because of what they been through."

Mama"s voice soothingly told me, "All girl children hate boys at one time or another but trust me, they will like them when they get older. As far as the pushing and hurting, let them know that liking and hurting don't go together. You ain't supposed to hurt to be liked. It is too early for love connection talk. We can wait until their womanhood approaches and then explain what's to be expected and how theirs is special. There are some things children are not meant to know at their age. We'll help you with that in a couple of years. They may need to talk to a problem solver that deals in them kind of things."

"Your Mama knows! Chile, hers been special to her for a while, the weekend special." Grandma chuckled.

Back at my weaving, I decided that James was going to look just like he had when I first saw him on the bus. My stitches moved swiftly across my rug. In fact, I stitched him inside one of the bus windows. I had it in my mind to also stitch him walking with the kids from church.

The hours flew by when I heard the children ringing the bell and excitedly laughing through the mail slot. I went down to the door and there they stood with a blue first-place ribbon tacked onto their project. Glory was waving a Polaroid picture in her right hand. "Look at this!"

I reached down and looked; it was a picture of them with their project and wide grins on the faces. "Well, look at my babies. I knew y'all project was the best, I just knew it." I'm so proud of them.

"You ain't seen nothing yet. Look at this." Grace rejoiced. She swung a big box of chocolates from behind her back

"Ummm, hum, we got candy for the rest of the month!" I laughed with them.

"I want all the ones with the white filling in it," Glory said.

"It ain't but two of them," Grace said, and me and auntie will eat the rest."

"We can share. Love means you share. Get on in here and let me see where I can hang that project."

It's the simple things in life that you can learn a lesson from. Today it was a blue ribbon and a box of candy.

All the noise had awoken Ms. Malinda. She yelled "What's going on out there?" Grace and Glory ran to her bed and showed their blue ribbon award. She was thrilled for them. She shouted "It's party time up in here!

James came through the front door quietly, thinking his sister was still sleeping.

"Stop that creeping, boy. You got four women in this house who want to party tonight!" Ms. Malinda announced.

There was relief on James's face. "Madams your escort will be ready and willing as soon as I freshen up a bit. In fact, let's all get dressed to show off our winners."

We scrambled upstairs to clean up and put on some Sunday clothes. Then, I remember Ms. Malinda. I ran back down stairs, "Ms. Malinda do you need me to help you get dressed?"

"Girl, I've been dressing since you was Grace and Glory age. Now go change and don't wear one of them house dusters or them robes things you been struttin' in."

James took us to a nice restaurant, making sure Ms. Malinda was steady. He was opening doors and pulling out chairs for us. The children had on their party dresses. I had on a really nice red suit with red pumps. Ever since I joined church I've been learning to walk in heels. Ms. Malinda had not been out of the house, except to go to the hospital, in about three months. Now she wore her black mink coat over her rose-colored dress. Jewelry hung everywhere; her mink hat was high up on her head. She was absolutely beautiful. She had a winner's smile and for the first time in many hours, I had forgotten about the telegram. It laid unopened on my nightstand.

The restaurant was decorated for Valentine's Day with roses and heart-shaped candles everywhere. James kept saying most of the other places were booked for this evening and we only got this because we were early. We were led to a table by a short young black man in a tuxedo. Right away another one came. This was service. The twins were taking this all in. Grace asked the man filling our water glasses, "Are you the water boy?"

"I am, and the bread boy, and the coffee boy, and the clean-up boy too, my little princess. It's an important job."

Satisfied that she knew what his position was, she proclaimed, "I'm going to get me one of those jobs when I grow up and then be a doctor."

We smiled and looked over our large menus. A smiling waitress approached.

"Habibah!" Glory shouted almost spilling over the water glass in front of her.

It was Habibah. Her hair was straight now and she wore a black and white uniform. She pinched the girls' cheeks and spoke pleasantly to both Ms. Malinda and me. She only nodded at James. She took our orders and switched her way behind the closed doors to the kitchen. While the children played games on the paper place mats, I peeped at James and Ms. Malinda. He looked down at the table but his eyes was much deeper, farther away than the table, his lips and chin picked up a sheen of sweat. "Jesus God," I heard him groan softly. Guilt was written all over his face. Ms. Malinda had a look of confidence on her face, her back straight, lips rolled in as if she was studying nothing but the dessert menu.

Dinner was good and Habibah attended to all our needs. James kept the conversation lively. Habibah even brought out cupcakes for the children in celebration for their blue ribbon. Things went well until we was about to leave. James asked for the bill and Habibah handed him a note on a white napkin. He unfolded it like it was something to be proud of but his face expression changed when in big red letters it read: *How much is my freedom worth? Pay that bill.* He sucked in some air and quickly folded up the napkin. But I was sitting right next to him, I saw what it said.

Ms. Malinda missed that one or she pretended that she did. She whispered something to Grace, looked up and asked Habibah," I hope this job doesn't mean you have given up on doing hair?"

"No, I still braid hair on my days off from here. Just call me anytime. I'll fix you right up."

A greenish-brown coloring rose from James's neck and covered his face as we left the restaurant. Grace caught the mood but Glory spoke up. "Habibah was nice to us but she don't like you no more, Uncle James. What did you do to her, and how come she ain't awoke no more?"

We laughed. Them kids noticed everything. Ms. Malinda sat up front with James and rolled her neck. "Things change and sometimes it's nobody's fault. We'll be friends again. As for her hair, when you grow up, you're going to try different styles too." James's voice was choppy.

Sensing that James was feeling down about his note from Habibah, I kept the conversation going on the ride home. Grace had french fries at dinner and now sported a large ketchup stain on her party dress. I leaned over and said, "Don't even worry about that, it's only a tomato strain. Let me tell you my tomato story. I was about fifteen and tried to work in a canning plant in Chestertown, Maryland. What a disaster that was! I couldn't keep up with the assembly line and more tomatoes landed on the floor than in the cans. I lasted four hours."

The bosses said, "You're not suited for the job."

"That stain is no match for me and my washing board. I've been handling tomatoes a long time." Grace gave me a high five. 'Course then Glory wanted a high five. "Don't leave me out." Ms. Malinda said. She lifted her hands up and behind her "Give me ten." We did. She looked at James and said "Not you, buddy. Just keep driving with your hands on the wheel," while laughing.

James pulled the car to a stop at a light. Just then a thin dirty man approached the driver side window yelling, "Yo, my brotha, where you been? I got what you need right here." He looked as if it was an effort to keep his eyelids open. Even his standing up straight was a real chore. He was scratching, twitching, and pausing. James tried his best to ignore the man but he was tapping the steering wheel with his right thumb and rubbing the inside of his right arm with his left hand. Look like a yearning to me. James sped away.

As we reached the house, I told James and Ms. Malinda I had something I wanted to speak with them about. After settling the children down in their pajamas and helping Ms. Malinda hang up her fine clothes, I called James into Ms. Malinda's room and pulled the telegram out. I could see James needed something to take his mind off what he was wanting to do. I handed over the telegram to James and told him to read it out loud. I just knew it was bad news.

He opened it and read it to hisself first and said, "It's not anything we can't handle."

"Read the damn thing, James," Ms. Malinda said.

"Almena Johnstone, I have been trying to reach you. You must come back and attend to your property business. For years I have tried to shield you from some of our family matters, but what is done in the dark is about to come to light. The county and others are going to take away our property if you don't appear here and claim it as your own. Also them children may own the property across the road. It looks like you have abandoned this land and it has become a hazard to Elktown. Call me, so I can set things straight. I only want the best for you...Sadie. My number is (301) 429-4287."

I sat on one of the chairs, thinking. *Here I go backwards again.*

Ms. Malinda thought a while and said, "We can take care of this. It's not so bad. But, if she knew how to reach you, why didn't the county just send you a notification? What is this family matters mess? I thought you didn't have no kin?"

"I don't have no kin. None I ever met. Sadie is the last person I want to handle anything for me. We had a bad argument when I left town."

"I wonder what her motives are. Do you want to go back to Elktown, Almena?"

"Maybe I will someday but not now. We've only been gone about four months and we have a lot of bad memories back there."

"This Sadie sounds like a hound with nothing to sniff on. What makes her think she can telegram up here and upset you? Is she related to the children?"

"No. She's the town know-it-all." My knees began to shake.

"Let me think about this tonight," Ms. Malinda said. "James, I might need you to take a little trip. Don't worry, Almena. We from the country and we can smell a rat before he can piss on cotton."

James gathered me up in his arms. "If I save you, will you please, please, please...?" He broke into his rendition of a James Brown song. We laughed.

If you could keep your mind off that man on the corner, things might work out. It felt so good to be held by him, I shuddered. *Oh Mercy!*

Even though Ms. Malinda and James told me not to worry, it still bothered me. I tossed and turned that night. Unable to sleep, I felt like I was being pulled back to Elktown. Backwards, that's also what I had been called. I looked in on my two sleeping little angels, they looked peaceful. *Stop imagining the worst,* I reminded myself. I didn't want to take them back to a place full of nightmares. I had promised Grandma that we would visit her home in the summers, but that was a lie. I never wanted to see Elktown again. It held Coral's family secrets and that is where their secrets should stay as far as I was concerned.

Coming down the steps early the next morning, I heard Ms. Malinda on the telephone giving instructions to someone in a rough voice. She would hang up the phone and then call someone again and give a new set of instructions. I knew it was about our problems. Working up my nerve to knock on the door, I tapped lightly and went in. She was sitting in bed with a pad and pen taking notes. She held up her hand for me to be quiet until she finished writing something down.

"Curtis Gibbs will be here in about an hour. Just make up the bed and fix us some coffee and warm some danishes. We'll talk about the telegram with him. However if there are any surprises that you might want to discuss with me, now is the time. I detest surprises." My stomach bubbled over as if I had taken a large dose of Alka-Seltzer.

The only thing that stopped my guts from spilling forward was the large lump in my throat. "I'm going to get my rugs, Ms. Malinda, I'll be back down. My rugs will speak for me."

My heart was thumping. Sweat broke out on my forehead as I lugged my life down the steps. I stumbled at her door but I got them rugs inside while Ms. Malinda gave me a puzzled look. She moved to one of the French chairs and sat like a judge waiting for the truth. I couldn't look at her anymore.

"My life as an adult started its downward spin in 1975 just after I graduated from school. It hadn't been good even as a little girl so I guess I should start from there. My rugs tell the real story so I'll begin with this."

I uncurled the blue rug. Right away the soreness returned to my lower stomach. "This rug with its light to navy blue with almost black thread shows how Wallace, my mother's husband, played a grown-up game with me for almost three years. I was eight years old. See how big the little girl's eyes are. A person might think, 'My, her eyes are big.' But that's fear and pain, not just size in them eyes."

I heard a sharp intake of breathing coming from the French chair. Yet she said nothing. Walking around my darkest days, I uncurled the red rug next. My legs felt like jelly so I sat right in the center of it.

"This rug is bright red as it gently fades into maroon. During these years I wanted to be just like what I had heard about my daddy. So when I got my completion certification from school, I signed up for the Air Force Reserves. They accepted me after I applied six times. Oh, I was so proud. This meant I wasn't too slow to serve my country and the recruiter said I wasn't going to be no secretary either. No, sir. I would be directly involved with country-saving operations. Well, I was a receiving clerk at Dover Air Force Base. One night, a huge plane came in full of black rubber bags. There was two receiving clerks on duty. Me and a wise-ass acting guy named Nathan. Nathan always ordered me around. He made fun of me no matter how hard I tried at things. He told me to go into the hangar and check one of the bags to see if it still contained the grain fertilizer it was supposed to contain. I went in. The smell was very, very bad. I unzipped a bag and before me was a swollen-up body. Its neck had busted open and rotting flesh took over my eyes. I was surrounded by over 900 body bags. I was the only one breathing in that hangar. I screamed and ran to the hangar's doors. Nathan had latched and locked them. I beat and banged on that door until my hands was bloody and my mind ran away. It was the winter of 1978, this was the return of the followers of Mr. Jim Jones. I spent a year in mental care before the government sent me home. I got an honorable discharge with what they called special needs. Notice the purple fringe at the end of the rug. It stands for how I was told he killed them and for the rain in my life. Every day during this time was purple to me, the time just before dawn and you are the only one breathing."

"Oh, sweetheart," Ms. Malinda said, "You don't have to finish this. It's too much for you. You've got chills."

I didn't realize I was trembling so much. Ms. Malinda's voice came at me like an echo. Running my hands over my partial life, I knew I had to finish. Still not looking at her, I knew I had to finish."Please, let me be me. I can't pretend it didn't happen, so I put the craziness somewhere to free up space where my mind used to be." In the distance I heard an "umph...umph...umph."

I got up off my mind-disturbing rug and laid out my yellow rug. At least it was bright. "One day, when I needed air, I left Grandma's house and rode the bus to Baltimore, Maryland. There in a bar I met a man who was full of fun and saw things in an unusual way and he loved the world. He put flowers in my hair and gave me wonderful names, like Sunflower, Lily of My Field and Lotus My Love. Every day he would give me just a little piece of paper to suck on. It was much better than my nerve medication. It gave me dreams in colors. Life was good, until one day he went out to sell some potholders and knitted flowers I had made and didn't return. I searched for him as best I knew how, for two weeks. Having no money I was put out of our room and on the streets of East Baltimore. Once again I ran into a deal in the form of a man. One I couldn't resist. I don't really remember a lot about this time in my day-to-day life that's why this rug has this fuzzy white border around it." Cloudy life days.

I heard water being poured from the water pitcher and Ms. Malinda made a big sipping sound. "Almena, it's a beautiful rug and we all have done things—"

I cut her off. "You ever been to federal jail? A place where the government say you wrong, the whole country's government. No, I don't think you have. It's under and beneath down feelings. This here rug is proof." I uncurled my many-colored rug.

"The man I couldn't resist drove me all the way to California. He said he was teaching me to see the country as never before. I was to take my time, because I had been through so much. We stopped and got me a driving license but I was not a good driver at all. He was patient with me. I remember he was handsome but his face, well, it's been gone from my mind for a long time. His name was Leon. I saw palm trees and an ocean wider than any I could ever dream of. People were easy with life. The sun kissed your body for breakfast and lemons hung on trees. I was never going to leave this place. This was heaven to me. We stayed in California for maybe two months when his daughter called and said she was sick. Nights on end Leon stayed up worrying about her. He couldn't return right away because he had come to California for some very important business. When he asked me to go on back on the bus and give her a hand, of course I said yes. He never used my body and I was so thankful for that. I would do anything for him. What I saw in him was kindness and acceptance like never before. I was rested so it wasn't a big deal. He told me to bring his daughter back with me. He even gave me more money than I had ever seen at one time. I don't know till this day how much money he gave me. What I do know is that when the federal police stopped the bus in the state of Texas, the only bags they wanted to search was mines and I was sent to prison for being a mule, an ass, and a drug smuggler. See the bars, guards, and hopelessness all mixed up in this rug. Much of this time blends together, but still I remember so much of that time. It took me four more years to get back to Elktown. And all I had to show for it was proof that I was unfit. Sadie knows most of this. She might try to take my—"

I opened my mouth to finish but the two last words was so hard into my chest that a silent cry hung in the air. I couldn't go on. Looking around the burgundy room, which now contained the pus of my life, I was afraid of what I would see on Ms. Malinda's face. The room went limp. When I did look up, she was rocking back and forward on the French chair. She reached for me and I crawled to her arms.

She stood up after a while, holding on to my quivering chin "You have nothing to be ashamed of and nothing to fear. Hold your head up, girl. You're a survivor. Life is trying, Almena, and you have had a lot going on in yours. But you are still one of the most honest, caring, and might I say, strongest women I've ever met. You came here in search of a better life and I'm going to help you achieve that."

I felt like the air in my lungs had been let out. A good feeling, like I wasn't tight no more. "You're fit, Almena. Your life ain't over. Trust and fight with everything you've got."

The doorbell rang and we both jumped. I wiped my face with a wash cloth on Ms. Malinda's towel rack and tried to collect myself. Ms. Malinda fanned herself with both her hands and said, "Have him wait for me in the parlor. I need a moment."

Mr. Gibbs walked in, smelling like he had bathed in Aqua Velva. "We meet again, my special one." He bowed and winked at me.

I wondered who told him that I was special. "Good morning," I said to the floor. "Ms. Malinda will be with you in a minute." I took his coat and led him into the parlor just like Ms. Malinda said. All the while looking at the floor. She entered the parlor about five minutes later. Her face was strong and steady, no signs of shame anywhere.

"Changed your mind, Malinda," he said.

"No! I'm certain the decisions in my will are sound ones. We have another legal matter we'd like you to look into. She handed him the telegram and told him to read it. She explained to him that at this time it was impossible for me to leave and attend to it. She wanted him to look into it and to ascertain (*I like that word)* who owns the property and just what was of interest to the county and just what Sadie was up to.

"Curtis, get right on this. I will be sending James down there. You can give him whatever legal papers he might need to straighten out any and all problems. We don't want our Almena unnerved about any of this now. Do we?"

"No, why I wouldn't dream of letting anyone disturb our fine sister. If you want, I'll go and clear this up in a day or two myself." He turned to me. "Now, my dear sister, do you happen to have a copy of the deed or of your grandmother's will?" I was still not myself. Numbly, I said, "I believe they are in my personal belongings upstairs."

Well, he said, "Why don't we go out to dinner this evening and you bring the papers and we'll settle this. There may be some more information I need after I look over them."

"Curtis, cut the bullshit! She ain't going out to dinner with you tonight and any information you need, you can get it from me," Ms. Malinda said, very sharply.

He snickered. "Malinda, the dear sister said they was in her personals and I just thought maybe she wanted to search for them at another time."

"I know you did. Almena, go see if you have the papers."

I went slowly, *Lord don't let me give up, I can't let them kids down.* Upstairs I pulled out the boxes of stuff I had brought from Elktown. I found it. I ran my fingers along the edges of the leather Bible. Opening it up, the letter from Mama fell to the floor. Inside it was the deed and further down behind some old pictures was Grandma's will. It was as if what I needed was lying there waiting for me. Coming back down the steps I could hear laughter and Ms. Malinda calling Mr. Gibbs a hound from the day he was born.

I gave the papers to him. He glanced at them and then at me and said, "I will study and verify them and get back with you tomorrow. Don't worry. I'm sure we'll be okay. The worst trouble you could be in is a little behind in taxes." He kicked his foot out and hooted, "I'm the man when it comes to real estate."

I saw him out. As I followed Ms. Malinda back to her room, she gave me her instructions. "When James comes running in here for lunch make sure he stops in here to see me. Call Sadie later on. I want to hear what she says and how she says it. Take that sad look off your face. If I tell you something's going to happen, it is. Bring your weaving down when you get done with your housework. You look peaceful when you weaving. Leave these beautiful rugs right where they are, too."

The morning crawled by. With my cleaning done and lunch prepared, it was time to join Ms. Malinda during her soaps time. I rapped lightly and walked in to find her asleep. All the activities of the last twenty-four hours had caught up with her. I pulled up her blanket to make sure she stayed warm and backed out of the room.

James came bouncing in. I held up my finger to let him know Ms. Malinda was sleep. He caught me by the hand and led me into the kitchen. "Almena, do you think we could start over?" He was playing with my fingers. *Whoohoooo, it felt good!*

"James, I got other things on my mind. This is not the time to start your foolishness."

"Girl, I ain't playing the fool. After this property matter is resolved, can we try it again? You know, I heard you panting the other night when I held on to you."

"Maybe when you finish your business with Habibah."

I pull my fingers away and turned my back to him while closing my eyes.

"Awwww, sookie, sookie, I'm done! Done! Done!" He danced around and stood right in front of me. "Give me a quick kiss, just one, a little bitty one. Okay, that might be too much. Just say my name, baby," he whispered and held on to my waist so gently.

I stepped around him, grinning from ear to ear and said, "Quit being a clown and eat your lunch, and I think maybe you better wake your sister up on your way out. She did sound like it was important that she speak with you."

"Yes ma'am. How about a rump roast for dinner!" He winked at me. *James has a way that makes me smile.* I turned around to wash some fresh turnips I was going to fix for dinner.

James knocked on Ms. Malinda's door, awakening her. I heard her give James his instructions to take off from work on Thursday and Friday. "Take care of this property business. Hopefully it's bullshit," she said. I walked in the room and she went on." Curtis will tell you what you will need to do. Drive down and that will save time. You may probably have to charm Sadie. Keep us informed of any unusual developments." Ms. Malinda winked up at James.

"No problem," James said. "I'll have her eating out of my hands. When I finish with her, she won't be sending anymore telegrams." He reached over and squeezed my hand.

The phone rang and I answered it, "Hello my fine sister," Mr. Gibbs said.

"Good afternoon, Mr. Gibbs."

"Almena, it looks like your documents are in order. I'm waiting for a call from a Mr. Willis to see what the county concerns are. Now, can I speak with Malinda?"

"Yes, she's right here and thanks for your help."

I handed Ms. Malinda the phone and they talked. "I see... we had planned on sending James down there this Thursday. Oh, if you think you should go then of course do it. Cost isn't a problem. Let us know." She hung up the phone, smiled at me, and said, "Curtis is going with you, James. This is going to be quite a trip."

"Gurrrrl," James rolled the word around in his mouth, "Only for you." He left out the door blowing air kisses as he returned to work.

"Almena," Ms. Malinda called. "Listen, let me say this. Girl, you are excellent at suffering and excellent at running away from your challenges, too. Now let me see if you can follow what I'm going to ask you to do."

I sat there, taking in every word. About five minutes later and after taking several deep breathes, I reached for the phone and called Sadie. I had been so nervous, but as soon as I heard her voice my fears disappeared.

"Good afternoon, Sadie. How are you? This is Almena. I have been meaning to call you. Ms. Grey told me of your call and thank you for the telegram and your concern. Sadie, I know it must be something important if you took the time to wire me so I have decided that I will be back in Elktown next Monday. The children are fine. We've found a wonderful church. I look forward to finding out what is so important. Sounds like you've changed. I'm working now so I can't stay on the phone but we will catch up on Monday. Good-bye for now."

I didn't let her get a word in. I hung up the phone and looked at Ms. Malinda who gave me the thumbs-up sign. Ms. Malinda had switched her mind. She didn't want to hear Sadie's tone of voice after all. Control the conversation and you control the situation, that's what Ms. Malinda had told me. She called it getting a back bone.

I could just see Sadie's face. *I wonder how long it had been since she talked to a person and didn't get to say a word or ask a question.*

CHAPTER TWENTY-THREE
James & Curtis – *On the Case*

I drove toward I-95 South with a sleeping Curtis beside me. It was 6 o'clock in the morning. When I picked him up, he carried on about not being a morning person. I turned the radio on and then off. Nothing is on except the traffic reports and the grim news of the morning, which might wake him up and start him talking. It wasn't that I disliked Curtis. He is the kind of brother who thinks he knows everything and his breath is kicking this morning. As far as I am concerned he can sleep the whole seven-hour trip.

My life has been a helluva of a ride. It's 1985 and here I am still riding up and down the roads. I know it is past time to settle down. Who would've guess that a little country woman with two kids would mean the world to me. I've wasted a lot of time. It's happening, changes. I don't ride the highways for nothing but a poker game. But since my baby, things ain't what they use to be. My day ain't right if I don't see her. It's better than a dream come true. I have never felt about a woman the way I feel about Almena. I'm ready to tell her just how much she means to me. I need to tell her some other things too, and the thought of the other things makes me cower. I hope I don't fuck this up.

Stopping to pay the toll at the George Washington Bridge woke up Curtis. Stretching and yawning, he said, "Man, stop at the first rest stop you see. Big boy is calling."

I wondered if he could have made it as a comedian. He certainly had the looks and his last statement had to be a joke. I pulled into the next rest area, let him out and got gas for the rest of the trip. He returned with two cups of coffee and two big sweet rolls and a piss stain on the front of his pants. Yep, this Negro could have been a star.

We rode on through New Jersey, past signs to Atlantic City, and finally into Maryland. This was where it got confusing. We was going to the eastern shore of Maryland and it had a lot of little towns within a county. When we asked for directions to Elktown, nobody had ever heard of it. I reasoned having a map and asking directions to the closest main town would work. Elktown was a dot on the map and the largest town near it was Salisbury. I gave the map to Curtis, just so he would have something to do. We stopped a couple of times to ask directions. Curtis, with his proper talking self, could not get answers from anyone down this way. They couldn't understand him and he was getting uptight. He was certainly out of his element. These folks was walking away from him the minute he said, "Pardon me my good man? Could you direct me to...?" One black man narrowed his eyes at him with a look that said, *If you don't know where the hell you at, what you asking me for?*

It was funny. I could hardly keep myself from laughing out loud. I was enjoying this spectacle. This is a scene I have to tell my sister when we get back. She likes it when I tell her about my road trips. Looking up I see another man give Curtis the finger.

After four missed turns, we finally see a sign that says "Welcome to Elktown." It was unbelievable. Picture Dodge City from the westerns on television and you had downtown Elktown. Curtis had already set up an appointment with Buck Willis at the county building, about ten miles away from downtown. I did a drive by, down Main Street to locate the post office, where I would be getting what information I could from Sadie. I took Curtis to the county building and went back to town.

A head moved up and peeped out the post office window. I parked across the street. I took my time and did the manly cool stroll to the door. There was two other people in line when I walked in. I leaned against a table in the middle of the room. Crossing one foot over the other in my Billy Dee Williams stance and smiling, I picked an imaginary piece of lint off my jacket collar. Then, arching eyebrows up and pulling my neck back, I stared into her eyes and held them until she miss counts a customer's change. *I think I got her.* She quickly got rid of her other customer. I licked my lips and continued to stare before moving in closer to her counter. I think to myself, Almena had described her dead on. Her dark complexion was dry and her slanted eyes frowned back at me eagerly. Sadie's large lips have peeled so much they are uneven in color. Her mixed gray hair is brushed back and in no particular style. She looks displeased with life. Her need for male attention is evident in the wishing way she looked back at me.

"My, my, my, it is true that precious things can be found in a small town," I announced to her.

She giggled and ran her hands over her fly-away hair. "Can I help you?"

"Of course you can. But, *will you* is the question. What's your name Miss or is it Mrs.?"

"My name is Sadie and it is Miss."

"Miss Sadie my name is James." Leaning into her counter, closer to her than she is probably used to. I continued to arouse her. "Lady Sadie, can you tell me where I could find a soul food restaurant around here?"

"There aren't any in Elktown. Over in Salisbury there's a nice one right off Route 301 called Benny's."

"Miss Sadie, what's the best dish they have there?"

"I like the ribs and potatoes salad myself. They're tasty," she said.

She wants to talk to me, I can feel it.

"In that case, that's what I will have. If I may be so bold, Miss Sadie. I just have to say you have a stunning, natural, country beauty about you. I hope I'm not out of order."

Sadie smiled and began tapping a pencil against her counter, so I continued, "By the way I'm from Sumter,

South Carolina. I'm a very nice, mannerly, single man and only in this area attending to some business. I know you don't really know me but I would be honored if you would join me for dinner. I mean, when you leave your job that is. I hate eating alone. I promise I'm harmless and just hungry."

"Well, this is a government position I have and all so I get off at 3pm, about an hour and a half from now. It would be nice to dine out. I've been so caught up lately. James, I think I would like to go over to Benny's for a quick dinner."

She said this but her eyes let me know she would shut that post office down if I wanted her to.

"This is just too good to be true. The saints have smiled on me, and I thank them that I'm alive! I'll pick you up at three, Miss Lady, or would you rather I pick you up at home?" I gave her a dreamy look. Eyes down, smile up, women loved this look.

"Oh, right here would be just fine." She drummed the pencil down again. "But James, what kind of business could possibly bring you to this town?"

"Miss Sadie, my business is south of here. I'm attending to an aunt's funeral arrangements and, to tell you the truth, being around family is often upsetting, so I drove up this way. I need to get things off my mind, sweetheart and I think I've found just the person to make me forget. My breath of fresh air, don't change your mind on me. I promise this dinner will be pleasant for both of us."

"I'll be here, James."

I left the post office with Sadie's eyes watching my every step. I pulled away thinking, I still have the touch. This is going to be one informative dinner. Then it hit me: the tags on the car. All my lies might blow up in my face if she saw the tags and connected the dots. This was starting to get complex. I quickly eased down the street and out of the little town area to see if the short man had any luck.

Curtis was not outside the county building when I first

pulled up. This area was busy with stores; a car dealership, Howard Johnson hotel, a bank, and a F.W. Woolworth Five and Dime. I parked and entered the dime store. A brother was standing in the back of the store stacking boxes and I made my way to him. "Good afternoon, brother."

"Hey, man." He mumbled and continued stacking small boxes of soap on the shelf.

"Listen man, my license plates fell off somewhere between here and Delaware. Can you give me a piece of that cardboard so I can write down my tag and put it on my car."

"I know you ain't from around here. That's not a good idea. Man, just leave it off. If these crackers see you with a homemade tag, you be stopped and investigated for car stealing. You've got your registration ain't you?

"Yes, it's in the glove box, but I thought..."

"I'm telling you, better to have fallen off than to be explaining making one up. They slow about investigating around here. It might take days, while you setting in a holding tank waiting for their investigation." He gave me a nod and thumbs up sign.

"I see what you mean, thanks for the advice. I nodded and left the store.

Back at the car, I opened the trunk, got out the screw driver, and as brother man said, just removed the plate. I threw it inside with the rest of the tools.

Two or three other black folk pass by the car as I wait on my heavy duty partner. One young woman was very attractive. She was dressed in a dark business suit with a trench coat swinging over it. She entered the bank tossing her flipped up hair. *A couple months ago, I would have sprinted to open that door for her while trying my lines on her. Not today. All my lines are for Sadie. Maybe I should sing her that song by the Spinners, Sweet Sadie and then ask her what the hell she want with my woman. No, I don't think that would work. Besides, I can't sing. What do I know, not much. But I do know that here's a woman who didn't even want to freshen up after work to go to dinner, who has accepted my invitation without really knowing me and who makes my woman shake. I don't know her yet but as tight as my game is, I will before I leave here. My conversation must not be too obvious. Think, man! How can I bring up the subject of Almena to Sadie without causing suspicion?* I start to step back out of the car to purchase some flowers but I see Curtis busting out of the county building.

Sweat dripping down his chin and eyes ablaze, he almost ripped the door off the car getting in. "James, our darling Almena may have come upon good fortune. I must call her to see how she would like to proceed."

"Just spit it out, Curtis. What happened?"

"First, I went to the tax bureau to find out if any taxes were in arrears on our dear sister's property. Taxes were due, but the amount was very small, which I paid without hesitation. Still thinking ahead, I asked and got the latest assessment value of the property. Then on to my meeting with Mr. Buck Wills; who was very surprised at my being a friend and counsel of our dear sister. Seeing that not only did I have the latest assessment—the paid in full tax receipts and the power of attorney from Almena—he had no other choice than to inform me that the county is interested in the purchase of her property, and they would offer her the full value." Curtis was clapping his hands, like he had sealed the deal.

"My man, he will forward their offer to my office, and if Almena accepts, we are finished here. Now I could not assure him she was no longer interested in keeping her homestead, but I let him know that whatever, in cases of realty, I move with the quickness. We're done here James. I feel like you should buy me a drink." With a flair for the dramatic, he wiped the sweat from his chin and dabbed it on his forehead. If Curtis wasn't such a hound, I would swear he was a sissy.

"You're on, Curtis but I need to make sure that's all there is to it and just how Sadie fits or doesn't fit in. I have a dinner date with her in about a half an hour. You check into this Howard Johnson hotel and have a drink on me while I handle my business. We need to rest before we drive back anyway."

Curtis chuckled, "James, you are shameless! And they call me a dog? Go ahead and impale yourself if you must. On second thought see if she has a friend." We laughed, and as he got out of the car, I said a prayer that we got back home before I lynched him somewhere on a country road.

I arrived back at the post office at about 2:35p.m. Sadie was looking out the window. I took a towel out off the back seat and wiped down the outside of the car and dusted off the mirror, giving her a full look at my well developed body. *It's the truth.* Then I walked in, gave her a wink and announced, "Your chariot awaits you."

A smile appeared on Sadie's face. "I have some undeliverable mail to send back, and then we can be on our way," she said. Some people just up and leave you with their mess and the government still wants me to follow up on their mail." Sadie tied up a sack of mail and started to lift it. That's when I sprung into action.

"Let me help you with that." I lifted the sack. It seemed very light when I tossed it in a bin labeled Lost and Found. I noticed she had applied a heavy coating of startlingly bright red lipstick. Just then, the door opened and a stocky white man with a police uniform on came in.

"Sadie, you all right and ready to close up in here?"

"Yes I am, and today I got me some help. This is my friend James from South Carolina."

He said, "Nice to meet you, James," extending his hand. "I'm Deputy Ray Packer. Are you staying with us here in Elktown?"

Shit, I don't like talking to the po-po. "No, I'm just here for a day or two and staying just south of here. This is a nice town ya'll got here and who knows what might help me stay on." Sadie turned away but I knew she was smiling.

"I see. Well, it's nice to meet you. We're a friendly small town. What do you do for a living, James?"

"I'm a barber by trade." *Here he go, getting in my*

business.

"That's nice. Yes sir, real nice. I always stop by at closing to help Sadie out but I guess she don't need my help today." Turning back to Sadie, he said. "I got another call from that fancy guy up north. He needs Almena Johnstone's address. You didn't give it to him?"

"Well, no I didn't 'cause she has moved. I was waiting to hear from her with the new address." My ears had perked up at the mention of Almena's name. *Sadie ain't above lying to the law I see.*

"When you git it, give it to me. I have his card. He can be as pesky as a fruit fly. He called me today and yesterday, too. He ain't no law man. I do hope all that murder mess is over and done with for that woman. It's a damn shame; she just wants some time away. Lock up good, now. And again, it's nice meeting you, James. Real nice of you to help out our Sadie."

"It's a pleasure to help our Sadie out." I said, standing there. *Did he say murder?* Then I bit my bottom lip to keep myself from cracking up because Sadie was smiling like a teenage girl with a new boyfriend.

On the ride to Benny's, Sadie gave me the history of the town and talked about how she was ready to leave but her job was holding her. "Communication is so important you know," she explained.

The third button on her blue postal shirt screamed for mercy, leaving a clear view of her bust line. It appeared to have suffered an earthquake. The collar of her shirt had a dingy ring around it and although she licked her lips, they still looked dry. This woman needs some work but I didn't come here for that. Finding out what she planned for my sweetheart was my only concern.

You could smell the smoke barbecue from Benny's about a quarter mile down the road before you saw it. It's a bright yellow low expanded building, with ten rocking chairs placed on the front porch. The front door was painted red and due for refurbishing. Paint chips flew off with every opening and closing. Benny's was between lunch and dinner service, therefore just about empty.

Walking in, you could feel the stickiness of the floor, a ripping noise accompanied us as the soles of our shoes separated from the floor. The ceiling was uneven and slanted inward. This restaurant felt dangerous. A waitress pointed to a table and said, "Y'all can have your pick, and I'll be right with you." The slow hum of outdated music played in tune with our shoes. I led Sadie to a side table covered in red and white oilcloth.

The menus sat behind the salt and pepper shakers and as I opened one up, a huge gang of well-fed flies immediately assaulted me. I didn't know how I was going to remain charming when my digestive system was reeling in protest. Sadie sat looking at the menu like she had never seen it before. She placed two fingers at the sides of her blood red lips, running them down and around them, and I saw the blue ink underneath her nails. That did it! My stomach flipped. I excused myself to wash my hands, remarking that the steering wheel of the car had left my hands so dirty. Once in the restroom, I gathered myself and repeated, "This is for my Almena." I could not bolt now. I know Almena had mentioned the kids' parents were dead. But murder? Who? What? When? I needed to talk to my woman way more than I had been. Just when I thought I had it all together two large roaches stared me down at the wash sink. This was not going well.

Back at the table, Sadie was ready to order. The waitress chewed a gray chunk of gum and had a pencil behind her ear. Besides her stained barbecue apron, she wore a pair of black Keds with light tan nylon stockings rolled around her ankles. The name tag on her chest read Esther. I let Sadie order away.

"I'll have the ribs, greens and potatoes salad with iced tea," she said.

"I'll try some of your ribs," I told Sadie. Looking up at our waitress, I added, "I think I'll have the fried fish with macaroni and a large glass of lemonade."

"Good choices." Esther smiled exposing the lack of her four top teeth.

I reached for Sadie's hands and covered them with my

own. "So, postal lady, tell me about you. How come you help out complete strangers in need of a meal and good conversation?"

"James, I sometimes wonder myself why I'm so caring. I grew up that way I guess. My mother always helped out people and I got that from her."

"Are your parents still living around here?

"No, they long since passed, but I've always lived by their teachings."

"Aren't you lonely out here in the country with no excitement to stir you up? I didn't even see a church in the town. No, let me guess, you're the kind of woman who can't deal with city life: the noise, the crime, the fast life."

"There's a fine church in the back woods that everyone attends. As for excitement, you would be surprised the excitement that this little town holds. Not that I'm a gossip, but it's just like it must be in your city of Sumter. Crime included. We have the same things here as elsewhere. Why about four months ago, a father murdered his whole family."

"What happened? Did somebody forget to milk the family cow?" I tried to joke.

"Oh James, stop making fun. This family was new to our area but anyhow, the father just up and chopped up the mother and her sons. The only ones that didn't die was the baby girls 'cause, by the grace of God, they was staying with my good friend, Almena."

"You mean to tell....Oh, I'm sorry to hear that. I guess meanness is spread all over the world."

I was damn near choking on my lemonade. I decided to turn the subject just a little to what was really important, so I said, "I heard that deputy say that name, Almena." She's popular here I guess."

"Only if you like slow misfit people." Sadie smirked and then she added, "She went up North, but she'll be back next week. Folks always come to the post office to find out where missing people are. About a week ago a man came looking for her. The county department is looking for her too. I really hope she is not in any trouble. That girl keeps me worried. She took those kids with her and now, like I said, this Mr. Baldwin is searching for her. It must be some mess 'cause he come all the way down here from Boston searching for her. He left some kind of appraiser card with me. She ain't really equipped to take care of situations or children. I may have to step in and foster them kids. Almena don't really think before she acts.

"Do you want kids, Sadie?"

"Not really, James, but what's a person to do. Anyhow these kids are big enough to take care of themselves. One of them has a smart mouth already."

"Well, you could have fun making your own....I'm just kidding."

"Hush. I've got enough responsibilities at my job," she said, pursing her lips. "And occasionally I have fun."

"I just bet you do!" I started to ask her when the last time was, but I was getting off track here.

I turned to the juke box selection arm mounted on the wall just above the table, flipping through tunes that I didn't recognize. Sadie was going full force, but murder statement stuck with me.

"She's my friend but she can find trouble." Sadie was caught up in her good intention spew.

"You mean this Almena?"

"Yes, I've helped her out before and I'll help her out through this too as soon as I can get to see her. I worry about those children she's got with her. I knew her mother and grandmother. They would've wanted me to see about her. She hasn't been herself since they died. Come to think of it I don't think she ever been right bright, but a good old soul, if you know what I mean."

"I'm a good old soul, too. What kinda help can I get, Miss Lady?" I winked at her and I swore my right eyelid stuck together.

"You never can tell," she laughed, licking sauce from her fingers.

Now, I had the information I needed. A man named Baldwin from Boston and the county department. Simple enough I thought. Then again, that was easy. Too easy. The unthinkable thing is Sadie doesn't want Almena to have Grace and Glory. No wonder my baby is fearful of this savage.

Sadie talked on and on but I only took in parts of what she was saying. This woman told me what she knew about any and every person in town.

I might have Curtis stop in to see the deputy and get the man from up North, full name and number.

As I watch Sadie destroy her ribs and potato salad, the inky nails dripping with barbecue sauce once again made my stomach flip. I found Al Green's "Love and Happiness" and dropped a quarter into the jukebox. Swinging my head in time with the music, I ask, "Does this make you want to do wrong or right, Miss Sadie?" I was laying it on thick now.

"Oh, I just do what's right."

"Girl, you sure know what to say. Ain't nothin' slow about you. Listen, sweetheart, how many barbers they got in this town?"

"Just one and plenty room for another one."

"Girl, stop. You are going to make that deputy come after me for kidnapping the postal lady."

"Oh Deputy Ray? He don't do nothing. He hangs out in the back of the grocery store next door to the post office. The only thing he does is listen to the highway patrol radio. He's not really the law. We still have to wait for the sheriff to come from the county offices if there's trouble. Lord, that was a good meal," she let out a loud belch. "James, you've hardly touched your food. Didn't you like it?"

"I'm sure it's great but my stomach's a little twisted right now. I guess I'm still thinking about my feuding family. I'll take it back with me and eat it later. Thanks for taking my mind off things and maybe we can get together when all this funeral business is over. Now that I have a friend in this part of the country, maybe I'll be able to stay awhile. If it's all right with you."

"Anytime, James. Anytime. There ain't many people who can recognize good people but I can."

I paid the bill, got my food to go and walked Sadie to the car. "Which way to your house, Miss Lady?"

"You can drive me back to the post office. My car is there. Would you like to stop by my house and settle your nerves down a little more?"

"I would love to but I know my relatives are wondering where I am by now." *Help!*

"Do you know, James, I don't even know your last name."

"James Grey," I said without thinking. "What's yours?"

"Wilson," she replied.

"Miss Sadie Wilson, it has been a pleasure." I moistened my lips.

She leaned over as if she expected a peck, but I couldn't bring myself to do it. "Miss Lady," I said, "Them some juicy lips I'm looking at but if I don't get out of here now, I'll be sitting in your lost and found bin forever."

I let Sadie out about ten minutes later beside a dark green Chevy parked slightly left of the post office. *That was close.* I wondered if she would make the connection between my last name and the name of the woman she spoke with on the phone in New Haven.

Curtis had checked into the hotel. Before I could get in, I knocked three times loudly. "Man, it's me," I called out.

Curtis finally opened the door, "Running from a quickie, my good man?"

The smell of whiskey filled the room. Two identical beds sat with a nightstand affixed to the wall between them. Not only did Curtis get a drink, he had gotten the bartender to sell him a fifth of Dewar's complete with ice and two cocktail glasses to celebrate the swift and impeccable work he claimed he had done.

"Hell no, I ain't running and a quickie never entered my mind. Now listen to this."

I relayed what I had learned from Sadie. Curtis sat listening and stroking his chin hairs with his forefinger. My plan is to speak with the deputy and get the unknown appraisers information. That meant an overnighter, which I would rather not do but the town was closing down. I looked over at Curtis who I now realized was drunk, not just tipsy.

"Lie down, Curtis. I need you to be fresh and alert in the morning so we can leave this town with all we came for."

"My good man, I'm in full control of my faculties. I'm well known in the Boston area and we might not have a problem finding this appraiser guy on our own."

"Man, I know you are well known, but a complete name and number would make me feel better. I want this shit over with." I knew I had to stroke Curtis's ego every now and then. I just bet he was well-known in Boston among the ladies of the evening.

"Are you hungry?"

"I had a fairly good steak and grits downstairs at the restaurant. I thought you just came from dinner."

"Man, I'll tell you about that part later. I'm starving. Give me the key in case you're asleep when I get back." He tossed me the key and fixed himself another Dewar's on the rocks.

I ordered a steak and baked potato with a side salad and thanked the gods the hotel restaurant was nothing like Benny's. While waiting for my food, I called home. Malinda answered.

"Big sis," I said. "You sound strong, girl!"

"Hey, baby boy! What's happening?"

"Everything is better than good. We're going to rest tonight and come on in tomorrow evening. There's no need to feign at all. In fact, it's good news. They want to buy Almena's land, but I'll leave that for the king of real estate to explain. Sis, we thought we was country. This is country. Where's my innocent future wife?"

"Let me get her. She's been waiting all day for your call."

Almena was on the phone in seconds. "James, how are you? Did you see Sadie? I ain't in no trouble, am I?"

"Hold on, hold on! Throw me a kiss."

"Your sister is sitting right here. Now quit teasing and tell me what's going on."

"Everything is fine. You're not in any trouble and yes I've seen Sadie. One question, are you friendly with the deputy down here?"

"Oh, yes, he helped us get our tickets up here."

"Okay, sweetheart. We'll talk in detail when I see you tomorrow and I don't care whose sitting there, throw me a kiss," I said and she did. My heart skipped a beat and I heard Malinda's delighted laugh in the background.

Early the next morning, Curtis and I began our last bit of information gathering. I parked across the street from the grocery store. I figured we had about half an hour before the post office opens and I might have to face Sadie again. I hope to be long gone before then. Curtis made his way across the street and into the store. I saw through the window as he picked up a bag of chips and got two sodas out of the refrigerator case. Reaching the counter, all of a sudden he moved out of my sight. I sat in the car wondering what was happening for all of three seconds. I didn't trust Curtis's moves. This morning he seemed hung over. So I went to see how he was doing. I entered the store, carrying the road map with me. Curtis's items was on the counter and he was standing close to the deputy who had yet to look up from his radio duty. The store clerk, a small pale man with thinning hair, came limping up to the counter.

"Can I help you?"

"Yes," I said, "I'll have a quarter pound of baloney and one of those dill pickles, if you don't mind, sir." His cataract-weakened eyes squinted at me. He nodded and hobbled to the meat counter to slice my order. While he went to get the baloney, Curtis delivered his pitch to the deputy.

"Good morning, sir. Your uniform tells me you are an officer of the law. I believe you are who I'm looking for. My name is Curtis Gibbs. I'm a representative sent by Ms. Almena Johnstone to obtain the name and number of a certain gentleman, wishing to contact her."

"Morning," Deputy Ray said, eyeing Curtis "You from up north, aint ya?"

"Yes, I am in this area on assignment. When I told Ms. Almena how close I was to her hometown, she asked me to look in on you or a Miss Sadie. She sends her regards and told me to thank you, once again for your help with the children."

The deputy gave Curtis another once over, "She knows she's welcome and I certainly do have that man's information right here behind the counter." He flipped the card from under a shelf and gave it to Curtis. Curtis was talking on and on about how the children had grown and since school was in session, Almena could not come home at this time. *Lying big time.* All the while I was thinking. *If he don't bring his fat ass on out of here.*

Curtis continued, "She also wants me to give you her phone number so you will have it. Ms. Johnstone says she feels it's proper for the law enforcement to really have this information on hand at all times. She will be back this way during the summer when school is out. She hopes she hasn't been a problem to you."

"You real polite, aint ya?" Deputy Ray said with a crooked smile that reminded me of a snarl. "Just tell her it was no problem at all. However, let her know this fellow is worrisome. You tell her and them children that we send our best."

"Here's my card and on the back of it is Ms. Johnstone's current phone number. This is a lovely area. No wonder she misses it so." Curtis studied the card the deputy gave him. "I'll see her this evening and make sure she calls Mr. Baldwin right away." Curtis was sweating, triggered by lying and the after effects of Dewar's. He paid for his bounty and left the store.

Before I could bounce out behind him, the deputy called out to me. "Morning, James. You a bit too early for Sadie. She won't be here for another twenty minutes at least."

"I see I'm too early. I've got to hit the road but I'll be back for sure. I want to make sure I'm going the right way. These back roads around here will throw you off. Route 301 will take me straight into 75 South, right?"

"You got that right, boy, and 75 will take you anywhere in the south you want to go."

I paid for the baloney and pickles but that "boy" remark had hit a nerve. *No! He didn't call me boy and in a deep southern way that made my hands draw into fist. Cracker like.* I bit down on my tongue and said, "I'll be back soon." I was fuming at Deputy Ray, but I got back to the car just in time to see, through the rear view window, Sadie's car turning onto the main street from the opposite end. Curtis sat in the car waving the business card like a Miss America winner.

Once again, I put my foot on the gas, putting distance between the post office and me. Looking in the rearview mirror again, I could see that Sadie was trying to open the door to the post office. About ten miles out of town, I glanced over at Curtis and said, "Get in the back seat and get some sleep. I'll drive home."

"I think I'm going to throw up," he bellowed.

"Yeah, you do look kinda green and all that sweating you doing might flood the engine out. Man drinking is not your thing."

"Might not be, but as an investigator I'm the best," he managed, holding a nervous hand to his mouth to push back his oncoming gagging. I shook my head. *This guy is unbelievable. Confidence is one thing but Curtis thinks he's Perry Mason.*

Six hours and fifty-one minutes later we pulled up in front of 240 Dixhill Avenue. Curtis slept all but the last two hours. Almena had fixed a big meal and Grace and Glory welcomed us like we was war heroes. There was no discussion of our trip in front of the children. Almena had asked that we talk after the children went to bed. She whispered something about memories of the past bring about nightmares. But she looked yummy.

After what seemed like a lifetime, Curtis in his flaming manner gave his account of all that occurred and added "My darling Almena, I can have your property sold in less than two weeks if you so desire. Just say the words."

"Mr. Gibbs, thanks is not nearly enough for what you

and James have done for me, but please accept it. I'm sure I want to sell the land in Elktown as soon as you can. Me and the twins will also be looking for you at church soon."

I had been smiling and posting my eyes on the woman I desired, but when I noticed Curtis looking at her the same way, I spoke up quickly. "My encounter with Sadie went well. I now know everyone's private business in Elktown. Almena, I can see why you was hesitant to deal with her. I'm sure if you call this appraiser in Boston we will also be finished with that business too. Have you ever been to a place called Benny's? It's a restaurant?"

She thought about it. "No, James. We rarely went to any places in the area."

"You don't know how that pleases me." Then I told of my dining experience with Sadie, I had the whole group of us laughing to the point of tears. Curtis got up to leave and I went to see him out. I didn't want to give him a chance to make a play for my woman now that she was so thankful. "Goodnight, counselor," I said firmly, almost pushing him through the front door.

When I turned around, loving arms wrapped around me and hungry lips met mine. I accepted them both. A peeping Malinda clapped her hands softly and I was sure she went to bed remembering how wonderful love feels.

‡‡‡‡‡‡‡‡‡‡‡‡‡‡‡

Almena and I walked back into the parlor. Logs crackled in the fireplace. The lights of the flames danced around the dim room. We sat on the sofa holding on to each other, breathing each other in, and talking long into the night. Her voice took me to feelings I never knew I had. "James, I really want good for us all." It was only then I realized how unselfish this woman was. Drawing herself up on my lap she asked, "Have you ever wept inside your mind? What I mean is, do old sorrows from the past pull at every fiber within you?"

"I don't think so but I have been ashamed of my past."

"I told you that the twins didn't have anyone but me

and as far as I know, that is true. Their parents are dead but what I didn't tell you is how they died. Fear can silence you and I was afraid to tell the whole horrible truth. My friend Coral, the twin's mama, was murdered by her husband right there in Elktown. He also killed the twin's brothers. On the bus that day, we was running. The twins didn't really know all this then and when you offered us a place to stay, I was so grateful. I didn't see the need to lay all our dirt out for people to judge us. I always had a problem with the way people seem to see me."

"Sadie told me about the murders. She almost bragged about them. Where is the father? In jail I hope."

"No, the sheriff killed him in the backwoods as he tried to outrun his crime. Coral had let the kids stay with me on that awful night. And I believe that she did that because she was planning to run away from his meanness. She gave me those kids to shelter them until she could git away that night and something musta went wrong. Malcolm, that was her husband, was a secret type person but in the days before the killings, I saw Coral praying like never before. Sometimes I wish I had paid more attention to things. Maybe I coulda helped her git away. You see, in my life I've made some mistakes and when I made them, I accepted them. I accepted that I was not able to think smart like other people. I can't really blame it all on other people; I was a part of my dumb-acting ways too. It hurts now but I found safety in not being smart. Folks never expected me to do the right thing and the sad part is I let them go right on thinking that way."

"Sweetheart, we all shift things sometimes in life if it's advantageous to what we want to do or if we want to please others. 'Easy' was often my nickname and 'sorry' was always coming out of my mouth." I held her tighter.

"But Coral never doubted me. My slowness never came up. She was a strong woman and never said a mean word about Malcolm to me. She loved each one of her children. I will never really know what happened in that house. Yet she gave me the most important things in her life, her babies. It's up to me to bring them into the kind of life Coral dreamed for them. The murder was terrible. More than that murder is the daily killing the children would have suffered in that town in the name of pity. It's rough being thought of as less than. My past doesn't have success written all over it. So we left. Folks like Sadie may make me fail at raising them."

"She's a spiteful person. We had a terrible argument about my leaving. I get nervous just thinking that she will go looking for kin of the twins. I would crumble like a piece of long forgotten bread if I lose them. I can't be without them. They are my life, my purpose and my friend's last request. Her final words to me was 'Do you think you can handle them?' I said yes then and I say yes now."

"I can help you with all that."

She placed her fingers between mine, moving them back and forth. It was softer than a kiss on my heart. He eyes strolled over me, knowing me...and my imperfections. I felt powerful and mission bound. "I thank you for your offer but I can't weep, grieve, wish, hope or have others save the day. I have to weave our way. This is our living rug. What you can do is be my witness as I complete my greatest piece. Me and the twins are going to finish this."

I wanted to make love to her but I knew that at that moment she needed me to be a listener. This woman is going to be the finisher of her fate whether I'm on board or not. She has resolved to succeed in raising those kids. I had a winner sitting on my lap. Her head resting on my chest; her mind in no way divided. My little sweet, country woman was in control.

An uneasy silence took over. I cleared my throat. *Ok here goes.* Taking a deep breath, my tongue finally moved. "We both have things we have to overcome; you sound like you're more than determined. I believe you will make good at anything you do. But there is nothing wrong with having a support system. I want to be that for you. Right now I'm glad you're strong. You are not alone. I have a war going on too. Sometimes when you think I'm going back to work or running off to do other church work, I'm going to drug counseling meetings. I try to make at least two a day. I had not relapsed in ten years but when I saw the helpless state of my sister's illness, I used that to do what take me out of reality and into a world that to me seems carefree. All I'm asking is that maybe we can be on the same side. I'll earn my stripes."

I stood up to hide my shame. She slid off me into the sofa cushion. I moved across the room and placed another log on the embers. It burst into licks of flames, sending more light into the burgundy parlor. When I turned back, Almena was curled up in a ball with her thumb in her mouth, innocent yet forceful. I knew then that I loved this woman. She had grown right in front of my mess, and had become strong and sure, right in the middle of my mess. It is amazing to witness the strengthening of a human spirit.

"Girl, I will stand in whatever shadow you need me to be in." I stood there shaking my head with my body at full attention. Easing down on the floor just below the sofa and turning to hers, I managed to say "I'll love you for the rest of your life. You do what you've got to do." She smiled, first in her eyes. She put her arms down around my neck whispering, in a breathy voice, "Thank you, 'cause I got this." She stretched out and we watched the fire dance until the sun came up.

CHAPTER TWENTY-FOUR
Showtime

There isn't much happening the last week of February except folks waiting for spring to make its entrance. Spring had an early start around here. It was still bone-deep cold but I didn't mind it as much. I felt alive and able to take on the world. It wasn't just what James and Curtis had done. There was a change in me. When I looked in the mirror I found things about myself I liked instead of all the faults I used to hang on to. Perhaps it was being in love with James. Love isn't nearly as complicated as I had made it out to be. There is power in love and I'm on overload. In fact, love makes your soul crawl out from inside and show up right on your face.

Every day after getting the kids off to school I spent three hours in the library learning words and how to say what I wanted to say. I knew my life was moving forward and I now had to get prepared to go with it. The staff at the library was still very friendly, yet I had heard nothing regarding the job.

Later in the week, Ms. Malinda took a call from Sadie. She left her number again. Sadie would not go away. She's not that kind of a person. I would have to deal with her directly. Never did I want Sadie to know where we was but now that she did, it kept me on edge. So, although Ms. Malinda thought I shouldn't, I called her. Sadie couldn't hang around in my life like an axe waiting to fall. There was a pay phone in the basement of the library. I decided I would call her from there just in case Sadie got long-winded or sassy. The phone sat on a wall next to the ladies room. After finding enough change in my purse, I made the call.

"Elktown, post office," Sadie answered

"Hey Sadie this is Almena, I'm returning your call.

"Almena! I thought you was coming down here to take care of the problems you left here girl...Hold on let me wait on my customer." I held onto the phone while I heard her sell some stamps and not even thank the person for coming in.

"Hello, Almena gurrrl....this is important and as your nearest relative, I'll just have to let the authorities know that you aren't being responsible."

"My representative has already attended to my affairs and what are you talking about with that as my nearest relative stuff?"

"Yes...Deputy Ray told me you had a fancy man stop over to see him. But we got other things to straighten out. So, bring your ass down here so we can settle our estate and see to the welfare of them children."

"I don't have a lot of patience right now so unless you let me know how you a relative to me or my kids, this talk is over."

"Alright, I didn't want to do this on the phone but, I will. Wallace Arthur Clemency is my father as he was yours. We sisters, girl!" Sadie's voice jumped as if she was pleased. "Gurrrrl...I been wanting to tell you this for a while now. He told my mother that he helped pay for your grandmother's place. When you came back from the service you had lost yourself and out of the goodness of my heart, I thought maybe I'd wait till you wasn't so crazy. Then it was that jail thing you had going on and bless your heart, your mother passed so I let it be. Now it's time for the truth to be told. Gurrrl, how them children doing?"

Anger and confusion gushed through me. I took the phone from my ear, closed my eyes for a moment and placed the receiver in the center of my forehead. Hearing her call out my name, I put the receiver back to my ear, "Sadie...I'm coming Saturday morning and you and me can remember things together."

It was Tuesday. In four days, Sadie would find out

things wasn't what they used to be. I wasn't nervous about seeing her. In fact, I welcomed this meeting. I wasn't scared, not about this lie she was trying to sell me but then again it could be a trick. Hanging up the phone and going into the ladies' room to gather myself I saw my eyebrows were up around my hairline. Could it be true? No, I know she's not my kin. Why does she hate me so? Why does she want me back in Elktown? And why does she keep asking about the kids?

Her words were festering in my head. I couldn't study today, the thought of putting on a pair of headphones to listen to the correct pronunciation of words and their meaning wasn't where my head was. Sadie was an outright liar. Today she had told the biggest lie ever. What reason would she have to go to that much trouble? Had she called the authorities or had someone come looking for the children? I remembered I had been wrong about my father being a weaver but I know Wallace was not my father. Light headedness returned. Now I know how a spider feels caught in somebody else web. It ain't full of hospitality. Secrets are the biggest dust balls in life. It is time to clean house.

Walking home from the library, I didn't even notice the cold. Reaching the house, I took a deep breath and prayed that once I saw Sadie, this calling would stop.

I must have had a serious look on my face 'cause the house seemed to hush down. Ms. Malinda, James, and even my twins was tiptoeing around me. Standing next to the sink in the kitchen and looking out the window, the day had turned gray. "Grace, Glory!" I call out to them as I heard them playing bowling in the hallway.

"Friday and Saturday I want y'all to spend the night with Ms. Malinda. I need to make a run down to the old house. I'll be back by Saturday evening." They stood there in the doorway of the kitchen and Grace gave me an evil eye. She bit down on her bottom lip to keep from crying and said, "Ok, but you coming back, right?"

"Right. Right back. You won't even know I am gone."

"Why can't we go with you then," Glory whined.

"Cause it's grown people business. Tell you what; I'll call you on the phone two times on Friday night and on my way home on Saturday."

That night, I heard Glory whisper to Grace, "You think she going to heaven to be with Momma and them?"

"Hush, Glory," Grace said sharply. Didn't she say she be right back?" For the next two nights Grace peed in the bed. That almost made me change my mind. After all, I was all they had. Sadie's mean ways had caused trouble again.

It didn't make sense the way Grandma's chair was rocking back and forth on its own since the day I talked with Sadie. Whatever Grandma and Mama had to say about this I wasn't in the mood to hear. I needed to handle this business myself. I would not sit in that chair or touch my weaving. This was personal.

Checking the bus schedules, I found there was a local bus to Elktown leaving New Haven at 8 pm on Friday. That would be perfect. It would give me time to have dinner with the twins and since the ride would take eleven hours there was time to put the finishing touch on my plan. Facing up to your past was scary but somehow my feelings of being tired of smack downs overrode my fear. Besides it's time to move on.

Pushing the trip from my mind, I cooked a meal Thursday night like it was a holiday. I started cutting up the kale and collard greens about 10 o'clock in the morning. Dinner would be herb roasted chicken with cornbread stuffing, greens, butternut squash and apple casserole, whipped potatoes, glazed carrots and hot butter rolls with apple butter jam. For desert, I would stir up Grandma's famous coconut cake. By the time James came home for lunch, he hollered, "Lawd have mercy, it smells good in here. If I didn't know better I'd think this is the last supper." *Now why he had to say that?*

"No, James. This is just a sample of things to come." He gave me a deep kiss and his hands got loose. I had to stop him but I could feel the temperature in that kitchen go up about ten degrees.

"I can't wait for dinner," Ms. Malinda yelled out. "Leave that girl alone before she burn something up." I knew she was teasing us.

When James left to go back to work, it come to me that James had just what I needed. I went into his room, it smelled just like him. I ran my hands over his suits and stiffly starched shirts and there on the top shelf was what I had been looking for. I got what I needed and as I put the box back, he burst into the room. "You missing me so much, you in here waiting for me?"

"No, just making sure you've got enough shirts to wear while I'm out of town plus this room smells just like you."

"Smell hell, you can have the real thing. Just say the word, nod your head or wink your eye and we can make it happen." He was holding me around the waist.

"I thought you was going back to work?" I pushed out from him.

"I forgot my keys. I can be late if you like." He had that silly grin on his face. "And, you know. Maybe smell on you a little bit."

"You are not right in the head." I ducked around him and ran back to the kitchen. He found his keys and gave me a peck and went out again. That was close. He almost caught me.

We destroyed that food at dinner. When I brought out the cake, they all clapped. I had put one candle on it. "This is our celebration of strength and my quick return from Elktown." Glory had been smiling, her smile melted away as quick as the wax atop the blazing candle. She got up from the table, covering her eyes with her hands and stumbled out of the kitchen.

"James, serve the cake please." I went after Glory.

I caught up with her in the hallway. Tears washed her face.

"Glory, have I ever let you down?"

"No, but I'm 'fraid."

I took her in my arms and we walked to the parlor. "Glory sometimes grown-ups have to do things. There is something I forgot to take care of. This thing I got to do will make a big difference in our lives. It's like cleaning out your old toy box. There are some toys you just out grow so it ain't no need to hold on to them. I want you to promise me to be a big girl and take care of your sister. She's afraid too. I love y'all more than life. Now give me a big hug, I'll be home in two days." I held her for a couple of minutes then whispered, "We better get back to our cake before James eats it all." We ran back to the kitchen and joined the others licking coconut icing from their fingers. Ms. Malinda gave me a wink. Grace was on her second slice.

James drove me to the bus station. If he told me once, he told me twenty times to call him. After checking my bag, he pulled me to him. "Just come back. You don't have to be a hero."

The bus stood waiting for me, exhaust fumes pumped from its rear daring me to get on. I hopped aboard with a hard lump in my throat. There was many young college kids on the bus. From what I heard, it was the beginning of a school break. They was excited and most of them carried a pillow or a laundry bag full of clothes with them.

Stepping over luggage and pillows in the aisle I managed to find an empty seat way in the back with no seat mate. My shoulders felt heavy. Maybe some sleep would help. Well, my best laid plan hit the shitter when a short black woman dressed in a well-cut woolen suit pushed her way toward the empty seat next to me. She placed her large bag overhead, sighed heavily and said to me, "Ooh weee, I thought I was going to miss this bus. Hold this, will ya," dropping a greasy bag full of food in my lap. She took off her jacket, sat down and grabbed the bag and came out with a fried chicken sandwich. You could smell the Crisco. She was out of breath but she took a great big bite of that sandwich. I turned to the window, wiped sweat from the window and stared at her reflection. I could tell she was going to be a talker by the way she was sizing me up. I closed my eyes and leaned my head into the cool windowpane. I was trying to let her sense I didn't want to be bothered when she said, "Baby, I'm sorry, my name is Rose. You want a sandwich? I'm so rushed I forgot my manners."

Raising my head slightly, I answered, "No thank you ma'am, I'm Almena." I tried to sound sleepy.

"Listen to you," she chuckled. "Ma'am and from the bottom ain't you. Where you going?"

"I'm going to Maryland." She was really a nice lady but right now I didn't want to feel friendly.

"I got family in Baltimore, 'course I'm going to Atlantic City. I've been winning at aces all week. I think I'm ripe for a big win this weekend and when I do, I'm going out West to my daughter's place. I ain't use to this cold; makes my arthritis act up." She patted her knees and continued. "I'm just running off at the mouth. You go ahead and get some sleep. I'll watch out for you."

"Thank you."

She don't even breathe when she talks. I laid my head back and closed my eyes and drifted into my plans for Sadie. The bus pulled off pressing my head further into the coolness of the window frame. I looked out as the headlights of the bus pierced the New Haven night. Although Rose was twisting around and pulling things out of her bag, I managed to fall into a deep emptiness.

A sudden shaking forced my body to slip toward the edge of the seat. Interrupting my peace. I was laid out completely on the seat and a red rose was lying in my lap. The bus made a sharp turn into the Salisbury, Maryland bus terminal. I sat up, looked at the rose, and remembered my seatmate. I hope she hits the jackpot.

"Twenty minutes. Rest stop," the driver announced.

Quickly standing, I go to refresh myself in the ladies room. Looking in the mirror I noticed my braids look neat. I scratch my head where it itched just under my bun. My eyes are clear and my clothes near perfect. I had borrowed Ms. Malinda camel hair coat so I was stylish. Just a quick brushing of the teeth and I was set to go.

The bus pulled away on the last lap of my journey. I reached in my purse and there in a hidden pouch was a program from my church. I glance at it. The title for that week's sermon was "The truth shall set you free." Ain't that something I thought? Sadie needs to hear this one. Creaming my hands with lotion, the smell of lavender fills the back of the bus. There was only about ten people still on the bus. Minutes later the bus pulled away from Elktown leaving me standing on the curb directly across from the post office. The air was dead tired. For just about three seconds my world wobbled.

Back again...arriving where I started.

Looking at my watch, it was seven-twenty in the morning and the only thing open was the grocery store. I picked up the medium-sized bag, crossed the street and entered. There's something about this town that never changes and that something is change doesn't happen. A buzzing sound came at me from the rear of the store and the smell of pickles in a barrel made my eyes swim. Blinking my eyes clear, the leather strap of my purse around my neck snapped me forward tugging me in the right direction like a leash. Although his back was to me I could see that Deputy Ray was listening to the radio.

Clearing my throat loudly, "Good morning Deputy." He turned quickly and gave me a hard stumped look. "Good morning, miss."

"You remember me, Almena Johnstone?" His face blossomed into a cheeky smile. I knew my hair and clothes had changed but until now I didn't really realize how much.

"Of course, I remember you. My goodness the North sure do agree with you. Ms. Almena. You looking well and you looking bright as anybody. I wasn't looking for you until the summer, how's them children of your'n?"

"They fine, in school and growing faster than corn." Mr. Johnny, the store clerk came out of the back room and peeped at me. He frowned.

I want to say I'm the one you use to watch so carefully. But I don't. Mr. Johnny is an old white man who could never understand why anyone would have a conversation with a black person. His dislike for darkies, as he called us, was written all over his face. He fiddled with the register, squinting through his glasses at me. I don't pay him no mind and turn back to Deputy Ray. "I thought maybe I'd come take a last look at the place and see Sadie."

"Sadie ain't due for another hour or so." Deputy Ray said shaking his head. "I can offer you a lift to your grandma's place if you like. You selling the place?"

"I'm thinking on it and thank you, I need that ride out there." We left the store and Mr. Johnny still had not made out who I was. He stood behind the counter nodding his head. Five months ago he would have asked, in a hurry up fashion, what I wanted in his store.

Before getting in the deputy's car, I tacked a note on the post office door just for Sadie.

The car was a mess. He had stuff covering the back seat from food wrappers to fishing equipment. Placing my suitcase in the back seat among the junk it comes to me: this man has been in my life during two deciding times. This time would be the last. He drove slowly and got me caught up on all the stories about the new highway coming through but I was hardly listening. He was talking with a Chesterfield cigarette dangling out of his mouth. It's a wonder he hadn't choked his life off before now. As we come up over a large hump in the road that signaled that Graham Alley Lane was next, I took a deep breath.

"Deputy Ray, I want to walk toward the house from here. I am fine; just want to walk it. I got some thinking to do. I'll see you back in town. Thanks again." He pulled over. I got out, got my bag, and started to close the door when Deputy Ray said while coughing, "I understand, Ms. Almena, you go ahead and say goodbye. This will always be your home." I fanned myself as he pulled off.

The lane looked the same, hard, brown and more like a worn-out path than a lane, and though I saw the house, I was not warm or soothed by it. As a child and a woman I had watched eagerly as my grandmother and mother walked this path. The sun was not shoulder high yet tired. This is not home. Glancing across the road the tract houses were gone, as they should have been. Big yellow road trucks looked back at me. The houses had been wiped from the face of this earth. Everything is so broken; sadly this brought a gentle order to things. I exhaled.

Passing the oak tree which is choked by winter and reaching the porch, a duck let out a call that made me jump but I knew I was too close to run now. Fishing around in my bag for the keys, my eyes rested on the porch swing, the one where my father told me his story of abandonment. The truth. The one I was going to hold on to. What a good day that was. A good day in a hard place. My shoulder began to ache, feeling like they longed to bend forward and come together. *Just a little while longer.*

Inside, the house appeared hazy. Dust lived there now. My shoes sounded like thunder on the linoleum floor. The sofa and chairs was covered with the same sheets I had thrown over them. I walk through the living room to the kitchen and tried to turn on the hanging light over the table. Met with no electricity, I reached under the sink and pulled out a kerosene lamp and lit it with matches from the kitchen drawer. Peeling contact paper that lined the drawers caught my eyes. I pressed it back down. I didn't know why. It just seemed like the right thing to do. Streaks of winter morning sun angled through the kitchen window which made the room bright enough. I sat down at the table waiting for an unforgettable memory; a memory that would pull upon my feelings. Instead, I felt like I was sitting and reading an alphabet chart. A for the apron hanging off the oven door, B for the back door locked with two bolts and C for the long crack running up the wall in back of the refrigerator. The box of grits in the open cupboard gave me no warmth. I sat for what seemed like an eternity waiting to want, miss or cherish being here. I reached out and picked up the salt shaker and threw some salt over my shoulder. Just in case. I blew out the lamp and walked to the back kitchen door. With my bag in hand, I started a brisk walk backwoods to where I had to go. I passed a duck pond. I had often wondered where the ducks came from and where they lived. Just like me, they spent time there without thought to their direction. They also ended up where they started.

The sign on the church door said "Seek Perfection" with a large cross in the center. As I turned the doorknob, the hinges on the door made a whining, swooshing sound. The door snapped back quickly and the smell of pine sucked me in. Walking through the small front hallway I passed two doors, one on each side. That's not where I wanted to go or even be nosey about. A bulletin board posted to the right declared Friday night as Testimony Night. Making a mental note of that, I looked straight ahead to the platform and altar before me. It was beautiful. Light wood surrounded the platform and the altar looked to be made of solid mahanoy. The carpet was deep red and the rows of seats smelled like they had just been oiled. Strong streaks of light danced from the stained glass windows. They had some unfamiliar symbols on them. I'm sure they mean something to the good people of this church. I couldn't make it out. On the back wall was painted the most prideful lion I had ever seen. His mouth was wide and his hair was golden. He's wasn't scary. He reminded me of me. He could handle it.

Sitting in the front row, taking it all in, with my bag by my side, I couldn't compare it to my church in New Haven. It looked like a stage, maybe because Testimony Friday was last night. There was no pulpit stand holding a Bible, no columns on either side and no plants or flowers. It was peaceful and warm and I didn't mind waiting. In fact, nothing is wrong, absolutely nothing. At this particular time I feel like this is the only place to be.

I wasn't waiting long before she came. She took long swaggering strides up to the front and she looked down on me. An underlying chill is lent to the warm room. She stood there in her two-tone blue postal uniform and said, "You look nice, baby girl."

My eyes rolled and the tension in my back locked.

"Sit Sadie. Make yourself comfortable. I picked the church 'cause I know that your granddaddy built this building. He did a mighty good job too. It is very serene here. This is a place for folks to let go and wash themselves with the truth and love. Talk to me."

"Yes, my grandfather did build all this." She sat down, jittery, along side my bag. "I know this may come at you strange but what I said on the phone is true and many people know it. Wallace is your father and we are sisters. My mother was married to Wallace and your mother came between them. I was five years old when he left us. I don't blame you for that but my mother never forgave him for that. I guess I was hard on you 'cause you had my father and he was providing for you and your family.

"Oh, so you do know you was mean to me and you meant to be? Don't you know that rejection is a living death?" The smell of a familiar rot sent goose bumps up and down my arms.

"Now, let me finish. I'm sorry.... but, when Daddy did stop by to see me, he always said that because of your mental state he couldn't come back to us. You didn't develop like other babies did. I went to a lawyer so we could get started on selling our property. I realize you shouldn't be saddled with these kinds of matters. It's time we come together as a family. Wouldn't you like to have a family? No one should be alone. You and them kids are like my kin and I plan to do right for all the wrong our parents brought on us. I'll see to it that you and those children get whatever you need. When I think of those children, well it just breaks my heart. Does the Child Services know about your conditions and all? It's a wonder your state of mind hasn't become fuzzy, then what would happen to them children? Your past is not suited to raise children and you know that."

"Thank you for your concern." My nostrils had flared. I faced forward, not wanting her to see the contempt I held on to. Placing my hands down on both sides of me, I gripped the bench to balance my voice.

"I'm not alone and your heart need not break for my children. I do hope you don't have a hard time with the truth. You see I know who my father was. I got to meet him on one of the best days of my life and he wasn't Wallace. I hate to rupture your rapture but, your father,

Wallace wasn't who your mama told you he really was. You do remind me of him, perhaps that where all your cruelty comes from. I'd like to say I've forgotten all about him, but I haven't. I'm working on it, though. It is with great pleasure that I surrender him to you. Life goes on after Wallace, but not as it should and as for my state of mind this morning it's clearer than ice. I brought you a present." I stood up and unsnapped my bag and uncurled my blue rug. "This is for you."

"Chile....listen, I don't need no rug. I need you to sign these papers." Her words was impatient. She pulled some papers out of her jacket. "I got a government job and I need to get back to it. Girl, you look good but you still confused. Still walking around with rugs." She sucked her teeth and pushed down them four frown lines she carried around on her high forehead.

"This one is just for you, since you want to remember your father. Stop all that teeth sucking in the house that your granddaddy built." She leaned up.

"Don't even think about moving. Look at it!" Through clench teeth, I almost screamed. I laid the rug across the altar. "That man holding the little girl's hand is your father, Wallace, and he is leading her to his favorite game. He was the castrator of my innocence. He suffocated my dreams and he robbed me of my childhood." My voice rose high now but the hurting lumps in my throat was beginning to dissolve.

She sat there with a smirk on her face and her right hand held up as if she was about to stop this telling. She started to rise from the bench. That would be a mistake, "Heifer, you best be still, words have never been able to contain all my pain until now. Studying vocabulary and kindness have helped me to express myself and now I'm able to get out what my rugs hold. I put up with your belittlement and signifying all my life. If you move I will carve you down!" I pulled the straight razor I had slipped out of James's room from my pocket.

"No need for that, please." Her fish eyes began to buck and I could see her knees shaking. "No," she moaned softly, "Please, don't....I—"

"Sit still, you lying bitch." I cut her off 'cause she was going to hear about her special father. My hands was trembling with the blade real close to her left cheek.

"You want a memory of him? He was the boogey man who darkened my bedroom door at night and in the daytime too. He liked little girls and the smell of baby powder. He was the dehydrator of my youth. He had a personal affection for the helpless. He drove me to seek solace in dangerous places later on in my life. Now, you want me to claim him? Sadie, I had him in the most intimate ways. He was my first problem and it will please me greatly if his offspring is my last."

She choked back a sob as I moved the blade closer to her throat. Her face sagged and her mouth formed a perfect circle with her lips frozen in a yet-to-be-heard scream. Her arms folded back like chicken wings against the back of the bench. She was holding on for her last breathe. I press the tip of the blade underneath her chin. As I pressed inward, a line of blood slithered down her neck. Just a quick flicker of this blade and her troubling ways would be history.

Don't do it....Don't do it. You promise those children you would be back, keep your promise sweetheart. Let Sadie live with the truth! Grace and Glory, for Grace and Glory. Mama's voice had such urgency to it.

I dropped the blade and push edSadie's face back so hard her head bobbled. "Now, close your mouth." I pushed her chin again, shaking her overlapping jowls. "Take your papers, your father's rug, your lies and threats out of my sight. Don't ever call me again unless of course you want me to let the good people of Elktown know all about your daddy. I can come back on Testimony Friday and let them hear me out." I picked up the blade and put it back in my coat pocket.

Her eyes by now was as big as small cabbages as she put the papers in her jacket. She slowly began to slide down the other side of the bench. My chest rose up and down like skins on a just-struck drum. I stared at her, almost wanting her to mention my babies, but I think she knew that nothing would stop me from killing her if she uttered their names.

Reaching the end of the bench, she sprinted up and around the other aisle crying out, "You cut me, you crazy bitch!" Holding her hand to the scratch on her neck, "I'm having you locked up."

"No you not. You see you too important with your government position and besides do I look like I care?" I yelled back.

"You think you so smart with your big words and all, Almena! You ain't nobody. Don't you come back here starting trouble."

"Don't forget your rug!" Turning face forward and taking a steadying breath while easing back down on the bench, I could swear that lion winked at me.

#‡#‡#‡#‡#‡#‡#‡#‡#‡#‡#‡#‡#‡#‡#‡#‡#‡#

As I stepped out of the church two beautiful brown eyes stared at me. They are soft and sad and deep as well water. Before I'm even sure I have seen a deer; he tilts his head upward as if to say "get out of here" and tromped off into the woods.

Pulling my coat tight around me and adjusting my bag, I began the long walk into town. The closer I got, bile rose in my throat. Things could have gone real wrong in that church. If I had slit Sadie throat, folks really would have a reason to call me crazy. The thought of how close I came to coming undone sent shivers through me. I said a thank you prayer to Mama and another one to Sadie's prideful ways. Sadie's too important to be flawed or have a skeleton come tumbling out of her closet. That's what I'm hoping. Still, if the police is waiting on me, I will have a seizure.

When I git to town, the post office is closed, due to illness. At least, that's what the sign on the door said. I breathe out a sigh relief. Once again Deputy Ray gave me a ride, clear over to Salisbury, where I caught the bus north....*Home*. I'm feeling good....*Believe*.

CHAPTER TWENTY-FIVE
Peace

Many seasons have come and gone. What was a new start has become one more grateful day. I raise my head to puddles of sunshine that pour into our bedroom window. The birds sing out their spring serene songs as if right on clue to the tranquility at 240 Dixhill Avenue.

The New Haven area is still welcoming in the morning light. I did not rock on my decision to sell my past. I figured I had paid for it and owned it long enough. Curtis sold the Elktown property for twice its assessment value.

Calling Mr. Baldwin brought favorable news, also. It seemed that them dolls that Grandma had been so protective of was valuable. My grandma had been given them from the estate of a family she worked for long ago, and the dolls were twins. Mr. Baldwin came and inspected them, "These dolls are twins and in mint condition, numbered as the seventh and eighth of their kind. They are from France, made by Pierre Francois Jumeau. Very nice indeed. I have a buyer who will easily give you a handsome price." When he mentioned that they was twins I knew I would never sell them. I keep them stored properly now.

Before I go any further, let's get something straight; we, the twins and I, worked hard on our new start. There are some things in your future that bring about a fear of the unknown. You wonder if all of your efforts will materialize. *Will you get what you've been working for? Will one of the biggest dreams you've had actually become real? Or will you fail again?* With every challenge we faced, we never traded in our new for our old. We left our *what-was* behind. Backwards was not an option for us. We was not runaways or throw-a-ways. We was committed to our new start. We chose to see good. Even with poor understanding, going forward we knew we had to be still until we could fit what life was tossing at us into the rhythm of our lives. Yes we had big dreams, but sometimes you must snatch yourself out of parts of them before they become a nightmare. Cutting Sadie's throat would have certainly ended our dreams. I counted myself lucky, no, blessed. I can't believe I came that close to ending it all. I almost let our wounds get in the way. Thank goodness Mama's voice reigns me in and allows us to give our dreams our best shot.

Dr. Moss helped out with the twins needs for counseling. They understand much more about their body and relationships with boys. I believe my angels sent him but I'm the one that had the sense to balance the problem and be still until our help came. Chile, we had to break the chains of our yesterdays. In my stillness I found the will of the heart to speak its own mind.

James kept his word to Habibah and worked within the church community and immigration to get her permanent citizenship status granted but she never showed up for court. Just couldn't be still. Some say she went to New York and works in Harlem braiding hair. James works as a volunteer counselor for drug abusers and his barbershop is one of the best in New Haven until this day.

Ms. Malinda lived six more years, leaving her home to James and me equally. During those years, she redecorated her home, held the grandest wedding that James and I could ever dream we would have. Announcements went out as far away as Elktown. Pastor Joel was the best man and the minister. We danced the night away. Been laughing ever since.

Grace and Glory was thirteen years old when Ms.

Malinda went home to glory and she had been a loving grand-auntie to them. She prepared them for her goodbyes by having me do a rug of her on the French chair with them sitting by her feet, one of the most beautiful portrait rugs I have ever done. This rug serves as a certificate of completion. We put aside our grief, took root, and graduated as survivors who let nothing stop us from fulfilling our dreams. Healing happened on the way. Our history was not our destiny. There was a gap in the stitches of our lives that allowed mercy to come in. Course, it never hurts to have Grace and Glory by your side.

Chile, I've been working at the library for years. They tried out another more qualified person at first, it seems. Of course, they didn't work out. And yes, I'm very familiar with Mr. Dewey now. I work at the reference desk. I can find anything you need to know. It's all in how you start a thing that determines how you end up. Believe me, I got this. As the reference supervisor, I'm damn good. I will always be a weaver. Information is what I weave now.

Grace is well on her way to being a doctor, graduated right up the street from here at a school called Yale. She's going to be a doctor that sees only children and a very good one, too. Glory is an artist of weaving and quilting; she had one of them showings and included my rugs, too! People was walking around this large hall with wine glasses and all, commenting on my work and wanting to pay big money for our work. She wouldn't sell a one of mine, they're historical, she says.

Mama and Grandma are still hanging around in my head, fussing. When Glory wouldn't take the money for the rugs, Grandma started up with "I told you that girl still ain't got no sense." And Mama said, "She wish Grandma would find the everlasting."

Personally I wished they would find free because me and my girls have.

Miriam Kelly Ferguson is a weaver of words....

I believe storytelling is a way to map and explore the ambiguities of human experience. This motivates me as a fiction writer. Stories have given me a language to express the contradictions in my own experience. Writing them has often been a challenging exercise in sympathy and compassion. I have come to see storytelling as imperative.